RICHARD WILKES was born in 1943 in Kununoppin, near Merredin, in the Western Australian wheatbelt. His father was a member of the Darbalyung Nyoongar community of the Swan River. Richard was educated at Eden Hill and Mogumber primary schools where, amongst other more street-wise attributes, he showed an aptitude for writing, winning a trip to the 1956 Melbourne Olympic Games in an essay competition.

Leaving school after grade seven, Richard went to work with a tin ware manufacturer for three years. Despairing of factory life, he then travelled throughout the South-West doing seasonal work; fruit picking, potato picking, farm labouring. Richard met and married his wife, Olive, in the wheatbelt, and they later moved to Perth for the better education of their four children.

Richard Wilkes has been an active member of Nyoongar groups and organisations, at the same time working in various government positions. Most recently, Richard spent twelve years with the Health Department of Western Australia working as a welfare officer.

Bulmurn: A Swan River Nyoongar is Richard Wilkes's first novel.

BULMURN
A SWAN RIVER NYOONGAR

A NOVEL BY
Richard Wilkes

UNIVERSITY OF WESTERN AUSTRALIA PRESS

First published in 1995 by
University of Western Australia Press
Nedlands, Western Australia, 6009

National Library of Australia
Cataloguing-in-Publication entry:

Wilkes, Richard
    Bulmurn : a Swan River Nyoongar

    ISBN 1 875560 41 6.

    1. Nyungar (Australian people) – History – Fiction.
    2. Aborigines, Australian – Western Australia – Swan River
    Region – History – Fiction. I. Title.

A823.3

Front cover image features a photograph of Nigel Wilkes taken by Victor France

Publication of this title was assisted by the Commonwealth Government through the Australia Council, its arts funding and advisory body.

Assistance was also received from Department for the Arts and Aboriginal Affairs Department, Western Australia.

Editorial consultant: Helen Bradbury Publications Management, Perth
Design by Brown Cow Design, Perth
Map on page 219 by Ros Davies, Creative Cartography, Perth
Printed by PK Print, Perth

DEDICATION

I dedicate this story about Bulmurn, a Swan River Nyoongar, to my forefathers through the ties of my umbilical cord which extend from now, February 1995, back to the time long before the white colonists came here and trapped us into the slavery we still suffer from. One day I hope we will be free to live in harmony with other Australians.

This novel is also a tribute to our patriotic Nyoongar leaders such as Midgegooroo and his son Yagan, both murdered in 1833. Despite valiant resistance, Midgegooroo was killed by a firing squad in Perth. Yagan was shot through the head on Herrison Island by a twelve-year-old boy. Yagan's head was hacked off, smoked dry and shipped to England where it was placed in the British Museum. Nyoongar people are now negotiating with English officials for the return of Yagan's head to Western Australia for a proper Dreamtime burial.

This novel is also a tribute to other leaders, such as Yellagonga, Mundy, Waylo and Banyowla, and other Darbalyung people. These are the people who took the brunt of the force of the colonists, colonists who invaded by treachery and with the power of the gun: a might that my people could not match. Against the odds, my people fought with great courage when they could and had to.

I also pay tribute to my great grandfather Nungat, my great grandmother Tilbich, my grandfather Edward Wilkes 'Wilak' and my grandmother Munderan, my father Edgar Wilkes and my mother Enid Mumunbulla, my deceased brothers Eddie and Ian, my youngest brother Peter and sisters Jane and Yvonne, my sisters-in-law, Judith and Sandra, and my brothers-in-law Frank Davis (dec.) and John Winmar.

I thank my wife Olive Winmar, my children Warren, Edgar,

Linley and Alison, Alison's husband James Kearing, and all my grandchildren. This is their story forever.

Thanks to all those other grans and grannies and all the other elder Nyoongar for their wonderful stories which I have been able to use in this novel.

I give a special thanks to granny 'Knayel' Winmar and my father-in-law Billy 'Beep' Winmar who comes from Quairading, a little town east of Perth. They were the people who showed me the rock and sacred site of *bikuta* which features so strongly in this story. It is believed that Fred Knayel Winmar was the last prisoner to escape from Rottnest Island jail, the death camp of hundreds, perhaps thousands of Aboriginals. Granny defied the odds in escaping. He swam through heavy seas over the twelve-mile distance, only to be captured on Coogee beach near Fremantle. As he lay exhausted his tormentors said, 'Don't run or we'll shoot'. The authorities took him straight back to the island jail. Granny Knayel's courage typifies the strength and tenacity of so many other prisoners of war in trying to escape, only to lose their lives.

I would like to thank these organisations, critics and friends, as well as the people who read *Bulmurn*:

- The Aboriginal Arts section of the Australia Council;

- The Department of the Arts, Western Australia;

- Mr Daniel Sprague. Thank you Dan;

- Mr Geoffrey Narkle, Aboriginal elder;

- Mr Craig Sommerville, Aboriginal Affairs Department;

- Mrs Elaine Mazzini;

- Mrs Patricia Drayton;

- Members of the Nungka and Murri Murri dance groups.

Also a special thanks goes to the University of Western Australia Press, especially Janine Drakeford, Jane Crawford, Joanne Berens, Ian Drakeford and Cate Sutherland.

And thanks to my editor Helen Bradbury, my champion. I'm certain Bulmurn was able to 'sing' you to do this story, otherwise other people might not have had the opportunity to read about Bulmurn, a Swan River Nyoongar.

I, as the author, sincerely hope that whoever reads the novel enjoys its passage back into the years of the eighteen hundreds.

Richard Wilkes
(Nungat Mumunbullawilak)

Bulmurn Boylla Gudjuk

Bulmurn crouched down beside the swift stream to drink the cold flowing water that ran through the hills of the Murrn Morda before finding its way into one of the larger rivers that flowed to the coastal plain below the hills.

Bulmurn drank the water slowly because time was something he had plenty of. In fact, he didn't hurry at all. After he had slaked his thirst he stood up. He had good height. His body looked slim but he had muscle on his wiry frame showing his strength.

He wore a *buka*, a cloak made from a *yonga*, a western grey kangaroo. The *buka* was draped over his shoulder. The other garment he wore was a *julup lup lup* which covered his crotch area. Around his waist he wore a *nulbarn* which is a belt woven from the fur of *kumarl*, the possum, or made from human hair. Tied on his *nulbarn* was his *goorrit*, a bag containing his own secret concoction of herbs used for healing purposes. Bulmurn was a *Mobarn Mamarup Boylla Gudjuk*; a powerful man who had special powers to heal his people. He was an Aboriginal doctor.

In his left hand he carried two barbed *keitj*, his spears. In his right hand he carried his *miro* which was used by all the men to propel their spears with great force. The spears were his source of protection and food, wherever he went. He needed them now because he had been travelling overland quite a distance, and was going home to his own people.

Bulmurn's hair was dark, long and curly. He had a large forehead, dark eyebrows and black eyes, high cheekbones, a large flat nose, and a rounded jaw that was hidden under a beard that complemented a handsome face. His arms and legs seemed extra long, but they fitted his body frame. Four large scars ran from the right side to the left side of his breast, for he was a *bugar*, a champion of the Darbalyung Nyoongar people. He strode with grace, with pride in his movements.

Bulmurn belonged to the Mooro, the Nyoongar people of the Derbal Yerigan, the Swan River area of Mandoon, Guildford. Bulmurn was a proud Nyoongar man. He was well respected wherever he went and everyone sought his healing. The reason Bulmurn had left the Guildford area of the Swan River was because he had received a message from Jumulga Kerring, the leader of the Balladong Nyoongar people, who lived in the York area, to go there.

The message was a request, from Jumulga, to heal a close family member of the Balladong people. Bulmurn did not hesitate, he went as soon as he possibly could. It was to take him many days to achieve a cure for Jumulga's relative, who the Balladong people thought was going to die. In their eyes Bulmurn had performed a miracle, so he was asked to stay on longer with Jumulga's mob to heal others. While he was in the Balladong camp he was able to show their doctor improved ways of healing.

Bulmurn had enjoyed his stay with the Balladong mob, but he knew the time had come when he had to leave to return to his own people, his people, the river people, to heal them. This was the reason he was travelling home. He was following the direction of the sun which was travelling along the sky towards the west, where it would settle down to rest at the end of the day.

The sun was directly above his head. He knew this to be the middle of the day. Bulmurn thought of the path which the sun would take, and he made an estimation of where it would be before he reached his people. He estimated it would be low in the sky, but there would be daylight left when he arrived at the campsite of the river.

Bulmurn thought about sitting with Weejup, his friend and future father-in-law. He was also longing to catch a glimpse of Lulura, Weejup's beautiful daughter. Weejup and Minyon, Lulura's father and mother, had agreed that she would be given away to Bulmurn. They had promised her to him as his future wife. Soon he would be able to claim her. Soon he would be able to carry her to his *miamia*, his home, which she would be able to share with him.

As Bulmurn walked on, his thoughts centred truly on Lulura. She was some summers into puberty. Now was the time to claim her. Then he thought of his age compared to Lulura's. He reasoned that he was a few summers older than her, but that was all right. Weren't all men older than their young wives? Bulmurn knew that a man could have as many as three wives with him at the one time. That was an accepted tribal custom.

Bulmurn knew that when Weejup and Minyon decided that he was the right man for Lulura, proper consideration of their skin group was taken into account. Bulmurn's skin group was of the *Ballarok Martagyn*. Lulura's skin group was of the *Waddarak Martagyn*, therefore making her most suitable to be his wife.

The skin groupings were made of six groups: the *Ballarok*; *Drondarap*; *Ngotak*; *Nagonak*; *Dijikok*; *Waddarak*. Bulmurn coming from the *Ballarok* skin group, and Lulura coming from the *Waddarak* skin group, made them the least likely to be related through blood ties.

This system was used strictly by the Mooro, Beelu, Beeliar and other groups who had ties with the Swan River people. By making sure people took their betrothed this way the blood lines were maintained so that no inbreeding occurred. Offspring had less chance of being born with mental or physical disabilities, thus ensuring the tribe kept healthy.

Bulmurn thought about Lulura, picturing her in his mind. Lulura was as beautiful as one could imagine: tall, with glossy black curly hair, a rounded face, dark, clear eyes, and a nose that balanced her face. Her lips were a little on the large side, but nevertheless suited her looks. She had long slender arms and legs that complemented her firm breasts and strong hips.

Lulura was somewhat of an up-and-coming young woman. The other women liked especially her willingness to learn the women's role of food gathering. Whether it was collecting herbs, berries, yams or the potato-like *quarn*, or kicking over the *balga* tree then foraging through it for the succulent bardi grub; or whether it was catching small lizards or goannas, or helping to take fish out of the fish traps, Lulura was only glad to learn quickly from the other women. She was careful to never overstep her role by pushing the other women aside. The women carried two bags: the *goto*, used for general purposes and the *gundir*, in which their small children were carried.

'Yes', Bulmurn thought, 'soon she will be mine'. His first *yorga*, his first given wife, had died a few summers back, leaving him devastated with grief. Rather than marry again he stayed single. Sometimes he shared other women who were offered to him. Bulmurn reasoned that now the time was nearly right for him to take Lulura, and he would do so when the proper time arrived. His instinct would tell him so.

Bulmurn's mind drifted to York and the Balladong people, how he had cured Jumulga's relative. He smiled to himself, thinking of the many friends he had made while he was there. He knew his own people, the Mooro, would have heard already how he cured the ailing person and of the others he healed. He knew this would make others seek him for his help. He knew this would enhance his image as a *Mobarn Boylla Gudjuk*, a fitting title for a traditional, spiritual healer.

Bulmurn really hadn't noticed that he had come down off the Murrn Morda. This was because he was deep in thought, but now he noticed he was close to the Swan River. He decided to stick close to the bush to avoid the *wadjbulla*, the white settlers who now lived around the area. The last thing he wanted on this day was for him to be seen by or to have any kind of confrontation with them.

Then all of a sudden he was at the Mooro campsite at Mandoon. As he approached the camp, the *dwerrts* yip-yipped his return, people rushed out of their *miamias* and then they ran towards him, shouting out his name, telling others he was back home. '*Bulmurn kullark! Bulmurn kullark! Bulmurn kullark!*' they called. Bulmurn has home. Men grabbed his arm to greet him. Women smiled at him. The *kulunga*, the children, walked alongside him, trying hard to imitate his steps as he took his long strides.

Some of the children would fall down laughing because they could not keep in step with him, but that wouldn't keep them from getting up and having another go at it. Bulmurn smiled as he walked onwards to Weejup's place.

As he neared Weejup's *miamia* he glanced at someone who had caught his eye. He looked her way, it was Lulura. He felt his heart almost miss a beat as she smiled at him. Bulmurn smiled back at her, but didn't stop. He knew that their time of being together as one was near. But first he had to go to Weejup's place to show his respect. At Weejup's place they would share food with him. They would sit and yarn until he knew everything that had happened in the river campsite while he was away in the York area.

Weejup was sitting near the door of his *miamia*. He rose as he saw Bulmurn approaching and smiled, acknowledging a greeting, showing that he was pleased about Bulmurn's return. Soon both were yarning as if the *Mobarn Mamarup* had never left the area at all.

Weejup told Bulmurn how the tribe had fared while he was away: the young boys were being taught how to track and hunt game animals; the women were teaching the young girls to gather herbs, foods of various kinds, how to prepare the gathered food, how to serve and share the food to make sure everyone was fed each day. Weejup said, 'life is good at this time. We have had no trouble within our tribe, no deaths, no bone pointing, nor death singing. No trouble with the Beeliar or Beelu people, other neighbouring groups of the river people. 'Yes', Bulmurn', Weejup said, 'life has been very good.

'You know, Bulmurn, we've even had no trouble for a long time now from those *wadjbulla* people, none of our people are being taken to jail. But I fear for our people because the *wadjbulla* are squeezing us off our land, our land where we have lived and roamed for a long, long time, long before they got here. But we have to put up with them.'

Bulmurn acknowledged what Weejup had said, pleased everything was going well. 'I'm glad', he said, 'the young people in our tribe are learning our ways so well. You know, Weejup', Bulmurn said, 'I'm a great believer in our young people learning everything they can about our ways to pass onto their children so our Law is passed down. Learning makes our people strong. It makes me pleased to know this.' After a pause he said, 'We must try to keep our people out of the way of the *wadjbulla* people if we are to survive'. Weejup nodded in agreement.

Bulmurn changed the subject of discussion by asking about Jubuc, the other healer within the Mooro mob. It was not uncommon for one tribe to have two or three healers within a group. Weejup said, 'Jubuc has been doing a good job of looking after our people's health while you've been gone. No task has been too big or too small for him. That one, Jubuc, he's a good man all right, he helps everyone. I'm glad. I'm glad in my heart that Jubuc has learnt the craft of healing. I always knew he would be a good healer for our people, I always knew he cared.'

Bulmurn asked Weejup about each individual member of the Mooro people. In turn Weejup was able to tell him all because Weejup was the leading tribal elder of the Mooro people.

Bulmurn then asked Weejup about Lulura. 'You know, Weejup, your daughter Lulura must soon become my woman. She must soon join me to come to live in my *miamia*.' Weejup nodded saying, 'Yes. She is promised to you. Soon she will be able to join you, to live with you in your *miamia*.'

'Now', Weejup said to Bulmurn, 'we will eat'. Minyon, Weejup's wife, brought a spread of food — *yarkinje*, the long-necked turtle, its eggs and Swan River mullet, speared by Weejup and other men that morning. After eating, Bulmurn rose from a sitting position to stand before his hosts. He thanked Minyon and Weejup for their hospitality. 'It is good you have shared with me. Now I must go to my *miamia* and rest. I am tired from travel.

14

I will do no more today. After a good night's rest, I will meet with you, Weejup, and all the other elder members of our council — Jubuc, Yumbun, Yobby and others — to discuss the needs of our people. *Kwabba jidaluk, Weejup, Minyon.*' They wished him good night and he left for his own campsite.

It was nearly dark when he approached the *miamia* that he had made before he went away. It was made of thick bushes on top of a wooden frame tied to forked posts that he had cut with his *korcho* his stone axe. His home was about chest high, made in a circle, with enough room for him to lay in or for three or four people to sit in. The door was small with a kangaroo skin tied at the opening, to keep out the night air or the chilly cold of inclement weather.

Just as he approached his home he saw a small fire in front of the hut. As he entered he noticed by the firelight how tidy the inside looked. Bulmurn smiled. Only Lulura would have come over to make the fire in front of his camp and clean inside and outside the *miamia*. He walked out of his hut and looked for her, but could not see her.

The dawn had not long broken the night into daylight when Bulmurn awoke from a pleasant sleep. He stretched his body, coughed a couple of times. Then he stirred the live coals out of the fire ashes of his well-made campfire. He threw dried banksia wood on the live coals to rekindle the flames. Even though it would be hot later in the day, Bulmurn needed the warmth of the fire until such time as the day warmed up. Later he would eat. Then he would meet with Weejup and other tribal members to discuss all that had happened while he was away in the York area.

After the meeting he would meet with Jubuc about the health of the river mob and about tending the sick and ailing. After the two meetings, he would consult only the worst cases with Jubuc, who was Bulmurn's assistant. Jubuc's power was strong, but at this stage not as strong as Bulmurn's. Jubuc was a good Nyoongar healer who had done his work well when Bulmurn was away in York on his mission of mercy. Jubuc, in his own right, was a good healer, but he never dared to question or criticise any of the methods or ideas of Bulmurn. Everybody of the Mooro people of the Swan River area knew Bulmurn as an all-powerful man who could *murak* any would-be victim by 'singing' them or pointing the bone at them — an act that could result in death.

Stories were told of Bulmurn's prowess as a *Mobarn Boylla Gudjuk* by the Nyoongar people who had seen him change into shapes of birds, animals and solid objects. Yes, it was true: they believed he could make any change at will.

Such was Bulmurn's power, he was fast becoming a living legend amongst his people. They feared him and were in awe of what they thought he could do. Amongst the river people it was rumoured that often Bulmurn changed into *wardang,* the crow. They also claimed that he could change himself into *balga*, the grass tree that grew around the Swan River in abundance, or into black stumps, also plentiful in the area. The Nyoongar people argued that Bulmurn could turn himself into *minga*, the black ant, as well. Some argued that there was no limit to Bulmurn's power.

Such discussion about Bulmurn's ability to change form always ended up with tribal members agreeing that Bulmurn seemed to favour changing into *wardang*, the crow. Nearly all the Nyoongar river people agreed that the *wardang* was his best camouflage. So whenever members of the Mooro saw a crow near their home, they were very careful of what they said and did. Each person was very cautious because they could not be sure if it was truly Bulmurn or *wardang* the crow near their *miamia*. Somebody always plucked up enough courage to call out to Bulmurn or go to see or hear where Bulmurn was. If Bulmurn didn't answer, the people kept out of sight of the crow or cautiously watched the bird suspected of being the healer.

If Bulmurn answered back to them or he appeared before them, showing himself to them, showing them the crow was not him, they would breathe a sigh of relief. Then out would come their *keitj*, the barbed spear, or the *kylie* boomerang, the curved throwing stick. The weapon would be thrown at the scavenging black crow. When challenged, the scavenger crow would fly away in great haste.

Bulmurn, Jubuc and others in the tribe were thought to be able to 'sing' and point the bone when requested, and if a request was about correcting a wrong through this mode of punishment, then it was done. Great respect was given to those people who the tribe thought could point the bone. People even avoided looking at such people. They made as little contact as possible, only going near the person if they needed their magical healing powers or their medical knowledge.

Bone-pointing and 'singing' was usually done at night. In a secluded place only the accuser and the *Mobarn Boylla Gudjuk* met to point the bone. The bone usually used was minute and shaped like the head of a barbed spear. It was nearly always fatal. Once the bone was thrown, it would need only to hit any part of the body to become a deadly missile. On piercing the body, it would enter the blood stream and travel to the heart or the brain. When the bone reached either of these organs, it would explode, killing the victim instantly.

The travelling of the bone in the body determined the length of time it took to kill the victim. If the bone travelled fast, the victim had a fast death. But the bone was nearly always designed to travel slowly. If it travelled slowly, the victim would go into a trance followed by a slow, agonising death. He or she became something like a sagging, sick plant without nutrients or sustenance. Nausea, vomiting and starvation followed. The body withered, and the victim lost the will to live.

The victim, as well as relatives, even the whole tribe, would know this act had been done and were usually powerless to do anything to remove the curse of the bone. However, if anyone knew who it was or suspected the identity of the person who had performed the deed, then revenge could be sought by having the bone in turn pointed at that person.

However, usually when the bone was pointed most of the family of the victim accepted it because the victim was known to have broken a sacred law. Every precaution was taken to have the identity of the singer or bone pointer kept secret, just as the act was done in secret, and with grave responsibility. So the *Boylla Gudjuk* was the enforcer needed against offenders to keep them from breaking their traditional laws.

When a man wanted his young given woman to come to him or to his home as a wife, he would sing the woman. The singing was usually done when the female was unwilling, or was too immature to realise that she had a certain role to fulfill to make sure the tribe kept growing. If the female kept resisting her lamenting suitor's singing or advances, then action would be taken against her. The suitor would approach and ask Bulmurn or Jubuc for help. They would be asked to take over the singing because of their position as *Boylla Gudjuk*. They would be asked to use their magic powers to sing the woman because usually the man who asked them didn't have any power himself.

When the *Boylla Gudjuk Mobarn Mamarup* took over he would send the suitor home telling him not to worry. Then the magic man would chant and sing over a small fire. He would lean towards the fire as he sang so that the heat waves could carry the message of love of the suitor to the woman, persuading her to join him at his home.

As he sang into the fire, the *Mobarn Mamarup* would look into the flames picturing the image of the woman's face and mind, so that she could see her anxious suitor waiting for her at his *miamia*. He kept repeating his singing, humming his message into her mind. He would keep singing and chanting until he felt her resistance give way so that she would become filled with the feeling of want for her given man. She would become filled with the feeling that she must go to his *kullark miamia* to share his home with him and with his other wives.

An initiated man could have as many as three wives. Sometimes a man's death could mean the passing of his wife onto his elder or another brother. The wife would thus be able to keep a position of status within the tribal group; also she would be protected from other men and other jealous women in the tribe. It was an accepted law in the tribe that she should do this. Usually nobody objected; it was done so that there were no single women in a tribal situation, as single women could be the cause of conflict amongst the men. A single woman could cause trouble within marriages. Drastic measures could be taken against her or any married man who sought her favours and was found out.

However, sometimes a given woman who kept on rejecting the man to whom she had been given, would become a victim herself for not accepting the role she was expected to perform within the tribal structure. It showed that the woman wasn't prepared to accept her full responsibility, and as a consequence, could be made to pay the supreme sacrifice, which could only end in death by bone-pointing.

The only persons who could remove the curse of the pointed bone were the people who had strong powers to do this. People such as Bulmurn and Jubuc had this power. Sometimes other *Mobarn* men of other tribes who lived nearby could be approached, but this was seldom done because of the friction it could cause between the law men of each tribe. This in turn could cause inter-tribal conflict, feuding amongst the people concerned, which in turn could cause a full-scale battle.

After Bulmurn had had his meeting with the Council of Elders, he met with Jubuc to hold council about the health matters of the Swan River people. Both Bulmurn and Jubuc decided they would see any sick people who needed treatment. Soon the word spread that the tribal doctors were available to anyone who needed their help.

Sick children were seen first. A concoction of herbs mixed with cold water was used to cool down and ease the pain of burns that were caused by sleeping too close to the campfires or by treading onto hot coals of dying campfires. Bulmurn also treated cuts, and if the incision of the cut was deep, he then used clean ashes from the campfires to fill the wound. By filling the wound with clean ashes, infection was prevented and when the wound healed, it would leave a much admired scar on the body.

If a headache developed, the head was very tightly wrapped with dried flexible strips of animal skin several times around the forehead area to relieve the pain.

When babies were sick, Bulmurn encouraged mothers to give milk from their breasts. Mother's milk was used to cure earaches, also inflamed, sore eyes.

Sometimes just the touch of Bulmurn's hand was enough to cure his people's aches and pains. If a patient's sickness was internal, Bulmurn would massage the area that caused the most pain. He soothed the patient with words of kindness while rubbing the infected area to draw out the evil within the body of the sick person, preparing the patient for an operation.

Bulmurn would massage and knead the infected area most gently until the infection was near the surface, then he would suck the evil out of the body, filling his mouth. He would spit out the *badjang*, yellow pus and blood, spitting it into a *coolamon*, which was always nearby to be used for such a purpose during an operation.

Bulmurn could do this without breaking the skin. When he performed such an operation, he usually took out all the evil illness that was within the body of the ailing person. An operation like this always brought out the best in him. During the treatment, all the people would be tense, most expecting the worst. But they need not have any fear of Bulmurn failing because he was an expert healer, and with a helper like Jubuc, Bulmurn could hardly go wrong and lose a patient. So far, Bulmurn had never lost a patient, young or old.

Each time Bulmurn carried out an operation, his fame spread amongst the river people and into outlying areas, north and south and east over into the mountain areas. Nyoongar people from other groups, the Beelu, the Beeliar, like the Mooro, belonged to the Swan River groups. The Moorara and Wailabinje people belonged to the north. The Dowerin and Balladong people were the mountain people that lived in amongst the Murrn Morda, the Darling Range, out in the eastern areas of Toodyay, Northam and York. Tales of Bulmurn's healing were spreading everywhere. It seemed everybody wanted him to use his magic cures on them.

Things had quietened down since Bulmurn returned to his beloved river people, the Mooro. Tonight, however, there was excitement, and all around the campsite, people were moving towards the clearing where big fires burned. The clearing was comfortable enough to seat all the people as well as have enough room for dancers to perform a traditional corroboree, tonight in Bulmurn's honour.

Only he would be honoured. He would be officially given Lulura; tonight she would be his, tonight he would be able to carry her to his *miamia*. She would be his until he or she died. Only he could cast her out of his camp unwanted, she could not choose to do this. If she did she would die, for rejecting the role. She would belong to him as long as they lived.

These dance nights were very special to any tribal groups of this country. As each dance was performed in the corroboree, a message of the important event unfolded. The story of the event was learned through the dance so that the traditional significance was passed on to the younger members of the tribe. The story was retold and retold. Each corroboree was an important way of passing on tribal folklore.

Bulmurn looked around and marvelled at his people. In his heart he was proud. Tonight was a family corroboree. Husbands, wives and children sat in their family groups waiting for the dancers to emerge. Almost everybody was painted with white, red and yellow ochre especially for the night. The firelight played tricks on the eyes illuminating the lines painted on their bodies, making them look very colourful in the flickering of the flames. Tonight, thought Bulmurn, was indeed going to be a special night. Yes, a very special night.

Old Weejup and Old Yumbun, the two distinct tribal elders, sat each side of Bulmurn. Like other members of the tribe, like himself, the elders wore ceremonial *wilgee* ochre.

The whole group suddenly went quiet as the *inji* ceremonial dancing sticks began to click together with the slapping sound of the *kylie* throwing stick, that was also used as a musical instrument. Then a group of singers joined the musicians and sat themselves along one side of them. After they had seated themselves they joined the music in song. Their droning voices combined with the clicking and slapping of the dance sticks to introduce the dancers.

All of a sudden the dancers are there among them. They begin the *Kaabo* dance, about a planned kangaroo hunt by a group of warriors, hunting *yonga*, the western grey kangaroo.

As the dancers begin the story of the kangaroo hunt, their bodies sway to and fro, to the left and to the right. The hunters pause in mid-stride, looking ahead, looking to the left and to the right, following the tracks made by the *yonga*. The hunters step lively here and there, stepping around obstacles, then they slow down as they come upon an area where the roos are feeding. Other dancers are acting as roos in the area, feeding on lush green grass. The hunters move off to prepare an ambush to kill the animals.

All eyes are on the hunters as they dance off to the far side of the fire. The trap is set and is ready to be sprung by two hunters who are left behind. The two hunters step out. Then they throw their spears and step into the light. The hunters shout after they have thrown their spears. One of the singers makes the thumping noise of a spear impaling the body of a kangaroo. Then the dancers pause, silenced, only their swaying bodies moving to a quieter chanting of the singers and the clocking and clapping of the dance sticks.

The two hunters point and shout as the wounded animal hops with other kangaroos towards the trap set by the other hunters who are waiting to ambush the fleeing animals. The trap is sprung, other roos topple over as they are speared; they fall dead. Then all goes quiet again because the only roo left is the wounded one with a spear sticking out of its side. It sees the ambush and tries in vain to flee to safety. Then a signal is given by a loud clap of the clicking dance sticks. One of the singers makes a sound of a reverberating killer boomerang in flight as it sails through the air and hits with a resultant thump, killing the roo.

The instruments click and clap louder again. The singers join in. All the dancers bunch together now, dancing at a brisk pace. They throw their bodies high into the air. They step high until a crescendo of excitement is reached before the finale. The dancers slow and move apart. One of the dancers carries the real body of a dead roo past them, and places it into the fire where Bulmurn is seated.

Quickly and quietly, Lulura is at his side. His heart misses a beat as he looks at her. He sees excitement in her eyes as she smiles back at him. He sees Weejup and Minyon smiling at him. Bulmurn knows by these gestures that he has been honoured. Then Bulmurn stands. Everybody else stands and stops still. They all look at him. There's a great tension in the air. All his people are watching. They all wonder if he'll accept their dance. Bulmurn looks around at the faces of all his people; he can read in their faces that they are happy for him. Then Bulmurn raises his two hands in the air. He smiles and, as he smiles, they smile. Then they all shout out as one: 'Bulmurn! Bulmurn! Bulmurn!'.

*   *   *   *   *   *   *   *   *

The celebration dance was over, the roo feast was over. People began to disperse and head back to their *miamias*, all chattering merrily on their way. Children cried to be carried to their homes. Some were carried, the unlucky ones had to walk.

Left alone, Bulmurn's hand found Lulura's. He looked at her, and she looked at him and they kissed long and passionately. They pulled apart. Then he picked her up in his arms as if she was an emu feather and carried her to his *miamia*.

They kissed as he carried her to their home. Once inside the hut he lowered her gently onto the bed. Tenderly he kissed her all over her body, until his lips found hers again. Eagerly her tongue found his. Lulura's hands were on his body urging him to cover her. He knew this would be her first time. He would try to be gentle if he could.

Then almost as if by magic he was on her, searching to enter her. When he found her, he probed her willing softness. Lulura moaned and cried. At first Bulmurn was gentle and slow then he stirred as Lulura rose under him to meet him. He called her name; she called his in their own special dance. Then they peaked together, their love for each other spilling into their very souls. Lulura was his. No more would she ever be a girl again. Lulura was a woman, his woman, his woman he would love forever.

Bulmurn Sees the Change

Bulmurn had been living with Lulura for some summers and even though they never had any children, this was no great concern to them because their affection for each other was strong. Both knew that there was time enough to have a family. Now wasn't the time. Right now they were enjoying each other's company and their relationship was good.

Lulura would go with other women and children gathering as many types of food as they could for their menfolk and to share with other tribal members. The men would go hunting *yonga* and other game animals. Everything was shared by them so that nobody starved or went without food. Such was the way of the river people.

Since Bulmurn's return and during the time he had been living with Lulura, a change had been taking place within the Mooro and other groups. Both Bulmurn and Lulura had noticed the changing bloodlines of their people, more mixed-blood children were now noticeable. It could not be hidden. The white man was a spreading weed that could not be stopped. He was sowing his seed everywhere into black ground. Bulmurn and Lulura knew that killing, jailing and raping was not beyond these *wadjbulla*. If they couldn't barter or trade for the river women, they just took them by force.

Bulmurn walked along the banks of the Derbal Yerigan with his wife, thinking of how the change had come about, how the story of the *wadjbulla's* arrival had been told and had to be passed on to future generations of the Nyoongar people. Bulmurn thought of the two stories about the coming of the *wadjbulla* and their invasion of the land. How they came down the Swan River in their big boats; how Yellagonga's mob, the Mooro people, had seen the big boats come to rest off the foreshore of Goomap, where the whites now had a jetty. The whites now called Goomap 'Perth'; how the Mooro warriors were in front of the women and children and had moved down to the foreshore where the whites had come ashore; how the Mooro watched them beach their small boats; how these strangers marched two abreast with what appeared to be a stick which they had laying on their right shoulder held by their right hand and arm; how the Mooro carried their traditional weapons, their *keitj*, and *kylies*; how the white man up front raised his hand for his men, calling out for them to halt. Then he ordered them into a firing position. How the Mooro had stopped in close proximity of the strange white beings and looked on in curiosity and puzzlement at these pale strangers, who wore many garments covering their bodies. They wore a *kartabuka* over their heads and strange big *genabuka* on their feet.

The Mooro had never seen anything like this before, they had never seen pale beings as close as this before in their lives. To the Mooro these were bad spirits of *jenark*, *jimbar* and *bulyut* all rolled up in one. A buzz of muttered agreement went through the Mooro people because already they felt an air of mistrust towards their unannounced visitors. The pale one up front who seemed to be their leader called out to his men to aim. The pale ones aimed their sticks at the Mooro people. Then the pale one in the lead called out, 'Fire!'.

The Mooro people had heard an almighty explosion. Flame and smoke followed the loud noise that sounded like thunder and lightning. And it seemed to come from the long sticks the *wadjbulla* pointed at them.

The Nyoongars were stunned at the noise of the thunderous

smoking long sticks the *wadjbulla* held, and alarmed as river people fell to the ground with mortal wounds to the head and body. Again the pale leader called out to his men. Again thunder sounded out of the long sticks the pale ones carried. Again more Mooro people fell to the ground either mortally wounded or injured.

This was too much for the Nyoongars; they were gripped with fear that they were smitten by magic, a magic they had never faced before. They fled to the high reaches of Kartigarrup, the place the *wadjbulla* named Mount Eliza and Kings Park, abandoning their homes in Goomap. Under cover of darkness, Murro, one of Yellagonga's warriors would lead a party back. Under cover of darkness, they would be able to carry their dead away for burial and help the wounded up to their camp in Kartigarrup. 'Yes', Bulmurn thought on, 'It's been told that nobody slept when *jidaluk* the night came. There was too much grief and sorrow. There was much wailing. There was sadness as the Mooro made a corroboree for the dead so that the dreamtime spirits would allow them to enter the dreamtime world.'

Bulmurn sat for a while. He looked at Lulura, admiring her. Even her beauty could not stop him from thinking about the *wadjbulla*, the white men who now had all but taken over the river area and were spreading further out.

Lulura could see that Bulmurn was troubled and was deep in thought. She did not say anything. She knew he would speak to her when he was ready. Bulmurn was thinking of the other story of the *wadjbulla's* arrival at Goomap — how the Mooro people saw the boats come up along the river water; how the strange pale men lowered smaller boats onto the water, then rowed to the shore.

The Mooro people had seen all this happening and had decided they should find out who was coming ashore on their land. Bulmurn thought on — how they came down to investigate; how the warriors led the women and children away. The Mooro warriors carried their spears and fighting boomerangs wherever they went. They had to, it was their only form of defence. Now it looked as if there was a threat and they would need their weapons. They headed towards what appeared to be an unavoidable confrontation.

The pale ones had now landed and were walking two abreast towards the river people. Closer, closer and closer they advanced; the distance narrowed to what looked like a looming battle between the two groups. Bulmurn thought on. The Mooro people were awe-struck at the appearance of the white people. They couldn't believe their eyes. They thought the strangers were the evil spirits Jenark, Jimbar mixed in with Bulyut, the frightening pale spirit. To the Mooro people here was a combination of the three spirits together in front of them in broad daylight. Scared as they may have been, the Nyoongars had courage. Murro, the Mooro people's best warrior shook his spear at the strangers. The people did the same.

The pale one who appeared to be the leader of the strangers raised his hand and said, 'Ready. Aim,' but at the last moment he said 'Hold your fire'. He looked at the Mooro then he looked up in the sky. He looked at a flock of black swans flying directly over the two groups of threatening people. Then he took the stick he was carrying on his shoulder and he aimed it at the birds.

All of a sudden there was a mighty explosion as the stick belched out smoke and fire. All the river people were struck in awe and amazement at what they had just seen. To them, *marlee* the swan carried in its body one of the spirits of their dead people from the spirit world of their Dreamtime people. Now it was dead, plucked out of the sky by the magic noise from the white man's thunderous stick which threw out thunder and lightning. The pale one's magic was indeed very strong. This magic they made was too strong for the Mooro. It was too frightening for the river people of Goomap. They fled the scene of confrontation, running away to hide in the sacred high rise of Kartigarrup.

'Yes', Bulmurn thought to himself, 'I have considered the two versions of the landing of the unscrupulous white man. That landing has been passed down in story by our old people. Now all the land that the *wadjbulla* has camped on he has renamed with a white man's name. Even the Derbal Yerigan is now called the Swan River. Goomap is now called Perth. Kartigarrup is now called Mount Eliza and Kings Park. Now no more do my people, the black people, own the river area. The *wadjbulla*, he got it all.' Bulmurn thought bitterly, 'I know which story I believe . . . I know in my mind . . . I know also in my heart the true one . . . Yes I know.' He said out loud, 'I know'.

Bulmurn knew the river people of the Mooro, Beeliar and Beelu who shared the waterway and land around the river. The three tribes had all been affected by the white man's hunger for land. The river people had tried hard to keep the invaders at bay, attacking in small groups.

But the *wadjbulla's widji bandi*, the thunderous firestick they had, made them a powerful foe. Despite the bravery shown by his people, they were always beaten back or killed. Some of them were hunted and shot. Some campsites were burned to the ground. Nyoongars were massacred for any kind of resistance. Bulmurn thought: 'My people are being pushed further and further off their tribal lands. The *wadjbulla* has taken land from Mokare and the Bibulmun people of the deep south where all the tall karri trees grow, and from other Nyoongars at Nannup, Wannerup, Malalyup — everywhere.'

Bulmurn thought of the other tribes to the north: how the *wadjbulla* came to the Derbal Yerigan area where they first took over the Mooro land, Yellagonga's country, which the Mooro controlled from Walyalup to Goomap, up the coast and inland to link up with the Moorara people and the Wailabinje people, the neighbours of the Mooraras near Mogumber. Both tribes lived north around what the white people called the Moore River area.

The Beelu tribe lived south of the Swan River and were led by Mundy. The Beelu people were a neighbouring tribe to the southern tribe, the Kalyute. The Kalyute lived in the Pinjarra and Mandurah region. The Beeliar lived further south on the branch of the Swan River, known as the Canning River, on the southern side right down to Walyalup, which the settlers named Fremantle.

Bulmurn thought on: 'Now this invasion is spreading further inland over the Darling Range, into other areas in the interior. The whites are greedy. They have no respect for our territory. Nobody from the white settlers, particularly Governor Stirling, was prepared to talk with the Swan River Nyoongar elders. No treaties were ever made or sought by these strange pale people. They had no respect for Aboriginal ownership of the land. They just squatted. They took possession of any land wherever they wanted, as they pleased. If the Nyoongar people ever complained or showed displeasure or any resistance, they were seen as troublemakers. They were chased and were either shot or jailed over on Rottnest, the blackman's jail on Wagemup. Yes', Bulmurn said aloud, 'we have tribal boundaries on our land. We, the Darbalyung people, respect our boundaries, but the *wadjbulla* don't.'

Lulura walked over to Bulmurn and put her arm through his: 'What troubles you, my husband? You seem to be angry. It is not like you to be troubled. I know you as a good and gentle man, a strong man. Will it help to tell me what worries you?'

Bulmurn squeezed Lulura's arm and hand in his. Then he looked at her, looked into her eyes. 'You know just as much as I do of the changes that are occurring to all our people wherever they go.'

Lulura answered, 'Yes, I know of the changes that they have caused to our land and our people. I fear that they will keep on pushing us further and further away from our river fishing and hunting lands.'

'It has already happened', said Bulmurn. 'You and I know, because we have seen the *wadjbulla* walk around the Nyoongar *miamia* during the day. Sometimes they are like bees around a honey pot, bartering for young women, who they return for under the cover of darkness, for their pleasure'.

'They barter with food, clothing, jewellery. If they don't succeed with these things, then they use tobacco, rum and gin to trade with the men for their women, to allow their women to go with them. Yes. The *wadjbulla* always make sure that the Nyoongar males have their fill of the mind-boggling liquor so that their time used in copulating with the women is extended for as long as possible.

'You know, Lulura', Bulmurn said, 'this is why our people are developing an unquenchable thirst for rum and for gin. They use many ways to gain the services of our black women, whether it is by force or by liquor. Sometimes the *wadjbulla* just take the women away from the men under the threat of the power of their guns. No Nyoongar man can resist. Those that do resist find themselves hunted and their homes burnt to the ground. Our river people face being massacred, destroyed by the *wadjbulla* .

'Our people are being jailed for spearing the *wadjbulla 's* sheep or cattle or other livestock. Some are shot or removed if there is the slightest hint that they are in the way or they represent some sort of danger to the farmers or their families. Sometimes we complain but the killers are never arrested or found guilty by the troopers.'

All this Bulmurn hated. He saw the likeness of the white men in the mixed-blood children the black river women were now raising. In the same children, he saw the image of his people, the Mooro river people. 'I see an evil in this white side which is causing great harm to our people', he said to Lulura.

Everyday now Bulmurn was treating men, women and children of mixed blood. Even some of Bulmurn's family were of mixed blood. Some of the women were ashamed of their children's colour, while other women were not ashamed of their colourful offspring. They realised that what happened to them was not of their own choosing, therefore it made their situation easier to accept.

The white man's law and the black man's law clashed repeatedly, both parties ignorant of how the other law worked. The Nyoongar people were hunters and gathers, not tillers of the land. Often when the Nyoongar people saw the settlers' stock, they saw the animals as part of the food chain that belonged to them, so they killed the beasts whenever they needed food. But when the Nyoongar people did this, the white man's law prevailed over theirs. Always they were hunted down to face the new law they did not understand. They were always found guilty.

They were sent to the jail for Aborigines on Wagemup, Rottnest Island, the island jail known as the Quad.

Rottnest Island was the black man's jail. This was where they were sent for punishment, no matter whether the offence was large or small. The Nyoongar men feared Rottnest because when they entered the Quad, they entered the Jenark's *miamia*, the home of the evil spirit. Once in there, very few ever returned to their families or homes on the mainland.

The Nyoongar men feared Rottnest because of the atrocious conditions set by the jailers. The weather conditions contributed to their deaths. Others died in the sea trying to escape from Rottnest. These men who faced the sea either drowned or were eaten by sharks. While they were trying to escape, they ran the risk of being shot by the island's authorities. Very few prisoners escaped from the Quad. Very few escaped and lived to tell the tale.

The jailing of Nyoongar men served a twofold purpose for the *wadjbulla* within the growing colony of Perth, Fremantle and outlying areas. The white authorities knew that imprisoning the Nyoongars would keep the peace and protect many settlers, colonists and convicts alike.

Because of the influx to the colony of male convicts, men far outnumbered women in the settlements. So, the authorities turned a blind eye to the treatment meted out as punishment for the black men. The authorities knew that some of the charges laid against the black offenders would hardly stand up in court. Nevertheless the offending black man would nearly always be jailed on Rottnest Island, out of the way of the white men.

The authorities never fined the black offenders because they had no money to pay fines, a fact that didn't escape the notice of Bulmurn. 'But the real reason those *wadjbulla* jail my people', Bulmurn thought, 'is because they find out that Nyoongar men each nearly always have two women, some of us have three women.

'When the *wadjbulla* jail our men on Rottnest Island, he knows our women have no man at home. Then the white man comes and takes the woman, too. They say that she's got to go to jail, too, or she has got to work for the boss's Missus as a domestic. When the woman returns she is always heavy with the child of the Missus' boss.

'Yes', Bulmurn thought, 'that's the reason why they jail our men, so they can take our women. The more Nyoongar men are in jail, the more Nyoongar women are there for them to use. White seed is going into black ground all the time now.'

The Challenge

Jubuc, the other Nyoongar doctor, was a fairly tall man. He was not as tall as Bulmurn, but nevertheless, his height was good. He had a similar wiry build, like that of many of the Nyoongar men in the Swan River area.

One morning Bulmurn was approached by his first cousin. Her name was Myan. Myan wanted Bulmurn or Jubuc to treat her son, Marjuk, because he was ill. Myan told Bulmurn and Jubuc that Marjuk had eaten some bad plant which he had mistaken for a good plant, and it had made him ill with fever. She had tried her best to cure him with the remedies she had learned from her own mother to cure her children. She told them that try as she might, her cures had not worked, and she was concerned about his condition because now he was very ill and in much pain. Myan feared that unless he was treated with something stronger than the poison, he would die.

Bulmurn looked at Jubuc and then back at Myan. Then he said to her, 'Myan, Jubuc and I will go with you to see what we can do for your son Marjuk. We will do our best to save him. Lead the way Myan, daughter of my father's brother, and we will try to cure your sick son.'

Myan led the way to her *miamia*. She pointed to the doorway of the bush hut, beckoning them to enter into her home where the ailing Marjuk lay. Bulmurn pulled aside the kangaroo skin *buka* that was used as a door to seal the hut. They entered one by one and saw the ill Marjuk writhing in great pain. Bulmurn looked at Myan and told her to stand out of the way while he and Jubuc tried to cure Marjuk.

Bulmurn could feel the evil forces in the room trying to hold him back so he couldn't treat the ill-stricken Marjuk. As Bulmurn approached the sick youth, his image changed to Bulmurn *Boylla Gudjuk*. The doctor would need all the powers of his *mobarn*, his magic powers, to heal Marjuk, or the youth would surely die.

Bulmurn looked at Jubuc, and saw in his eyes and the nod of his head that he was ready to help him try to heal the boy. The two medicine men would work together. It would take all their power and skill to cure Marjuk, as the poisonous plant which Marjuk had eaten the day before had somehow provoked a previous illness. It had weakened an area in his stomach causing him great pain. Now an internal sore had developed. They would have to remove it. Bulmurn looked at the young man lying, covered by a *waral*, a rug made from a kangaroo skin. The boy was of mixed blood.

Bulmurn thought of his Nyoongar culture and cursed under his breath, '*Muyung*. This half-white relation of mine needs me to save his life.' He lifted the skin rug from the body of the youth and the escaping heat was like some evil force trying to push him away so he could not help Marjuk. But Bulmurn was calm. He looked at Jubuc with confidence.

Bulmurn cast aside the *waral* from Marjuk so he could begin to cool his body down. As he did this, Jubuc began to chant over a small fire he had built at the door of the *miamia*. Bulmurn nodded his approval. Jubuc sang over the fire to drive away any evil spirit lurking around Myan's home waiting to capture the spirit of Marjuk, and so kill him. The evil spirit could not do this if it could not get into the room to take his spirit out of the hut.

The Nyoongar doctor put his ebony hands on the boy's body. As he did so he noticed how pale was the boy's skin compared to his own colour, something he had not noticed before when treating other mixed-blood people of his tribe. It was as if his eyes were opened for the first time. Now he noticed the difference, and he didn't like what he saw. A feeling of hatred overtook him, welling up inside his body. Bulmurn realised how much he did hate the *wadjbulla* for what they were doing to his people, how they were changing the colour of his race.

All of a sudden a passion of hatred for Marjuk filled Bulmurn, his body shook with rage. Here before him was a part-white man and now, Bulmurn thought, 'I am trying to save his life, a life that could mean so much in the way of destruction to our culture and personal disharmony to my Nyoongar people'.

Bulmurn paused as these thoughts passed through his mind. Then he heard himself say in a low voice, 'I must cast these bad thoughts out of my mind and do what I have to do to help Marjuk. Am I not a traditional healer? I must help him to survive. For if I do not, then I will be as guilty of killing a helpless Nyoongar as one of the whites.'

Bulmurn's kindness overruled his bad thoughts, so with a clear conscience, he applied his healing skills to save Marjuk. Bulmurn looked at his father's brother's daughter Myan, who had just come into the room to check, as if she was suspicious of Bulmurn. Again Bulmurn's mind began to turn from good to bad, and he decided that he would help Marjuk, but he would not remove all the evil that was poisoning the boy. He convinced himself that it might be a good lesson in the values of life if the youth had to overcome some of the illness himself.

Jubuc sensed there was something wrong with Bulmurn and asked if he could help. Bulmurn's answer to Jubuc was just a shake of his head. He then spoke, saying he was all right, and that he would cure Marjuk as soon as he could. Again Bulmurn placed his hands on Marjuk's hot body, gently feeling the affected parts, probing the region with experienced fingers. Then his fingers began to go deeper, kneading the flesh, forming it into a lump. Bulmurn put his mouth to the lump he held between his fingers and began to suck. When his mouth was full, he spat out the *badjang.*

Bulmurn treated the infected area four times, first using his hands and fingers, bringing the area to a lump again, then sucking the lump and spitting out the evil. Each time he did this the lump became smaller. One more treatment this way would cleanse the area. But Bulmurn didn't carry through the last treatment. He left a small portion of evil in the infected area. Bulmurn looked at Myan and Jubuc, then said to them, 'I've done all I can for the boy'. Bulmurn failed to tell them that he had withheld his finest effort, allowing some of the poison to remain in Marjuk's body.

Bulmurn expected that the remaining evil in Marjuk's body would kill him. His reasoning for leaving it was to preserve the Nyoongar culture. It would be a way of teaching them to deal with the problem, to hate the *wadjbulla*. 'Yes', Bulmurn thought, 'the best way is to hate'.

Bulmurn burned with intensity as he fought his conscience, guilt for the boy and the issue of white versus black survival; how the white man was creating mixed-blood children more than the Nyoongar man was creating full-blood children. Bulmurn also knew that once a coloured offspring was born, the *wadjbulla* father would never claim it as his own. 'No', thought Bulmurn, 'they could never be found responsible, let alone be identified, as the fathers'.

There was great sorrow amongst the Darbalyung people. Marjuk lived only a further six days after he had received the treatment from Bulmurn and Jubuc. Marjuk had shown signs of recovery, but unfortunately, his condition deteriorated.

Within a short time of Marjuk's death, a *bokgal* was dug in which his body would be buried. His *bokgal* was dug by his closest male relatives. While the grave was being prepared, Myan, Marjuk's mother, was joined by other women, her next-of-kin, her close relations, who would comfort her.

The ceremony began as Marjuk's body was carried to the *bokgal* for burial. Myan and the other women were shrieking, wailing and crying out as Marjuk's body was wrapped in a kangaroo skin *buka*. It would then be placed for burial into a grave just over a metre deep.

The Aboriginal custom was, as with all other Swan River people, to dig the grave in an east-west direction so that when the body was placed in the grave, it was positioned in a slightly half-sitting position with the head facing the east. This was done so that the spirit of the dead could see the dawn on the morning following the burial. If the spirit was placed in an angled sitting position, it would see the new dawn's rays of light, and so be transported by the light into the spirit world of the Dreamtime.

When the body was placed in the grave, the male relatives then would begin to bury the feet and head with sand. Boughs of trees especially cut for the ceremony would be placed across the body. Then more dirt would be added, and more boughs. This would be done repeatedly until the grave was filled in to ground level. This preparation was called *Bokgal D Yuar*. Following this a mound would be made the length and width of the grave.

Whilst the ceremony was being conducted, it was Jubuc who took Bulmurn's place to carry out the final act of the ritual. It was Jubuc who took the role of the *Boylla Gudjuk* to sing and chant. Then Jubuc stopped and put his ear on the mound of the grave. All the mourners became quiet. They listened, too, while they awaited Jubuc's signal that all was well. Jubuc listened to make sure the spirit was in the grave, in the right position and awaiting the next dawn for the flight into the Dreamtime.

When Jubuc was sure that the spirit was in the right position and was content, he leaped high in the air in approval, therefore letting the mourners know that they need not worry. They need not worry anymore. Marjuk's spirit was ready to achieve the ultimate, to enter into the spirit world of the Dreamtime.

When this was done, the graveside ritual came to a close. The only thing left to do was to take Myan and her family away from the *Bokgal D Yuar* with the comfort that everything possible had been done for Marjuk. They had to relocate the camp so that if for some reason the spirit didn't go into the Dreamtime, it would not be able to find the new camp and haunt the tribe.

The following months seemed to be mixed with death and consequent moves to new locations in the vicinity of Mandoon.

Most of the people who had died were of mixed blood, but now full-blood men and women began to die as well.

When a death occurred and burial rites were performed, a marker was made so that the loved ones and other people would respect the area, see it as sacred to the Nyoongar people and not desecrate or defile it. If respect was not shown it could mean that the person or persons who desecrated the area could be cursed with haunting by the spirits of the dead. It could also mean bad luck to those people and their families. Personal belongings were sometimes buried with the deceased or burnt, and sometimes a totem of carved markings was erected or a column of stones was used to mark the sacred place and to indicate its importance.

* * * * * * * *

It was during these times of death that Jubuc began to realise that Bulmurn had been deliberately mistreating patients who had been in contact with the white settlers. Jubuc, a *Mobarn Mamarup* himself, had to challenge for the truth. Jubuc had already spoken to a full Council of Elders regarding his suspicions. After they had heard Jubuc speak, they had a discussion among themselves, then a decision was made. Weejup, their spokesman, said to Jubuc, 'Jubuc, we have all agreed there is something in what you say. It will be your duty to summon Bulmurn to appear before us and face the Council of Elders for judgement to be made of him and of his future in our tribe. He must be brought before us at first light tomorrow and the truth can be known.'

Jubuc rose early after a sleepless night. As he lay in his hut that night, he had thought of ways to confront the powerful traditional healer, Bulmurn.

Jubuc knew the strength of the power Bulmurn possessed. He had seen Bulmurn use it on many occasions and that's what worried him. He knew that Bulmurn, if angered, could cause much more pain and more deaths in the Nyoongar tribe if he so desired. Jubuc knew that once he challenged Bulmurn, Bulmurn could easily kill him through his powerful magic.

Jubuc hoped that he could talk to the powerful man without any kind of confrontation of physical or spiritual force. 'Not that I'm afraid', Jubuc thought. 'All I have to do is to deliver the Council of Elders' order for Bulmurn to appear before them.'

Then Jubuc thought back over past events that made him suspicious of Bulmurn mistreating the ill Nyoongar people. They seemed to get better, but their recovery only lasted a few days. Then their condition gave out. They deteriorated into death.

Jubuc also noted Bulmurn's reaction to his people's changing bloodlines. Jubuc was sure Bulmurn was not removing all the evil curse and infections from the patients' bodies, so that pain and sickness redeveloped.

While Jubuc had come to terms with the changing of the bloodlines among their people, Jubuc sensed Bulmurn could not. Jubuc believed and accepted that the mixed-blood people were still his people. The fact was that the mixed-blood people still had to obey the tribal laws.

The mixed bloods, too, had to hunt and gather food for the Mooro people. They, too, had to teach their children the Law and they too had to learn how to survive the heat of the summers and the biting cold winters. 'Just as we have all done', Jubuc reasoned to himself.

'Today', Jubuc thought, 'I must tell Bulmurn that he has to face the Council of Elders, including myself, so that we can make a judgement of him. Then we must decide what we should do with him or to him.'

Though Jubuc was worried about the outcome, he had learned to admire and respect Bulmurn. Jubuc also kept him in high esteem as a man and friend. 'No matter what decision is made, he will still be respected by me.'

As Jubuc approached Bulmurn's *miamia*, he called out, 'Bulmurn, it's me, Jubuc. I need to see you. I need to talk to you. It is of great importance.' Jubuc stood a few paces away from the door of Bulmurn's *miamia* waiting for him to appear. Jubuc waited for what seemed an eternity, but breathed a sigh of relief as Bulmurn drew aside the *waral*, to emerge from the hut. Bulmurn stood tall in front of Jubuc and looked Jubuc straight in the eye. Then he said, 'Jubuc, I knew you would come here to seek me out, to talk to me. Last night in my sleep, I dreamed I could see you standing, talking, holding council with Weejup and the other elders, to speak to me. In my dream, I could see the others seated with you standing before them. You were pointing my way. You were speaking to them about me. I saw you talking to Weejup, Yumbun, Murro, Dokun and others of the Council whose faces I could not see. I saw you stepping this way and that', Bulmurn said.

Bulmurn moved his eyes to the left, then to the right, indicating the way he thought Jubuc had moved. Bulmurn continued to talk to Jubuc about what he had dreamed: 'But I could not hear what you said about me. Now, you Jubuc, will tell me about the meeting. Then I will know.'

Jubuc was aghast at the powers of this man. He thought of his request of the elders to meet in secret. To do this, they had to make sure Bulmurn would not know or hear of their meeting. So it was decided that Weejup would ask Bulmurn to take a group of young boys out in the bush to teach them the art of tracking and spearing *yonga*.

Then Bulmurn's voice boomed out as he spoke to Jubuc: 'Speak. Speak, Jubuc. Tell me it all.'

Jubuc looked Bulmurn straight in the eyes, saying, 'Yes. It's true. Your dream is true. I have met in secret with the Council of Elders of our people. While you were teaching the young boys the skills of tracking and hunting, I met the elders about you. I have spoken to them about the treatments you have been giving our people. Now I have been requested by the elders to ask you to appear before them for judgement to be made of you.'

To Jubuc's relief, Bulmurn agreed. 'I will come with you, Jubuc, to face the Council of Elders.' Then they walked to where the Council of Elders sat waiting to judge Bulmurn.

The Trial

The Council of Elders sat in a circle, Weejup and Kalamund in the middle flanked by the others. It was Weejup who spoke first. 'The reason we have summoned you to appear before us is very serious. I will ask Jubuc to tell you of our suspicions. You can then have your say, and we will make judgment of you.'

Standing in front of the circle, Jubuc said, 'As you know, I, too, am a *Boylla Gudjuk*. I have powers similar to yours. I have begun to realise that your healing is not as good as it has been and many of our people who have had illnesses have died. First, our people of mixed-blood were let die, then the women who had borne mixed-blood children. Then you neglected the men who had bartered their children or women for a flagon of rum. Even though we cannot prove you killed them, many of our people have died. So now, our people fear you. We think you are trying to keep our bloodlines the same as before, with our kinship intact, so that we can safeguard our traditions, and face the *wadjbulla* as strong people.'

Jubuc spoke on. 'We now have many mixed-blood people in our Mooro group. We cannot change this. We may never go back to what we were. We may have to change laws to prevent more deaths of our mixed-blood people. Most of our people accept the pale babies. We believe they are still our own people.'

Jubuc looked at Bulmurn and back to the Council of Elders, then said, 'I have said my piece'. He then took his position in the semi-circle of the Council.

Weejup looked at Bulmurn and said, 'Now, Bulmurn, you have heard Jubuc. What do you say in your defence?'

Bulmurn looked around the tribal elders; they were sitting at ease in a crossed-leg position. Sitting this way showed that they were not uneasy or worried about the present situation, nor were they afraid of Bulmurn.

Bulmurn looked around them, then he looked into the eyes of all the elders seated before him. Again he paused, his eyes over them, showing no emotion or guilt. Then after what seemed a long time, Bulmurn spoke to them.

'I will admit nothing about killing any one of our people, including our mixed-blood people. Obviously in the eyes of some of my people I am guilty of such acts, but only I know if I am or not. I will say one thing though, my Mooro people have always come first for me.'

Then Bulmurn shouted, 'If I am guilty or not guilty, let the spirits of the Dreamtime decide'.

'You are right', Weejup said. 'Let the spirits of the Dreamtime decide your fate. Today you must face ten of our best warriors who will be hand picked to throw one spear at you. They will be our best spearmen. Some of these spearmen are related to the people who have died and I know some of them would hold you responsible. I, too, have heard the rumours, so I know they will hold nothing back. They will want to spear you to prove that you are guilty beyond any shadow of doubt. In the spear throwing ceremony, you will be able to use your own shield. If you succeed in parrying each spear, then we will know that you are not guilty.

'However, if you fail and are hit by a spear, you will not be killed, but only wounded. Then another ten spears will be thrown at you.

'If you are hit again, the spear throwing will continue until you are dead. However, if you escape the first round of spears, you will be banished from the Mooro. Some of our people mistrust you.

'Only the Council of Elders can decide if you can come back here to live ever again.' Weejup did not have to look around him. He knew every member of the council agreed with the decision he had just made.

Weejup's heart was heavy. Bulmurn was his son-in-law, the given man of his daughter Lulura. What would his daughter say? Nevertheless, he was the leading elder. It was his duty to be fair and just, otherwise nobody would respect the Law. Weejup knew the decision would hurt Lulura, but it had to be done. He would tell her of the judgement, somehow, before Bulmurn faced the ten best spearmen.

Two warriors walked each side of Bulmurn to a clearing near the Nyoongar people's campsite, where the trial of spears would be held. He would be guarded by them until it was time to face the ten spearmen. Weejup and the Council of Elders picked the ten warriors to throw the spears in the ceremony.

The scene was set for the trial of spears to begin. Soon, the spirits of the Dreamtime would decide if Bulmurn lived or died. If Bulmurn did win the trial of spears contest, however, he still lost because he faced banishment.

Weejup had made time to talk to Lulura and Minyon about the council's decision to test Bulmurn. 'You know I had to hand down the decision of the Council of Elders. It was not one reached easily. Both of you know it was not an easy task for me.' Lulura and Minyon understood his task and respected the decision, but Lulura's heart was heavy.

A wall of warriors lined up on each side of Bulmurn. It was just a precaution, should he try to escape his trial at the last moment, but they needn't have worried because Bulmurn had no intention of running away. He wanted to face the ten best warriors. Bulmurn stood some fifty paces away from the ten best spearmen. He was calm and watchful, ready to prove himself or die a guilty man.

Just briefly, he caught the eyes of Lulura. He could see her worry for him on her face, but he knew she could only watch. She could not say anything or do anything to help him. Bulmurn knew he was on his own.

Then Weejup stepped out in front of the now gathered tribes people and said to them, 'Today we must use the trial of spears to judge if a man is guilty or not. This is the man', he said as he pointed at Bulmurn. A gasp of surprise went up from the onlookers. Some of the people were heard to say out loud, 'It's Bulmurn! It's Bulmurn who has to face the trial of spears!'Again, Weejup spoke out: 'The trial of spears will decide. If one of the spearmen should hit him, then he will most surely pay with his life. It will prove to us that he is guilty of withholding his powers and letting our people die.

'If he should survive the spears, he will be able to keep his life, but we will banish him from our river tribe. As you well know, no other tribe will have him. Only we, the elders, can decide if he should be allowed to return to live amongst us again. Now I will name him. This is the man', he said. 'You all know him, his name is Bulmurn.' As Weejup said Bulmurn's name, a roar arose from the people as they chanted, 'Let the trial begin. Let the trial begin!'

All went quiet as Weejup put his hand high over his head. 'Let the ten warriors come forward to take their places.' Under Weejup's instruction, the warriors took their places.

'Are you ready, Bulmurn?' Bulmurn said nothing, nor did he give any indication that he was ready, but Weejup sensed he was. So he said, 'Jubuc, you will throw the *kylie*, the boomerang, around the contest area. When the *kylie* has finished its flight and returns to Jubuc, then the contest will begin.'

Jubuc threw the boomerang to the right hand side of the wind. Every eye followed its flight. The people were wondering if they were hearing properly because the boomerang seemed to be shrieking a whistling sound as it orbited around the arena. At last it completed the circle, returning to Jubuc, who caught it. A roar went up from the watching people.

The ceremony of the trial of spears began. Bulmurn knew that the men he faced were very skilled and were the elders' hand-picked best in the Mooro tribe. He sensed the first spear thrower would take his time before he threw his spear at him. But the next two would throw their spears at him almost immediately after the first. Then maybe the fourth thrower would take his time, trying to balk him. Whatever happened Bulmurn would have to be careful and alert.

The first spearman was Dulumbart, a fearsome-looking man. All of his body was covered in white ochre. Dulumbart lifted his frightening barbed spear into his *woomera*. Then he ran towards Bulmurn as if to throw the spear, but he was only bluffing, to lure Bulmurn into making a wrong move. Dulumbart feigned three times before he threw the spear at Bulmurn. He screamed as he let loose the deadly missile. Bulmurn could see that Dulumbart was about to throw the spear and he was ready. As the spear snaked its way towards him, he just stood still until it reached him. Then, coolly, he knocked the spear to one side of his body with his shield.

The next two spearmen came at him quickly, throwing their spears almost simultaneously, as did the next two and the next three. Bulmurn was able to flick and parry their spears away from his body, so they did not harm him. This only left two out of the ten warriors to throw their spears at him. The second-last spearman balked and Bulmurn took a step backwards to give himself a bit more room to move. As he did this he trod on a rounded piece of wood. This caused Bulmurn to stumble, lose his balance and fall. As he fell, he was just able to shield the most dangerous spear from his body.

The river people roared as Bulmurn fell. Lulura sensed his danger and shouted at him urgently 'Alliga allawah Bulmurn', meaning lookout, beware. Bulmurn had heard her warning cry as he moved quickly to pick himself up from his fall. As he was getting up, he could see that Jamurra, the last spearman had already let his weapon loose from his *woomera*. The spear was coming at him just like a snake, writhing its head from side to side. The barbs of the spear seemed like the fangs of a snake, sticking out the front, trying to bite into Bulmurn's body, trying to put its poison into him to destroy him.

Lulura screamed because she thought Bulmurn would be hit by the spear and be wounded. She knew that if the spear hit Bulmurn and he was wounded, the spearings would continue until they eventually killed him.

But Bulmurn was equal to the task of defending himself. It was only the awkwardness of his position that put him in any sort of danger. At first it seemed to every onlooker that he would be hit. Instead he righted himself just in time to put the spear to one side, out of harm's way. Bulmurn had passed the trial of spears.

Lulura ran forward to him, relieved he was not hit. She also knew he had won the battle of the trial of spears. But her joy was shortlived because Weejup blocked her way, stopping her from joining Bulmurn. The look on Weejup's face told it all, she could not go to him. Her heart sank, cold as stone. She felt helpless, she could do nothing for the man she loved.

Weejup looked at Bulmurn and then he raised his right hand in the air. He looked at his people and said, 'Bulmurn has won the battle of the trial of spears. Therefore the spirits of the Dreamtime have favoured him. They think he's not guilty. However, there are many in our group who still think he is guilty. My heart is heavy, but I must pass down the judgement of the elders.

'I, Weejup, will not change my mind because you, Bulmurn, have won the trial of spears contest. Because there would still be mistrust of you, you will have to leave our tribe. You must leave the Mooro people. You will live in banishment from your people, alone, without your wife. Lulura will go to Jubuc, who inherits your position of *Mobarn Mamarup Boylla Gudjuk*.'

Lulura looked in dismay at her father, then at Bulmurn, then at Jubuc. She could neither say nor do anything. A tribal decision had been made and she must obey. She knew that Bulmurn still had his warrior status because he had won the trial of spears contest. Only he could protest and take her with him, so she waited until he spoke.

Bulmurn looked around at his people. He could see mistrust in some of them. Then he knew what he had to do. His life was taking a new path, a new destiny awaited him. He looked at Weejup and said, 'I will go. I will go.' He looked at Lulura, then at Jubuc. 'I will leave my woman Lulura with you. I ask that you look after her because Weejup has spoken, but when I need her, she will come to me wherever I am. Later she will return to you. *Mar* the wind will tell her when I need her. Nothing can or will stop her coming to me. Not even you can stop her from coming to me Jubuc.' With those final words, he turned and left.

Jubuc, Lulura and all the other tribes people stood still. They watched Bulmurn go until he was out of sight. Jubuc felt sad that Bulmurn had to go. Jubuc knew that, even though his own power was strong, Bulmurn's was stronger, strong enough to take the life of anyone he chose; but still Jubuc respected the ordinary man in Bulmurn. He respected his courage.

Jubuc looked at Lulura, Bulmurn's woman. He could see the sadness in her eyes. He looked at her as she gazed in the direction that Bulmurn had walked to his exile. Jubuc remembered Bulmurn's words. He would look after Lulura. Jubuc felt a bond take place within him as he looked at her. He noted her height, her lovely face. Jubuc admired her slim body. 'Yes, she is beautiful', he thought.

In the past, Jubuc always had spoken to Lulura, whenever he had the chance. In fact, Jubuc had always admired Lulura from a distance. Now she was his wife.

Lulura would go away from him only when Bulmurn needed her. She would go off when *mar* the wind brought a message from Bulmurn. He knew that Lulura would go to Bulmurn no matter how far away he was. Yes, she would just go. Even if he knew she was going, Jubuc would not be able to stop her. She would find a way to go, despite him, but in the meantime, he looked forward to her joining him and his two other wives. Jubuc was sad about what had happened, because he felt they had banished perhaps the greatest of Nyoongar doctors, Bulmurn.

Bulmurn's Magic

Although life amongst the Mooro people improved immensely after Bulmurn left the camp and moved away, he was not forgotten. Many Nyoongar people reported Bulmurn's camps in different locations in the bush.

He had become a loner and was always on the move, especially if his secret camping sites were discovered. These sites ranged over great distances throughout the districts of York, Northam and Toodyay. Sometimes he would come down on the coastal plain and spend a night or two near the river, near his people, the Mooro, at Guildford in the Swan Valley. Sometimes he camped in the Darling Ranges near Kalamunda or Mundaring.

Bulmurn always took care to have his camp well hidden and if people found it, it was by accident. Nobody would actually see him, though most coming across a lone *miamia* would suspect it to be his, and would leave the campsite as fast as possible. They noted that Bulmurn was nowhere to be seen or found. The powerful man was never in sight, not once. And, even though he was nowhere in sight, each intruder had a strong feeling that he was very close, watching every movement.

As the hunter or traveller felt Bulmurn's presence, the hair on the back of his neck would rise, creating a prickling uneasiness, a feeling accentuated if *wardang* the crow landed on a limb of a tree near the camp of Bulmurn. Sometimes an intruder would be rooted to the spot like a tree.

Then *wardang* the crow would 'caw' at them in anger, in resentment of their presence at the camp. The unwelcome visitors would leave in great haste because they believed the black crow sitting on a limb in the tree to be Bulmurn, the great man, about to attack them. Anyway, no one was going to wait around to find out if it was him or not. They just fled the campsite as fast as they could.

Sometimes *wardang* the black crow flew after the unwelcome intruders. Sometimes the crow swooped down on them, trying to peck their heads. To protect themselves from the bird's attack, they would throw their *bonu*, a hunting stick, or their boomerang, at the crow. As always, they never seemed to strike the crow a blow, there always seemed to be near misses. This made the unwelcome visitors more fearful of Bulmurn. They simply believed he had a more powerful magic when he turned himself into a crow.

All the stories told about Bulmurn added to his fearful reputation. The Mooro believed that if he were able to change at will into a crow or other forms, then he must have more power than any Nyoongar alive.

A young Nyoongar warrior named Bujhub told the story of how he had come upon a lone camp which he believed to be that of Bulmurn. He told his listeners how the crow had watched him and how he was frightened at his confrontation with the angry bird. He told them he was sure the crow was Bulmurn watching his every movement all the time he was near the camp. Bujhub told them how he grew afraid for his safety, and how his only thought then was to get to safety as fast as he could. But he said to them, 'I wasn't going to run or show him I was afraid, even though my heart was pounding in fright'.

Bujhub said, 'As I left the site, the crow seemed to disappear. All around me the bush became quiet. I walked near a tall black stump I never noticed before. It was a stump of a burnt-out wandoo tree. The wandoo stump had one limb on it that was in an upraised position, as if it were ready to strike at any moment. As I walked under the limb, I heard the cracking sound of a splitting tree. Because I am young and agile, I was able to leap to one side without looking around to see what was happening.'

This kept Bujhub from being crushed or hurt by the limb. 'As I picked myself up off the ground, fear welled up within me, and I fled the place. I feared for my life because I kept hearing a voice in my mind saying to me, "Go quickly because next time I won't miss you. I'll kill you." I tell you', Bujhub said, 'I'm sure it was Bulmurn. That was enough for me, I wasn't going to wait around to see if it was him or not.'

Bulmurn had found out that whenever he moved and set up his camp, he always seemed to be able to find a sign, a message, near his *miamia*. Somebody would leave it in a position so that Bulmurn would be able to find it. Each time Bulmurn found the message stick, he would smile, thinking to himself that only someone with similar powers could come to his camp and leave a message without being seen by him, or by his trained crow. Bulmurn thought that the man had to be Jubuc.

Bulmurn still regarded Jubuc as his friend, regardless of him being partly responsible for his banishment. He felt that Jubuc was giving him the only friendship he could since being dismissed by the Council of the Elders.

Even though Jubuc had played a major role in his trial, Bulmurn knew the man had only been doing his duty as a healer and elder. Bulmurn felt that the elders really didn't want to banish him, but they had little alternative. So they did what they thought was best. 'It's best this way', thought Bulmurn, 'because I could never return to the way that they are living now. Our bloodline is disappearing fast, it's getting whiter and whiter every day now. I could never go back there and live among them again.

'First the *wadjbulla* killed our men and took the women. Sometimes they still do this. Now they jail our men in the jail on Wagemup, on Rottnest Island, and other islands so the men are out of the way. This makes our women readily available for their pleasure. The Nyoongar men are trading their women for more rum and tobacco. I don't want to be with them. They are fools.'

Then Bulmurn's thoughts returned to the travellers sneaking around his secret camps, and this made him smile. He thought back to the beginning of his banishment when he had climbed a tree to take a young *wardang* from its nest, so he could train it so that it might warn him of anybody approaching his hideout. The crow seemed to have developed a real desire to attack anybody who came too close. This made Bulmurn laugh out loud as he thought of the times the crow had actually driven off inquisitive visitors from his camping area.

Again he thought of Jubuc. It was Bulmurn himself who had taught Jubuc many of the secrets that he was now using to make him a powerful traditional healer. This friendship would not be destroyed too easily, Bulmurn thought.

Then Bulmurn thought of Lulura, the woman he had had to leave behind with Jubuc. He knew Jubuc had given Lulura a good home. Jubuc had looked after her, taking her into his *miamia*. Then Bulmurn began to realise how much he missed Lulura. Now was the time when he needed Lulura, when he wanted to see her. Bulmurn would sing her, and by nightfall she would join him in his own *miamia*.

Bulmurn sat in front of a small fire he had made just outside the hut. Then he began to sing his message of love, his need for Lulura to join him. As he sang, *mar* the wind began to blow a gentle breeze across his face telling him she would take his message of love to Lulura, telling her to come to him. He would keep her with him only for a short time, then he would send her back to Jubuc's camp.

Bulmurn pictured Lulura in his mind. He saw her walking away from him. His singing grew more urgent. Bulmurn asked her to turn and listen to him. Then Lulura stopped, looked his way as if she had heard his call. As she stopped, *mar* the wind blew Bulmurn's message of love to her, telling her of his powerful need for her company. Then she looked more fully in his direction, she looked as if she could see him. Then Lulura walked in the direction of Bulmurn's *miamia* .

Lulura smiled approvingly, so that Bulmurn would know that she knew of his request and would go to meet him. First she had to make sure nobody followed. She looked around to make sure all was clear, so nobody was suspicious of her leaving the Mooro campsite. Then when she was sure all was clear, she began to run towards the location where Bulmurn waited. Lulura would not lose her way, such was their communication. Tonight was theirs.

When Lulura stood before Bulmurn, she smiled, making Bulmurn smile. He marvelled at her beauty. She had not changed in the three or four seasons that they had been forced to part.

Bulmurn felt his passion for Lulura rise as she came closer towards him. Then Bulmurn pulled her to him. His lips hungry for hers, he kissed her with great passion. Lulura responded warmly to his kisses, then she wrapped her bare legs around his. Without really caring whether they were inside his home or not, Bulmurn covered Lulura, then he entered her. They each savoured the other's nearness with a rekindled love for each other, both of them moving slowly, meeting each other. Their lovemaking continued several times during the night, then in the morning he walked her near the river camp, where he left her.

Time passed. It was almost five nights since Lulura had been to see Bulmurn at his campsite near the Mooro people. Bulmurn had since moved to a new location further inland, due east of Perth near the Kellerberrin and Quairading districts. Once he had reached this location, Bulmurn set out to build a new *miamia* for himself.

After he had built his *miamia*, Bulmurn went hunting for food. He made his way carefully through the bush, treading cautiously here and there. Bulmurn was lucky because his hunting patience was to be rewarded. He came upon a mob of grey kangaroos grazing on the lower plains near the large rock where he was camped, and with the first throw of his spear, brought down a small young boomer.

Bulmurn carried the young roo on his shoulders back to his camp. He was pleased, he knew he'd eat well. He put the roo on the fire he had prepared, then waited for it to cook. While he waited, he placed his *warnbro* over his shoulders to keep out the fast approaching cool of the evening. His *warnbro* was a long cape made from the skin of the grey kangaroo.

Soon Bulmurn was feeding off the cooked part of the roo meat. As he ate the flesh he cut pieces of the meat which he fed to his pet crow. As Bulmurn ate, his thoughts drifted over his life and his people, and Lulura. He knew his life would always be a lonely one. He wondered whether he would ever be received back into his tribe by the Council of Elders, whether he would ever want to. He felt, with foreboding, that he never would.

'Tomorrow', Bulmurn thought, 'I'll go to my special place and spend time with the spirits of the Dreamtime. I will spend a day and night there. I will be able to recharge my body with more energy. I will sing and corroboree before the spirits of the powerful ones, who passed into the sacred Dreamtime many countless seasons ago. If they are pleased with me, then I will receive more power from their spirits into my body. I will be like a new man.' Bulmurn felt that once this contact was made, the ritual finished and with extra powers, he would truly be a great force.

After Bulmurn had eaten, he began to prepare his fire for the evening ahead of him, he stirred the larger sized coals, putting the coals together so the fire would burn slowly on the ends of the wood he had placed on the fire. He needed the fire to keep the night air out of his *miamia*.

Bulmurn was tired and he knew he would sleep deeply this night. A properly made fire would keep him warm. All Bulmurn's people had been taught to sleep lightly so that they would awaken to stir the coals of the fire and place the unburned sticks around the coals to keep the heat, yet prevent the fire from burning itself out rapidly. To the river people and other tribes, the fire was a precious commodity. They all made their fires as Bulmurn had made his. This way they could sleep out most of the night with the fire burning low, not waking them.

Bulmurn lay curled in his fur *waral*, his kangaroo skin rug. He needed the rug as well as the fire to keep warm. Just for good measure he added his *warnbro*, but he could not find a comfortable way to lie. He tossed and turned, then finally, as he slowly drifted towards sleep, he heard the night voices of *dwerrt* the dingo telling all was well.

Bulmurn rose early next morning. It was just daylight. Dawn had struck its brightness all around, pushing the darkness away from the surrounding horizons. He stirred the coals in his fire, placing dry grass and small sticks on the live embers. He blew the embers until flames burst from them. Then he placed larger bits of wood onto the blazing fire. Bulmurn warmed himself and stretched his sinewy body. The warmth of the fire felt good to him, seemed to give him strength.

Bulmurn looked towards the rapidly rising sun. He felt good about himself. He felt this day would be a special day for him. Bulmurn flexed his arms and legs to draw out any stiffness from his body and thought of his sacred place. Nobody knew this place but him.

Bulmurn ate a portion of the roo cooked the previous day and fed his crow. Then he paused and looked at the sun. He judged it was nearly mid-morning. Now was the time to set off on his journey to the sacred site. Bulmurn adjusted his *warnbro* about his shoulders, then he picked up his *woomera* and barbed spears. These weapons were for defence as well as for hunting. Wherever Bulmurn travelled, he carried his weapons near his body. Bulmurn was always alert to defend himself from any would-be enemy.

When Bulmurn left his campsite, he knew he would have to be careful. He didn't want anybody to follow him to his sacred site, so he put on his *genebuka*, his ceremonial shoes. These shoes were made from interwoven grass and feathers from *waitj* the emu, and sometimes other bird's feathers. The feathers would cushion his footprints and not allow them to show. They would help to keep others from following his trail. Bulmurn concealed his tracks well. As he travelled along, his mind went back to the first time he found the sacred site.

It was an early morning in late spring when he was out hunting *bikuta*, the red rock kangaroo, near a rocky hill. Bulmurn knew *bikuta* lived amongst the rocks during the day, lying under cover of whatever brush or rocks it could find to hide from predators. Some small trees grew on the rocks in patches of loam that collected in the crevices and sometimes the *bikuta* lay under these trees.

Bikuta came down at night onto the lower plains to feed. Like most animals when they get fat, the *bikuta* gets careless and lazy. When this happens it becomes an easy target to stalk and spear.

Bulmurn crept through the bush towards the hilly terrain, centimetres at a time. Patience was essential in this kind of hunt. He moved forward silently, assessing every rocky outcrop and bush. Then, surprisingly, he saw a *bikuta*, forward of the rocks and far away from the safety of the rocky hill. This *bikuta* was also careless in its eating habits, Bulmurn observed. The red rock kangaroo was so busy filling its mouth with the fresh green growth of grass that it failed to realise it was being stalked.

Bulmurn was skilled and moved effortlessly and quietly. Patiently he stalked his prey, as every careful step he took brought him a little closer so he could come into range of his spear. The last thing Bulmurn wanted was for the roo to see or smell him.

The hunter was equal to the task. He was so quiet nothing could see or hear his movements as he drew closer and closer. Then when he was close enough he positioned his body effortlessly, ready to strike like *dugite* the black snake. He raised his arm, drew it back and threw the spear forward with the barbed head aimed at the red rock kangaroo's heart.

The spear sailed through the air on target. The pointed barbs of the spearhead tore into the organs inside the animal's rib cage. *Bikuta* was mortally wounded. It staggered for a while, then fell to the ground as if dead.

'*Haryo yoki! Haryo yoki! Haryo yoki!*' Bulmurn's victory shout resounded as he jumped out of his hiding place and ran towards the fallen roo. In his excitement, Bulmurn had left his other spear behind. He ran back to gather it, then he calmed himself down from the rush of blood and excitement that the kill had raised. Calmly, he walked towards the fallen animal.

Bikuta, the fat and lazy one, was not there. It was nowhere to be seen, for badly wounded as it was from the barbs of the lethal spear, *bikuta* had somehow managed to get up and go towards the safety of the rocky hill.

The red rock kangaroo struggled to make its way to the safety of the hill. As it hopped away with the spear shaft hanging out of its body, as luck would have it, the shaft of the spear got caught between two mallee trees. This caused the animal to sway to the right so that its body weight broke the spear into two pieces, leaving a small section of the spear protruding from its body. The *bikuta* gained momentary freedom to move towards the safety of its beloved rocks. When it reached the outcrop, it could surely hide from its antagonist, now in pursuit. The animal could hear the hunter coming behind him, searching for him. Once concealed in the rocks, the roo would hide, rest, and maybe the pain in its body would go away.

Bulmurn was anxiously surveying the scene where the *bikuta* should have fallen dead. He wanted to know why his spear had not impaled the animal so that it could not move from the spot where he had speared it. Bulmurn wanted to find the *bikuta's* trail and follow it until he found the roo, so he could retrieve what was rightfully his.

'*Kiaya har! Kiaya har!*', he shouted as he found signs of the injured roo. The tell-tale signs of blood in large drops and the drag mark of the spear confirmed the strike.

'*Kiaya! Kiaya!*' he said out loud again. 'I must have patience following the trail of *bikuta*. His blood will show me where he goes. He is mine, he will not go far before he is *mirinditj* and going into the long sleep. I am a good hunter and tracker. This *bikuta* will soon be in my fire, his flesh will give me strength. Before this day is out, his flesh will be my strength.'

As Bulmurn tracked the *bikuta* among the bushes and rocks, the blood signs grew larger. Then Bulmurn came to the place where it had broken the spear between the two mallee trees. He found the end of his spear, broken from the spearhead which remained inside the kangaroo's chest. Bulmurn's confidence grew, because he believed now the animal must surely die before it reached the safety of the rocks; but the trail of blood lead him across the larger of the rocks, clearly showing him the path the injured animal had, somehow, taken. To Bulmurn, the tell-tale spots of blood seemed too good to be true. He climbed over the huge rock to descend the other side on a stepping stone and out on to a patch of brown loam.

Bulmurn tracked the roo over the brown soil, through bushes and sheoak trees onto the side of another large rock. The ground seemed moist, soft and cool.

To Bulmurn's surprise, all marks and the blood trail the *bikuta* had made suddenly vanished. No trace of its movements were to be seen anywhere. Bulmurn felt despondent and disappointed. He was almost ready to abandon the search. He sat down to ponder what he should do, whether to give up the search for his missing *bikuta*.

Then he felt a breeze fan his face as *mar* the wind blew around him. So suddenly had the wind come up that it gave Bulmurn the sense of an eerie message. He jumped up from his sitting position and chased the wind until he was right at the base of the second rock. As he approached the bushes at the bottom of the rock, a hole in the rock suddenly appeared.

Bulmurn's heart began to beat rapidly making him jump and shout, '*Kiaya! Kiaya!*'. As the wind blew the bushes apart, exposing an opening to what appeared to be a cave entrance, Bulmurn cried out, 'I have you now, *bikuta*, you are in that cave. You're mine. Today, *bikuta*, you will feed me and my people — we, who need your red flesh and your fat to keep our bodies strong!' Bulmurn got down on his hands and knees and crawled into the tunnel entrance of the cave carrying his other barbed spear with him.

The cave was dark. He clawed his way slowly along, feeling along each side of the tunnel for the furry body of *bikuta* the red rock kangaroo. Then he saw a light ahead of him. The cave widened, enabling him to stand upright and walk along the cave floor toward the source of light up ahead of him.

In the dim light, Bulmurn could make out the source of the light as cracks in the roof of the cave. He could see that as the day grew older, the sun would lighten up the cave more than it was at this moment. Then to Bulmurn's surprise, the cave opened into a sanctuary-like arena with steep rock walls on nearly all sides.

The only entrance appeared to be the way Bulmurn had come along through the cave itself. Amazed, Bulmurn gazed at the rock walls. There on the flat floor of the sanctuary lay the body of *bikuta*, the red rock kangaroo. As Bulmurn approached the kill, he suddenly felt a strange and unique feeling, one that conveyed the message to him that this was a place he belonged to.

Bulmurn's amazement stayed with him. Even though he had never been to this place before, he felt comfortable, as though it was his place. He felt he belonged here, that he had been in this sanctuary before, perhaps in a different spirit form.

Bulmurn looked very closely at his newly found environment. He surveyed the scene closely, not missing the slightest detail of any of the rock paintings protected from the elements by rocky overhangs. Bulmurn realised that the ancient paintings were drawn by the 'old ones' many, many seasons ago, in the Dreamtime.

There were paintings of different kangaroos, of other animals, of birds and fish, of human figures, also many different sized hand prints. There were other objects Bulmurn noted. The figures of Nyoongar men and women were done as the animals, birds and fish forms were done, in the traditional way, showing internal structure. There were shadow paintings. These forms of painting were very old and very much of Bulmurn's tradition.

Bulmurn walked around the scene in intrigued silence. He saw totems and burial signs and markings. Some he could understand, some he could not. He could see the graves where important people had been placed. Then Bulmurn knew that these were *mobarn* men. 'Yes, they were men like me. Now I know I was meant to be led to this place by the *bikuta*, the red rock kangaroo. *Bikuta* was the old ones' messenger sent to lead me to this sacred place.

'These *mobarn* men were led here before by *bikuta* the red rock kangaroo just as I have been.' Then he looked for *bikuta*, anticipating that he would prepare a fire on which to cook the animal's flesh, but the animal no longer lay where he had seen it when he had first entered the sacred place.

Bulmurn's thoughts began to race, then he cried out, 'It's true! It's what I thought. *Bikuta* is a spirit, he has led me to this special place. Now I must know the reason why.' Then all of a sudden, Bulmurn was compelled to walk towards a painted figure on the rock wall, a strong being with a rug-like covering over its body and a circle of light over and around its head.

Bulmurn inspected the painting closely. He gazed at a small yellowish-white circle near the heart of the painted figure. As he did so, the sun suddenly beamed a ray of light from overhead onto the same spot. The figure emitted a blazing light, momentarily blinding him.

Bulmurn gasped in astonishment. The golden light seemed to come from the circle on the heart of the figure painted on the rock wall. The light engulfed him, covering his body. Bulmurn felt himself becoming stronger and more powerful. Each part of his body seemed to quiver as the new energy crept throughout his every muscle and the sinews of his human frame. Bulmurn had never experienced power like it.

'I now know I have been blessed by the spirits of the Dreamtime', Bulmurn thought. 'It is indeed the strength of the old ones I am receiving, the ones who also were brought to this sacred place. Their spirits are no longer of this world. They are of the Dreamtime world', Bulmurn reasoned.

Bulmurn thought out loud, 'I am honoured. I am honoured that these spirits of the Dreamtime have chosen me as a special person to receive their gift of special powers. It is our Law that I must enforce. To heal my people, I must wisely use this new power. I must use it for the good of the river people and others who may need my help.

'Tonight I will stay here with the Dreamtime spirits. Tomorrow I will try to go back to my people. I will go and serve them as a special healer. I will try to heal their aches and pains. I hope to bring them cures. I will try to give them a new life energy.'

Then Bulmurn's thoughts came back from past experience to the present. His brow wrinkled because his life had now changed. Also his people's lives were changing, perhaps forever. He reasoned that their lives were being changed by the *wadjbulla* people, these new people who called themselves settlers, pioneers, adventurers, and explorers. These white people were brushing his people aside, they were taking the land as they wanted it. They were 'discovering' land belonging to his people. They were 'discovering' the land as if his people didn't live there or know about it.

The *wadjbulla* were too established in this land now to try to drive them away. Instead it was the reverse; the Nyoongar people, the rightful custodians, were being pushed further and further away from their river land. Bulmurn's people, the Mooro, the Beeliar people and the Beelu people, were feeling the pinch of the squeezing hands of the *wadjbulla* people, who were now taking away their hunting grounds and destroying sacred sites that were of special value to the Swan River people. Bulmurn's resentment of the white man and his brown-skinned children grew. He turned and left the cave for the second time, full of the knowledge of his banishment. He did not return to his people.

What Bulmurn would never know was that later Jubuc would also see the special *bikuta*, the red rock kangaroo. Jubuc would also stalk the roo and throw his spear at him. He would see the roo fall down, and like Bulmurn, would be distracted. When Jubuc looked for the roo, he would not be there. The red rock roo would disappear among the same rocks. Jubuc would track him down in the same way Bulmurn had done.

Jubuc, too, would find the sacred site of the Dreamtime spirits. He, too, would experience the new surge of powers into his body so that he would have powers to heal amongst his people. Jubuc would experience everything that Bulmurn had experienced while at the sacred site. The Dreamtime spirits would look at him and decide his fate, whether he was to follow the same trail as Bulmurn.

Bulmurn felt excited as he saw the outline of the rock and

approached the sacred site for the second time. Already his reserves of energy began to grow. He knew he would be able to experience the Dreamtime power once again. This would make him feel good. While he was in the sacred site, he would perform a corroboree dance. He would do his dance with the Dreamtime spirits as his audience. Bulmurn knew that *mar* the wind would tell them of his approach. When his visit to the sacred site was finished, he would paint his sign on the rock face, as other *Mobarn Mamarup* had painted their signs on the rock walls before him.

*   *   *   *   *   *   *   *

Meanwhile, a group of settlers were on their way back to their farm from the new town of Perth. They had been to the wool stores in the port at Fremantle to sell the wool clip of the last shearing season. The party of men was led by a farmer, Jim Rows, and consisted of foreman, Jack Harding, and workers, Ron Smith and Norman Lynch. The latter two were shearers whom Rows employed to do the fencing once the shearing season was over. Harding had been transported to the colony as a convict, but had been working with Jim Rows on his ticket-of-leave for nearly a year. Harding had known the worst cruelties.

Rows and his workers had been drinking at a tavern in Perth, after Rows had purchased needed provisions for his farm. Now after business, Rows felt they needed a break and rest before making their long trip through to Guildford, then north-east to Rows's homestead. After a fairly lengthy session in the tavern and other public houses in Perth, Rows felt it was time for them to make their journey back to the farm through the warm still night.

Rows was satisfied with the sale of his wool clip; the others had praised his efforts over the sale, and about the provisions he had purchased for the farm. They told him the 'missus' would be very pleased with the trade. Rows told them, 'Mrs Rows should be pleased because we have flour, tea, sugar, salted pork and bolts of cloth for her. She will be able to make dresses and shirts for us and curtains for the homestead and workers' cottages.' The men had also been able to purchase new boots, trousers and shirts. They did not expect to return to Perth for a lengthy period of time.

Jim Rows was in a jovial mood, a mood that made him want to relax with his men, even take a drink with them. Normally he would not join in with them — they were always demanding too much rum from him, and hired help in the colony was generally regarded by the new land-owners as difficult to manage — but because of his good fortune he wanted to drink and sing along with them on the way home. The noisy men would have ordinarily reached their destination in the foothills out from Guildford long before nightfall if they had not prolonged their revelry in Perth and stopped often on the track to urinate. Soon the band of mates would initiate an event that would change them from ordinary, hard-working settlers into criminals that even the likes of Harding avoided.

Harding drove the four-wheeled heavy wagon behind four huge Clydesdale horses. The men were happy and sang *Botany Bay* and other ditties as the Clydesdales plodded steadily in front of the wagon. The horses were relieved when Harding let the reins go slack, allowing them to make their own pace along the Guildford track.

They stopped singing to pass the bottle around and began to talk and yarn about where they had worked and how life had treated them since arriving in the new colonies at Swan River. Harding, however, fell silent and brooding, then suddenly swung the loud conversation around to the natives, in particular the native women, and what it was like having sex with the 'gins'. He recounted tales of bartering drink and food for women, how easy they were to grab and how sometimes he and his mates just took them. The others listened keenly, lurching in the motion of the wagon. 'I tell you, Mr Rows', said Harding, noting that Rows seemed not to have been with a black woman, 'they may look like savages, and smell different to us, but these gins, by Jesus Lord, are worth a bit of rum. You've got to try 'em.'

Rows had always been loyal to his lovely wife Julia and had

never thought for a moment that he would be unfaithful to her. But Harding's talk about the black women had aroused his curiosity. He had heard about other homesteaders siring 'half-breed' children from sexual activity with Aborigines around the colony. Sitting there in the rocking wagon, surrounded by the anonymous night Jim Rows let himself wonder what it would be like making love with a black woman, a wild savage. If he had the chance would he do it?

Jim Rows's question would soon be answered. He was the first to notice the smoke rising through the bush. He raised his arm charging his men to be quiet and called on Lynch to halt the cart so that they could investigate.

'It's a native bush camp Mr Rows', said Ron Smith.

'We can bloody well see that, Smith', said Harding, answering for his boss.

Maybe it was the rum he drank with his men, or maybe the good trading he'd done that day, or maybe the tempting conversation about black women that made Rows feel he had to save face and 'reward' his men with a native woman right there and then if he could. He made a decision. 'Hopefully men, there are gins in this camp we can bargain for to cap off a good day. We are well-provisioned to barter for any native women, but stick together. As we approach we'll stay close to the cart.'

Harding said, 'Boss, usually once their men see and smell the rum it's enough to make the trade'.

Rows knew what he had to do now. 'We'll not take "no" for an answer boys.' To reassure them he pointed to the guns they carried. The others readily agreed.

'We can take them anyway we want to', Harding said. 'I say, let's go in steadily and see what we can see, for I wouldn't mind a bit of black flaps to pass the time away. They just don't mind, these gins, once the trade is made.'

Each man's thoughts were almost identical. All wanted a black woman for the night ahead and all approached with the same desire.

Rows thought that a well-provisioned party such as theirs ought to be able to get the best women in the camp for a price.

He was willing to pay the highest price — rum and tobacco. Hopefully they would meet greedy men who would be willing to trade their women for these sought-after commodities.

As the *wadjbulla* men approached the campfire, they saw only two blacks in front of them, a male and female. The man was a very tall, thin, wiry Nyoongar, who stood in their pathway. In his hands were his weapons, his symbols of power, the spear thrower and two spears. In his *nulburn*, his hair belt, he carried a *korch*, his ancient but effective stone axe. Also in the belt he carried a *kadjo*, a stone hammer. It was not uncommon to see the men carry the *korch* and *kadjo* as extra weapons. Behind this man stood a young and quite distinctly tall, ebony woman who was very beautiful.

The drunken white men were foolish in their desire for her. Swaying slightly, each man took in the details of her beauty. They noted that her body was full of youthful beauty, a beauty that was not often recognised by the white men. Her breasts stood high on her chest, giving a sign that she had not borne many children. Her pubic hairs stood out between her legs like a shiny black flower. Her eyes glistened with interest in the white men — not fear, not excitement — just curiosity.

Rows and his men, to a man, could not contain themselves. 'She's too good a looker for this big-nosed, skinny black buck', Harding said to Rows and the others. 'I could live with a woman like that if she wasn't so black.'

The tall black man was unknown to the white men. Perhaps if they had known he was the brother-in-law of the powerful *Mobarn Mamarup*, Bulmurn, they would not have acted out the tragedy that was slowly unfolding.

His name was Binyung. His wife's name was Munyee. They had been joined together in Nyoongar marriage for several summers. Munyee was actually given to Binyung as a very young girl, with the approval of the Council of Elders. The couple also had the blessing of both their families. The two made a handsome couple. Munyee was some eight summers younger than Binyung and they were well-liked within the community of the Mooro tribe.

When Binyung and Munyee had heard the *wadjbulla's* approaching vehicle, they had instructed their only young son, Binyu, to hide. Binyung told him that no matter what happened he was not to show himself. Binyu was to remain hidden in the bushes and to make no noise. They told him he was not to be afraid. But again they said, 'No matter what happens you must not reveal yourself. The white strangers must not know about you.' Binyu nodded. He would do what his parents asked of him.

Binyung could see the *wadjbulla* men were already drunken and even though he was armed with his spears at the ready, he felt a cold chill run up the spine of his back. He knew that he and his wife Munyee were in grave danger. Nevertheless, Binyung's love for Munyee was strong, so he stood his ground as the strangers drew closer. Binyung knew his feeling of imminent danger was not wrong because the *wadjbulla* men did not look at him. He could see the look of lust on their faces as they leered at his beautiful wife, Munyee.

The intruders' eyes were wide open, all their faces expressing animal lust for her lovely body. Binyung's body frame stiffened with anger and fear for now he realised he would have to fight for his wife, his family and his honour as a warrior and as a man. Soon they would say what they wanted.

Binyung heard the voice of Jim Rows, 'G'day boy! We want to bargain with you today.' Rows pointed to the wagon. 'Lotta tucker, boy! Tea, flour, sugar, tobacco and rum, all yours boy. We only want your woman for an hour or two. What you say, boy? We only want to borrow her for a while.'

'You offered him a lot for his woman, boss', Lynch said.

'Shut up you fool', Rows said. 'You might spoil the trade. Anyhow look at her. She's worth a portion of everything I've mentioned.'

'What you say boy?', Rows said to Binyung again. Then Rows pointed at the goods. 'There, boy, what you say?'

Binyung looked at their wagon and he could see they did have much food. He could smell the tobacco and tea. His fear changed ever so slightly as his attention was drawn to the smells of flour. Thoughts of his family eating well flitted through his mind.

Rows sensed Binyung was having second thoughts, so he thought he might tempt the man a little more to win the woman from him. 'Mr Harding, open a bottle of rum and you have a swig, but don't give him any. I just want to tempt him a little more, the smell of rum might just do the trick.' Harding popped the bottle and drank deeply. When he finished his swig, he poured a little on the ground where Binyung stood.

Binyung saw the bottle of rum. He heard him pop the cork as he pulled it out of the neck of the bottle. He watched him drink, again he watched him pour some of the rum near him. He could smell its flavour. Binyung could almost taste the tobacco, too, and he liked its tangy wildfire taste when he chewed it. Binyung thought to himself, 'All I have to do is let them have Munyee, like the other *mamarup* in our tribe trade their women for these goods of tea, flour, sugar, tobacco and the rum'. He had seen others of his people drunk from such a swap. He had seen them falling about from drinking this rum.

Then Binyung looked at Munyee and to the place where Binyu was hidden. They were black like him. Then he remembered the mixed-blood relatives he had. Binyung weighed up the pros and cons of such a deal. Then, after long consideration, Binyung made his decision. He didn't want them to soil his wife. He loved her too much to have anyone else touch her.

Then he said to Rows, 'Me gut nuttin 'ere, boss, me sorry — nuttun to trate dis day maypee morrow'. Binyung looked up at the sky and moved his head in the direction the sun would rise and set. 'Meum mite hub sumtum morrow, boss to sull, sure gut nuttun dis day, boss.'

Harding, the foreman, said with a sneer, 'Boy we don't want no kangaroo skins. We don't want your stupid spears or boomerangs, nothing tomorrow either. Nothing like that, boy. You know what the hell we want, you black bastard. Sure as hell you know what we want. We want your woman.'

Binyung tried to play dumb. 'Noad me dun noad boss, me dun noad, boss', Binyung replied, even though he knew in his heart, his mind and his body that they wanted his woman, Munyee. *Muyung*, these *wadjbulla* devils, they were like animals.

They would have to kill him this night to take Munyee from him.

Then Harding said, his drunken voice filled with aggression, 'Corse you know, boy. You know! We want your woman', and he pointed at Munyee. 'That's what we want. We want your woman! We have rum', and again he waved the rum bottle. 'We got it, boy, that's what you blackfellas like. Well, boy, we got it all, flour, tea, sugar, tobacco. Boy, you can't say we not fair. That's a good bargain and you bloody well know it. You fuckin' well know it.'

Rows looked at Harding, nodding approval at what he had said to Binyung. By now he felt it his right to have the black man's woman. Gripping their muskets, both looked at Binyung to await his answer. As Rows and Harding watched Binyung, Smith and Lynch had got off the cart and were edging slowly towards Munyee. Munyee had not noticed them edging closer to her. She was intent on what her husband was saying. Then Harding moved his musket in line with Binyung's chest. Rows whispered to Harding, 'He looks angry with us. You had better get ready to shoot, especially if he goes for his spear.'

Binyung heard Rows whisper, although he did not understand exactly what he said. He now knew he had to defend his woman, Munyee, and himself. Binyung's arm was raised so quickly that there was no hint of movement as he placed his spear in his spear thrower, all in one motion. But this would be the last thing Binyung would ever do. Harding made sure of that. His gun fired. A bullet sped into Binyung's heart, deep into his chest crushing away his life before he could sink his spear deep into the white man's body.

Munyee screamed, then she ran to where Binyung had fallen. She tried to make him get up. Blood poured from the damaged heart of Binyung. Munyee put her hands onto his body as she tried to stop the blood from escaping the gaping hole in his chest. Crying she cradled him in her arms. Red blood still gushed, running down her own chest and abdomen.

Rows, Harding, Smith and Lynch were fascinated by the black's death, how the woman had run to him trying to save him. They knew she could not. They stood momentarily dumbfounded.

Suddenly, Munyee felt fear for her own life, for her own safety. She jumped up, she tried to run, but it was too late. The white men were already upon her like a pack of mad dogs. Now there was only agony in her desperation. Munyee was taken by the four men, whose savagery bore no decency, no constraints toward the dignity of her womanhood. They raped her, torturing her with their own crude methods. When they had satisfied their crude lust, they shot her, like her husband. They murdered her so that no one would ever know what they had done. Dead people tell no tales.

Jubuc's Sad Message

Enveloped by the dark night the white men cleaned themselves of the blood and mess that they had created in the murderous taking of Munyee and talked of the story they would tell the authorities. 'This is the best way', said Rows. 'We will report that the buck tried to steal a bag of flour from our wagon as we passed their camp. When we chased him, he attacked us with his spears. Then the gin joined in. She tried to get us with the weapon that she carried for her buck. Nobody needs to know what really happened. Do you all agree?' said Rows emphatically.

Sobering up, each man agreed with his employer, Rows. This was the way they would tell the story to conceal the dastardly deeds they had just committed. The authorities and the other settlers would accept Rows and his workers' story, and they would also let them off without any punishment, but the truth would be known to every member of the Mooro people living in the Guildford area of the Swan River.

What Jim Rows and his men did not know was that a small black figure had witnessed them committing the murder and rape of his parents. Binyu lay huddled in silence with tears running down his cheeks. Numbed with shock, he had not dared to move or cry out. It would be a long time before he could feel it was safe to come out from hiding and move away from the torturous violent scene.

Binyu had witnessed all that had happened to his parents and the lump in his throat threatened to choke him with emotion. Nevertheless, he had courage; he had to have one look at the shallow grave his parents lay in. Even though he couldn't see them he knew they were there. He crept out of the bushes and stood in horror beside the carelessly dug graves.

Binyu ran blindly through the night. His one thought was that he had to get to his own mob to tell what had happened. The very first person he ran into was Jubuc. It was to Jubuc that he blurted out his life's most hurtful story.

Binyu was totally exhausted with emotion by the time he had given all the details, so Jubuc took Binyu to the home of the boy's mother's sister, Beena. She gently rocked him on her lap by her fire and he fell into sleep.

At dawn Binyu was brought before the full Council of Elders to repeat his painful story about the murder of his father and the rape and murder of his mother. The elders reassured young Binyu that they would do their best to see that the evil white men would be brought to justice by the Mooro tribal lawmen. The Council placed Binyu into the care of his second mother and father, Munyee's other sister, Yiberu, and her husband Bindarp. They were only too willing to take Binyu into their home to look after and care for him.

That duty done, Weejup called the Council to make a decision about how they should avenge the death of the two people. They feared retaliation and hardship against their tribe if they tried to fight against the weapons of the *wadjbulla*. The Council of Elders decided that they would send Jubuc to find Bulmurn and tell him about the murders and rape of his sister and brother-in-law. The banished Bulmurn was the obvious choice. They reasoned that he was still one of the most gifted men living. His magic was powerful and he was a strong, capable man. He had much to gain by revenge, and because he had been banished the tribe could not be held responsible. Each member of the Council of Elders agreed that he should be the first one they should ask to right their law, to bring the bad white men to justice. He was ideal for this task.

Weejup instructed Jubuc to go out and find Bulmurn's secret camp and pass that message on, asking him to act on behalf of the Mooro people. The story that Jubuc would tell Bulmurn was of tragic proportions and Jubuc knew it. Jubuc also knew Bulmurn would set about destroying the white men involved. Jubuc planned to relay the message to Bulmurn exactly as it had been told by Binyu to him and the Council of Elders. Jubuc would confirm all the gruesome details of what had happened to Binyung and Munyee.

Jubuc would tell Bulmurn how he had gone back to the spot where the crime had taken place; how he had read the signs of the struggles that had taken the lives of Binyu's father and mother. Jubuc would confirm the story that Binyu's courage had kept alive. He would tell Bulmurn of his own sorrow and the Mooro people's sorrow over the horrible thing the wicked *wadjbulla* men had done to Bulmurn's family.

Jubuc arose early the next day. Before Bina, the dawn, he watched the rays of light spread over the night's sky, replacing it with the day. The high hills of the Darling Ranges looked as though they were sent from the spirits. It was a beauty that Jubuc always marvelled at. Bina, the dawn, never failed to inspire him. The wonderful birds were awake. Some were hunting, looking for food. Other birds sang their melodic songs, filling the bush and the valleys with their beautiful calls. Some played frivolous games of follow-the-leader, darting here and there from tree to tree.

Jubuc's temper became aroused over the murders. His sad face showed only the grimness of the duty to inform Bulmurn. To be the bearer of such tragic news was not going to be an easy task. Bulmurn's reaction to the bad news would be frightening. In Jubuc's mind, there was no doubt that Bulmurn's anger would burn. Jubuc felt he would immediately set out to take revenge for his family, his brother-in-law, his sister, and little Binyu, their son, and this would be in line with the Aboriginal Law. The crime would be avenged by punishing the bad *wadjbulla* men who had committed this act of evil against them.

Jubuc knew that if Bulmurn agreed to go after the bad men, he would try to kill them. Jubuc knew that if Bulmurn did kill the four white men, the police troopers would become involved. The troopers would set out after him. There would be no stopping them from trying to capture or kill him. Their pointed stick could kill a man from a great distance. He knew the *wadj-bulla* as relentless hunters when trailing a blackfella. Jubuc knew that Bulmurn would become an outlaw in the eyes of the white settlers, even though Rows and his men had killed and raped first. To them, no crime had been committed, Binyung and Munyee were only a 'couple of blacks', worthless in their eyes.

Jubuc had the trust of the Council of Elders to see that the tribal law was carried out to right the wrong that had been committed against the Swan River people. Jubuc knew that Bulmurn was the person to put the wrong right and to uphold the Law.

But the Council of Elders feared reprisals against Nyoongar families of the river people who were camped in the Guildford area along the Swan River. The Council of Elders feared that if they openly attacked the Rows homestead, then the white troopers would come out and take action against the river people which could result in many more deaths.

A whole lot of the river people could be massacred, like those killed at Gidgegannup and at the Battle of Pinjarra in which the settlers and troopers nearly eliminated all the members of the tribe of Gidgegannup, the people of Murrnmorda, and the Kalyute people of Pinjarra along the Murray River. These massacres took place for a lesser reason.

Jubuc reasoned that the river people were still lucky because each time there was a massacre, some members of the tribe in the conflict always escaped to tell about the raids by the aggressors, the newcomers, the now dreaded white settlers, and their troopers. Jubuc knew that the people of the next sunrises would know about what had happened to their people in the many summers and winters that would pass into yesterday.

Jubuc reasoned that it would be good to let Bulmurn get angry, then he would go after the bad white men to kill them. If he succeeded, the authorities of the white men's law would place the blame on Bulmurn. This is the way they would keep the blame off the river people, keeping them safe from harassment from the troopers when they came to investigate the killing of Rows and his men.

Jubuc visualised himself and the other councillors telling the troopers that they knew nothing. They would say that Bulmurn no longer lived amongst them. They would say that Bulmurn had been banished from their river tribe many summers ago: 'He made his campfire a secret, so nobody knew where he was.'

'*Kiaya kurah!* Long time ago. *Kiaya!* Yes, a long time ago', thought Jubuc. 'Let Bulmurn take the blame, I feel he owes us that much. *Kiaya*, he owes all the river people that much. It will give Bulmurn a chance to set himself straight with our people in our tribe. Yes, it will give him the chance to set himself straight once more.' Although it would place Bulmurn at great risk, Jubuc knew it would be a good tactic to keep the safety of the river people.

It was mid-morning when Jubuc reached the foothills of the escarpment near Toodyay. He climbed toward the top of one of the large hills of the Darling Range. When Jubuc reached the top, he gazed at his home location, then he looked toward the new settlement they called 'Perth', Goomap. Jubuc thought of the *wadjbulla's* big *miamia* there, and the big fire smoking all the time there. Jubuc shrugged his shoulders in a disgruntled manner, then turned and set off in the direction of Bulmurn's last known campsite.

Jubuc recalled how many times he had left message sticks, to tell Bulmurn he had passed by his *miamia*. Jubuc always did this when it was not possible for Bulmurn to see him. This time he must face the man, bringing tragic news. His mood deepened. Jubuc knew that Bulmurn would know he was coming, because he was being followed by a crow. The *wardang* was flying from tree to tree and cawing, cawing loudly as Jubuc walked towards Bulmurn's *miamia*. Then the *wardang* flew ahead and disappeared. Jubuc smiled because the crow had stopped its cawing, and he strode on knowing he was very close to Bulmurn's *miamia* which was concealed in the bush ahead of him.

Then Jubuc saw the camp. As he approached the *miamia*, Bulmurn stepped out of his home and his sudden appearance made Jubuc marvel at his stature and willowy strength. He noted that he had more thickness in his long arms and legs. The four scars on his chest stood out more than before. The look in Bulmurn's eyes was that of shiny gemstones, something like Jubuc had once seen near the sea, like a shell he found in the sand upon the beach when he went to the ocean with others of the Mooro people to swim in the sea.

Jubuc knew he was in the presence of a very powerful man. He didn't like the job he was about to carry out, delivering the sad message about the deaths in Bulmurn's family. What he carried in his mind angered him, for he was a messenger with bad news this day.

The two men, Jubuc and Bulmurn met for the first time after many summers since his banishment from the Swan River Nyoongar people. They stood about three paces apart from each other.

Bulmurn saw the grim look on Jubuc's face. Bulmurn realised something terrible had happened. Jubuc, being shorter and of lighter build than Bulmurn, felt slightly uncomfortable under Bulmurn's stare. Nonetheless, Jubuc stood his ground. He gazed deeply into the face and eyes of Bulmurn.

Jubuc spoke first, 'Greetings, Bulmurn. It is good to see you. Are you well? I need to talk on important matters.' Jubuc stood, waiting for Bulmurn to make a reply. Jubuc had to speak first because of the older man's importance.

Bulmurn smiled and spoke: 'It is good to see you, Jubuc, my friend. I knew you were coming because my *wardang* friend told me someone was on the way to my camp or past it.'

Bulmurn continued on: 'I knew that I would get a message today from a person like you, because I had a dream. I was being chased by the *wadjbulla* troopers from the bottom of this great hill. I also saw the Council of Elders in my vision talking to you, Jubuc, giving you a mission to carry out. Is that why you are here?'

Jubuc marvelled at Bulmurn's powers of perception, but he

still had to tell Bulmurn the bad news.

Jubuc could scarcely tell his story of horrors to Bulmurn. As he told each part, Bulmurn made sounds from deep within his body. Bulmurn spat in disgust on the ground in front of the two men. Jubuc told it the way Binyu had told them, adding his interpretation of what had happened after visiting the death site; how the Mooro had moved the bodies to a proper burial site on the hill near the swamp just out of Guildford close to the place where the swamp emptied into the Derbal Yerigan, the Swan River.

Jubuc held nothing back. He told Bulmurn how the Mandoon people had said they would not seek revenge, because the Council of Elders feared the *wadjbulla* troopers would come and kill them all.

'I have come on behalf of the Council of Elders to ask you to make the wrong right, because these mad white dogs have broken our Law. They have to be brought to justice; their deaths would even the score. That is why we are asking you to take revenge for our people. We are asking you to become an outlaw to the white people by killing the white men who killed our sister and brother.

'We realise that if you are caught by the troopers you will be hanged like others of our people, but Bulmurn, you are a man with many powers. Maybe you won't be caught. I hope not', Jubuc added, 'but the spirits of our brother and sister will never be free until we avenge their deaths. Until this is done there will be no dreaming for them. No!', Jubuc said, 'no dreaming for them until this is done by you'.

'Bulmurn!' Jubuc repeated. 'You know their spirits will have no dreaming until this is done by you. Their spirits will never be allowed into the land of the Dreamtime. They will never be able to rest, they will wander forever.

'These bad white men must die', Jubuc cried out aloud, showing his anger over the events that had happened in the last few days. 'Don't you see, Bulmurn, your strength is needed by our people? You must do it, Bulmurn. Only you can do it.'

Jubuc walked away from Bulmurn. He went a couple of paces still further then turned and said, 'I will wait over here for you while you think of what actions you will take. I will wait over here for your answer to the Council of Elders.

'If you cannot do it, I will ask the Council of Elders to sit in another meeting to determine who else is the right person to carry out action for our people.'

Jubuc was startled by Bulmurn's quick, easy reply, which was given in low tones, almost indistinguishable from the rustle of the wind that began to blow through the bush. 'Of course, Jubuc, you well know my answer. My decision is already in your mind. You did not walk all this way without knowing what actions I would take. That would not be like you Jubuc, your powers are nearly as strong as mine. That is how I know you know what my answer will be.'

Then Bulmurn shouted, 'I will do it! I will do it! I will do it for my sister! I will do it for my brother-in-law! I will do it for Binyu, my nephew! I will do it for our people, our river people and for the upholding of our own Law. I must carry out the Law. The bad white men must surely die or I will die attempting to kill them.

'The Dreamtime spirits will decide who's right and who's wrong and who has to die. I will avenge our tribal Law, upholding our people's honour. When this is done, Binyu can sleep in peace, knowing his parents' spirits are free to enter the Dreamtime world. Binyu will know their killers were brought to Nyoongar justice. Our whole tribal council, our river people, and those people in surrounding areas will bear the mark of justice on their will knowing that our laws, our life will continue to hold value to us all.'

After Jubuc had left him, Bulmurn went to the secret cave. In the cave he would gather *wilgee*, an ochre he would use to mark his body with ritual stripes, symbolising his power. *Wilgee* was an important material that he and his people used. The *wilgee* would give the medicine man an added spiritual significance to his appearance — red, white and yellow lines and splotches would cover his body. He would put it all over his body, especially where his hands and fingers could reach. Bulmurn would also make a head-dress that would increase his height, giving him an appearance of colour and power.

It was dark at the secret cave when Bulmurn arrived there. He stirred the old ashes where he had built a fire on a previous visit. He placed dried grass and twigs on it. He rubbed a pointy stick between the palms of his hands, kindling a heat to spark a fire that would give warmth and light. The wood he had stored nearby was added to the fire, and the fire's flames began to flicker their new light into the night's sky. As the flames licked the cold air, the light cast eerie shadows across Bulmurn's body.

Then Bulmurn began to paint on his body the splotches and stripes. He adorned his headgear. Then, as if it were a signal, his appearance began to take on mystical qualities. His figure began to take on longer and longer proportions, and the outlining of his body created by the red, white and yellow *wilgee* created illusions of several bodies united into the one human frame, 'Bulmurn'.

A breeze began to penetrate the sacred place. As it blew, the sounds seemed to carry messages from the spirits of the caves. It was this wind spirit that Bulmurn wanted to listen to. The sheoak trees overhead began to quiver and shake and a sudden quick twist of air created a deep howl from them. Gradually, as though the spirits had become agitated at being called forth for this occasion, *mar* the wind blew violently among the trees, which seemed to make them sway in frenzied disregard for the safety of their own branches and trunks.

Bulmurn was not afraid, he knew that the spirits of his Dreamtime people had come to speak with him, to watch and encourage him as he prepared to right the Law and take revenge for his people upon the evil white men who had killed his sister and brother-in-law. He felt he could count on the Dreamtime spirits to give him more power and cunning to bring punishment to the four.

Bulmurn felt the wind rush across his body, sometimes with fire, sometimes with the chill of death. A twisting column of wind moved him nearer the centre of the sacred site. In the changing light of the campfire, Bulmurn began to corroboree. He danced gracefully, purposely, he swayed his body as he lifted his legs, moving his arms and his hands. He threw back his head, chanting words in a rhythm that he had been taught since puberty.

As Bulmurn danced, the words started to revolve in his mind. On he danced like a brolga bird, his long legs seemed to penetrate the earth making dust rise, adding more to the slowly developing colourful scene. He swayed in the firelight's glow, dancing with precise steps here and there. The light of the fire seemed to be showing his body, then hiding it from any would-be audience.

Bulmurn danced more slowly now. Then slowly, his movements became faster, then he began to sing and chant.

Gnungar djuka gnungar gudjar gnulgar gnarnya mobarn mamarup
Ngarnyar yjul dargangacinj warra wadjbulla mamarup
Ngarnya yjul dargangacinj warra wadjbulla mamarup
Dargangacinj warra wadjbulla mamarup jengas
Yjul gwabba allar karranhudo yjul bangulbyina
Ngannilak nyoongar gudjur gwabbanyo gwidjar balgup

My sister and brother-in-law, me I'm a powerful magic man
Me I will kill bad white man
Me I will kill bad white man
Kill bad white man devils
I will right the Law, I will avenge our people and make it right for them

Bulmurn began to slow his corroboree movements down. He danced a slower movement around the firelight. Bulmurn looked around him, he could hear the clicking of his people's traditional corroboree dancing sticks and the sharp clapping of the *kylie* boomerangs being hit together. Both instruments were being played to blend in with an unseen singer, who sang in a low key. Bulmurn could see no singer or musicians. Then he fell to his knees as though the singer and musicians were singing and playing for him. As though the voice and instruments were summoning up an intensity of energy from within his very soul,

Bulmurn rocked back and forth waiting for a signal to tell him what to do.

All of a sudden *mar* the wind returned. To Bulmurn the wind seemed to have a face that he'd never seen before, a spiritual face that seemed to be part of the wind. The wind engulfed Bulmurn in a screaming funnel urging him to move. The face of the wind seemed to be talking to him, urging Bulmurn to finish his dance, for them both to reach a far greater height.

It was the signal Bulmurn was waiting for. Bulmurn jumped from the crouched position he was in. He jumped high into the air. The musicians and singers sang and played louder. The clicking sticks, the slapping boomerangs and the unseen singers blended in unison with Bulmurn's now urgent dancing, urging him to dance and sing at a higher pitch.

Instead of singing his words out loud, Bulmurn sang through his mind:

My sister and brother-in-law, me I'm a powerful magic man
Me I will kill bad white man
Me I will kill bad white man
Kill bad white man devils
I will right the Law, I will avenge our people and make it right for them

Bulmurn continued to reach new heights, and as he danced the words flashed through his mind once again.

My sister and brother-in-law, my magic will kill the bad white devils
I will kill the bad white devils. I will right our Law.
I will make it right for you to enter the Dreamtime.
My sister and brother-in-law, I will make it right for you to join our people in the Dreamtime world.

Mar the wind screamed around Bulmurn in the dim, flickering fire, creating an effect like a halo which engulfed his shimmering, sweating, ebony body, outlining his body painting which grew fluorescent lines of power right through his body, giving Bulmurn an awesome appearance in the moving firelight.

Bulmurn shouted, then he jumped high into the air throwing his arms outwards. His painted body seemed to spread in all directions in the flickering firelight. Bulmurn shouted as loud as he could, as if he wanted everyone who could hear him to know what he was going to do. 'Lookout you bad white devils. I'm coming after you to right our Law. Lookout, I'm coming after you to make our Law right.'

Then Bulmurn, his body spent, collapsed near the edge of the fire. He lay in what seemed to be a trance. He lay prone without moving for many minutes, with hardly a sound coming from his exhausted body.

After what seemed to be an eternity, Bulmurn moved. He glided to his feet all in one movement. He moved effortlessly without any sound coming from his body, nor any noise or rustle of the earth. He was silent. Bulmurn stood still. Suddenly a bolt of lightning streaked its flashing light across the sky, followed by the crackling rolling thunder which to Bulmurn seemed to be a million voices of the past giving their approval. *Babbangwin* the lightning and *mulga* the thunder and *mar* the wind had delivered the approval of the Dreamtime spirits for Bulmurn to act, to right the Law for their people, his family and the Mooro river people. Bulmurn looked around the sacred site. He looked at every nook and cranny expecting to see something or somebody, but he saw no one. Then the fire blazed as though someone had put firewood on it. Bulmurn smiled. He knew the old ones of the spirit world approved.

'Yes', thought Bulmurn. 'All the spirits have approved. Now I have all the power I need to right the Law, to bring to justice the killers, so I can avenge my family.' Now it was time for Bulmurn to rest and prepare for the trials that lay ahead of him.

Bulmurn entered his *miamia* which he had made earlier in the sanctuary of the special place. He lay down in his resting place, pulling his rug and cloak over him so that he would have warmth to ensure he would be rested and have a good sleep. Soon the rugs would be warm. As Bulmurn rested his body, he began to think about what tomorrow would bring. Tomorrow he would go and search for the killers. He would seek them out in the most cunning way possible. Then he would kill them, the killers of his sister and his brother-in-law. If he succeeded, then his nephew Binyu would have his revenge, too.

Revenge

Jim Rows called out to his workers from the verandah of the stone homestead he had constructed five years earlier. 'Breakfast is ready! Come over here and get into it, lads, so we can go out to work. We have a hard day ahead of us.' Julia, Jim's wife, had made a hefty breakfast for her husband and their three employees. They all had a serve of porridge followed by lamb chops, eggs from their own fowls, and toasted home baked bread, all washed down with large mugs of tea.

Julia Rows was a good woman in the eyes of most people who knew her. She was toughened in the ways of the Australian settlers' life. Julia Wilmott was born to a middle-class family who lived in Kent, south-east of London in England. Her father, Richard, was a general merchant who traded in goods of all kinds. Her mother, Anne, was a strict woman who gave Julia and her two brothers and two sisters a Christian upbringing, as well as a good education.

This education was to lead Julia to become a teacher and governess to well-to-do families in the area. Julia was a successful governess and her teaching skills were sought after within the county. It was through her work that she met Doctor William Edwards and his wife who had told her about their plans of starting a new life in the young Swan River Colony in Western

Australia. The Edwardses had spoken to Julia of their plans to make the voyage to this new land and they asked her to accompany them as governess to their four children.

This offer was something she had given a lot of thought to. She discussed it with her father and mother and brothers and sisters. Her family did their best to talk her out of what they thought was a mad idea of going to a new colony on the other side of the world. But Julia was not deterred by their concern of all the dangers she may encounter in the new world. She was determined to make up her own mind.

Then one day she knew what she was going to do. She had waited for the time when her family were having a Sunday evening meal. She said, 'Father, can I make an announcement to the people I love most?'.

There was not one sound. Everybody went quiet; she saw her mother look at her father wide-eyed. Her sisters put their hands to their mouths. Finally, after what had seemed an eternity, her father spoke. 'Speak then, girl, tell us what's on your mind. The sooner you do it, the sooner we will all know what it's about.'

Julia said, 'Thank you Father. As you all know, I spoke to you about the offer by the good Doctor Edwards and his kind wife to accompany them to the new colony in Western Australia as governess to their children, in the quest to start a new life over there. I want you all to know I have given this offer careful consideration and it is not a decision I have reached quickly, but I have now made up my mind to accept the Edwardses' offer. I am going with them.'

Julia's mother cried. Her sisters rushed to Julia's side. Her brothers sat and stared at her. Then her father, Richard, tapped the handle end of his knife on the dining room table and beckoned the girls to sit down. When they were seated and everybody was quiet, he said to Julia, 'Then that's it girl, you've made up your mind. There's nothing we can do to change it. You are the eldest and over your majority, and always you were headstrong, a bit like your mother I say. When will you be going to this new place?'

'We sail in two weeks' time, Father. Doctor Edwards will pay my passage and he also has given his guarantee that if I do not like it over there he will pay my passage back home again. I think this is a fair offer, that's why I want to go. I like the idea of a new adventure; perhaps while I am over there I will be able to make a name for myself.'

In the new colony Julia Wilmott would indeed establish herself as a reliable governess to the Edwards family and later a teacher to other children in the colony. She met her future husband James Rowland Rows, known in the settlement as Jim Rows, at the Governor's ball. After a brief courtship they married in the Anglican church in Perth, and commenced life together, farming Jim's property at West Swan.

In the early days when she and Jim had had to clear the land, it was grinding, back-breaking work, but they did it together. All settlers had to help one another in some way to improve their farms through hard work. Julia did her best to keep the men happy whenever they were back at the homestead. The only time she saw the hired workers was in the morning, then late evening when they came home tired and hungry. She cooked all their meals, and saw to it that their cottages were cleaned and their laundry done.

The Rowses had been successful in raising sheep and cattle. They had nearly five hundred head of sheep and forty-five head of cattle grazing on their thousand acres of land, and they were making an income from wool, meat and grain. Now because they had had a few good seasons, they were able to employ hired help.

Lynch and Smith had been taken on to work with their regular farmhand, now foreman, Jack Harding. Jim and Julia were very pleased with the work efforts of the men who were fencing new land near the escarpment of the foothills towards the Toodyay Road.

The men finished breakfast and got up from the table. Each in turn complimented Julia for the fine meal she had prepared for them, before departing to the stable to catch one of the horses to harness up the work cart. Lynch soon caught the workhorse. Harding and Smith helped to harness the horse and cart, readying the vehicle to take them down to the new fenceline.

Jim Rows approached the men and said to his foreman, 'I won't be going with you this morning Jack, however, I'll come over to the north paddock where you'll be working, later in the day. I'll use the light buggy for transport because I want to go around the sheep to check them for blowfly infestation.'

'Righto, boss', Harding replied, 'see you this afternoon then'.

Julia waved to Rows to catch his attention and Jim swung his buggy back towards her. He halted the horse as Julia came towards him.

'Jim, darling, would you be able to come this way later in the day? There's something I need to discuss with you. Why don't you come back to the house for lunch before you join the others at the new fenceline?'

Rows replied, as he bent down to squeeze her hand: 'Julia my dear, if I can I certainly will. Is it of importance that I do?'

She smiled up at him. 'I'll see you then.' When he came back for lunch she would choose the right time to tell him that she was pregnant, that she was carrying their child. How happy he would be, she thought.

Soon the men disappeared into the distance. She knew them all as hard workers and ignored their rough manners. Julia was aware of how the workers looked at her, admiring her, complimenting her with their looks. This made her feel appreciated, but she missed the company of women. Julia Rows was a tall, beautiful red-headed woman with a good figure. She mused how they would be with women, white women. She had heard them talk about black gins, how it was easy with them. What the settlement needed was more white women, Julia thought.

Julia Rows dropped her thoughts of men and women, putting them out of her head, so she could get on with her own work. After cleaning the house, she would go out into their vegetable garden to hoe and cull the plants, one of her favourite chores. She made sure that fresh vegetables were always on the table.

Meanwhile, the fencers were on their way in the cart to start work on the north paddock. Their conversation started innocently enough about the task in hand, about the good breakfast they had just had, about the nature of the woman their boss had married. They all commented on her beauty. They all agreed that Jim Rows was indeed a lucky man to have married her.

Then their conversation changed to the rape and the two murders of the Aboriginals, the man and his wife. Ron Smith was the first to comment. 'Jesus', he said, 'I can't get it out of my mind what we did to those people five days ago. How we killed that blackfella, what we did to his woman. And then we killed her just to cover our tracks! I say we didn't need to do it. Why the bloody hell did we have to do it? Why the bloody hell did we have to get boozed out of our heads? I tell you, you blokes, it's the liquor that made us do it. Lord, it made us sex starved, crazy madmen', moaned Smith.

Harding's nerves were as taut as a wire: 'Shut your fuckin' mouth!', and he punched Smith sharply on the jaw. The blow knocked him from the cart onto the ground. Smith lay there stunned, gasping for breath.

Harding, the foreman, jumped onto the ground where Smith had fallen and stood over him. 'Shut your loose mouth, you stupid bastard. You're a bloody fool to even think about it! We did it sure enough, we feel guilty as sin, but how in the hell can we shut it out of our minds if you go around whingeing like a stuck pig?'

Harding looked at Smith, then at Norman Lynch, then back at Smith, who was now in a sitting position. 'You both know we hid their bodies well enough. You both know we cleaned up the signs of the struggles. I reckon nobody, but nobody, will ever find those bodies now. We brushed the whole area to rub out our tracks after we dug the graves. We did a thorough clean-up job — nobody would know we were there.

'I don't want you, Smith, or you either, Lynch, to speak or breathe a solitary word of this incident to anyone again. You hear, Ron? You too Norman. If I hear that either of you has been popping off his mouth about this, you'll finish a lot worse off than today, Smith.

Then Lynch cut in: 'All right, Jack, you're right.' Lynch said to Smith, 'You'd better clam up about what 'appened, mate. We can't let an incident of this kind bother us out 'ere. This land is too wild, it's untamed. It was just one o' those things that 'ad to 'appen. Nobody's goin' to find those bodies. I say, let's go to the fenceline, so we can start earnin' a quid. Forget this silly business. I say, let's get some good 'ard work under our belts.'

Harding finished the conversation with a warning to Smith. 'You bloody fool, Ron. I've a mind to make you walk to the fenceline. A walk across the next two paddocks might do you some good. You've got to clear your mind of that garbage about liquor. Come on Norman, let the bugger walk.'

Lynch joined in with a boyish taunt: 'Yeah, let 'im walk the next two paddocks. I'm sure as 'ell that should quieten him down. It'll do him good to have plenty of time to think about what's 'appened and 'ow we should forget about the 'ole damn thing.'

Smith clambered to his feet rubbing his jaw. He wiped the dust from his trousers, looking rather apologetically up at Harding and Lynch. 'All right, Jack, you're right again', he said. 'Both of you are right. Maybe the walk will do me the world of good, whatever you say. But it weighs heavy on me now. I never did such a thing in my life before. It doesn't fit well with me. Even if time has passed since we did what we did, I have never done such a thing before, and it doesn't fit with me at all.'

Thankful to get away from Harding, Smith began to walk in front of the horse and workcart keeping a pace so they wouldn't see either the anger or the fear on his face. Soon he'd gone across the paddock, separating himself from the other two. As he walked and they travelled by cart and horse, the distance between them widened. They travelled their ways separately, one person cutting across the paddock to where he worked, the others travelling by cart and horse around the perimeter.

At the fenceline that separated the cleared land from the surrounding bush, Smith paused for a minute. He gazed over the land Rows owned and mused to himself about how much extra work the settlers had to do to kill all the big trees and hack out the smaller bush. Smith marvelled over the fact that a few hundred sheep could keep down any regrowth of bush vegetation. He thought to himself how good it was to see the land cleared by hard labour. He looked at the thick bush either side of the cleared paddocks, then turned to walk along the fenceline in the direction of the others. Suddenly, he stopped dead in his tracks. A gasp of surprise whistled through his lips. There, no more than ten metres away from him stood a very tall, powerful, heavily armed black man!

Smith's fear was instantaneous. He could not utter a sound. He froze in his tracks. He couldn't move even if he wanted to. The hair bristled up his spine to his head as a cold fear enveloped him. The painted body was awesome in its appearance.

Smith could do nothing with his body. The long silence of the scene was overbearing. He tried to talk, his mind said he had to say something. 'What do you want, boy?', he said in a strangely squeaky, quivering voice.

The only answer Smith received was a blur of movement from the black man, then he felt sudden ripping agony that came from a barbed spear as it tore into his chest. Smith fell heavily, impaled with nearly half a metre of spear protruding from his back, fresh blood spurting from the wound, spilling over his shirt, staining it red.

Smith's hands tried to feel the hole in his chest, but all he could do was grab onto the spear shaft. He tried to cry out, but there was no sound coming from his throat. His final thought was that somebody had seen them murder the blacks. Then his body convulsed, shaking all life away.

Bulmurn pushed the spear on through the body of Smith, withdrawing it, leaving the wound exposed to allow blood to flow freely. Then he lifted the body, and flung it on the fence to hang there, like the body of a sheep that he had seen hanging near a settler's house. Bulmurn purposely hung Smith's body in this manner, knowing that sooner or later, the others would come looking for this *wadjbulla* and when they did, he would be ready for them.

Jack Harding and Norman Lynch arrived at their work site on the new fenceline just about the same time that Smith had met up with Bulmurn. Harding and Lynch got down from the cart, then they set about getting to work. 'Hey! Norman', Harding said, 'I reckon without Smithy helping us, this is going to be hard yakka.'

'Yeah', Lynch said. 'You know yourself, Smithy isn't a bad fencer at all. Mind you 'e's one of the better workers around this settlement, I can tell you that . . .'

'Do you reckon I was too hard on him, Norm?', asked the now calm foreman.

'Maybe', Lynch said to Harding. 'He don't seem to feel too good about those blacks, but as a matter of fact, neither do I. I'm concerned myself, even though I've put it be'ind me. You know what, I reckon Smithy 'as got weak knees. 'E's a coward, that's what 'e is. I just hope 'im walking the rest of the way to this new fenceline will do 'im some good. I 'eard 'im shouting in his sleep last night. 'E's been feeling the strain for sure. He's got to get 'imself sorted out.'

'I know it sure was a grisly business all right, but as you, I and the others know, it happened', said Harding. 'We can't change it, we've got to put it out of our minds. After all, they were only blackfellas. It's not as though they were white, you know.

'Look Norm', Harding said after a short pause. 'Let's change the subject. Did you hear the thunder last night? You know I got up, I was feeling restless. I went outside for a smoke, to think a little. When I was outside, I saw tremendous flashes of lightning. It must have been the brightest lightning I've ever seen. Then the thunder rolled, bouncing across the sky. There wasn't much rain though. There must have been a hell of a storm somewhere last night.'

Lynch whistled: 'She sure was a beauty wherever she was. You know, I got up last night, too, and while I was up, the door was ajar. The bloody wind was flying 'round our 'ut. I moved towards the door to shut it. Then a scary feelin' came over me, I tell you true, it seemed like the wind didn't want me to shut that door. When I reached out for the door knob, the wind blew against me. I 'ad a 'ard job to shut it, I tell you. There seemed to be some force be'ind it. I tell you, I felt scared as though there was somethin' evil out there. I still 'ave this feeling of unrest as though something bad is going to 'appen. Maybe it's an omen.'

Then Harding cut him short by saying, 'Come on, let's get crackin'. This is good money Rows is paying us. He's not a bad boss you know.'

Lynch nodded in agreement and, walking towards the cart, began to unload the wandoo posts. He coughed and spat on the ground before he plodded further along the line to mark the spot for the next post-hole to be dug. When he marked the right spot, Harding began to dig. Norman Lynch returned to the cart to unload new posts and place them near the holes they were to be put in. He continued on down the fenceline until the cart was empty, then he returned to pick up a shovel.

The two men worked steadily for nearly three hours, then when they placed the last of the posts, they stopped. Harding said to Lynch, 'You go back to where we stockpiled the other fence posts yesterday. After you've loaded the cart, go back to where we dropped Smithy. He should have been here by now. Pick him up and take him with you to help load the cart at the stockpile in the other paddock. When you find him, ask him how he feels, he may be feeling crook. Maybe I hit him too hard. He might be groggy.

Get going or we'll never get any more work done on this fence-line today', said Harding, showing annoyance at Smith's absence. 'I'll put a billy on for a cuppa tea. Time you get back it'll be boiled, ready waiting for the pair of you. A cuppa tea might make everybody feel a lot better.'

Lynch snapped the reins across the rump of the work horse. 'Giddyup', he said to the horse as it began to trot away from where they worked. Lynch bumped up and down in the seat as the wheels rolled over the uneven ground. 'This is no highway', he laughed to himself. He would let the horse trot until it slowed down itself, then he would let it plod along at its own pace.

The horse started to slow down as Lynch turned towards the paddocks where they had left Smith to walk. 'Coo-ee!', Lynch shouted. 'Coo-ee! Coo-ee!' Lynch let his eyes search the paddock, but he could see no movement of anyone walking. 'Where is that bloke?', he said to himself. 'I'll go on further, then I'll give another hoy.' On Lynch went, passing a small hill along the fenceline. Finally he came to the paddock corner which led back to the homestead.

Becoming annoyed Lynch again called 'Coo-ee! Coo-ee! Ron! Where are you?'. Nobody answered. He muttered to himself that Smith was a fool to have gone elsewhere at this time of the day.

He turned the horse and cart around the corner up the homestead fenceline. Lynch could see something slumped over the wire of the fence, something that looked human. 'Yeah', he thought, 'looks human all right. Bloody 'ell that looks like a man for sure. Might be Smithy playing a trick on me – damn 'im!' He flicked the reins to urge the horse on. 'I 'ope he's all right, I didn't think Harding 'it 'im that 'ard. Maybe 'e is feeling the effects of that 'it. What would make the man prop 'imself up against the fence for?'

Lynch never for a minute thought of the man being dead. Indeed, he never imagined that it was Smith's lifeless body hanging from the fence, not propped up against it like he thought it was. If he wasn't so curious, he might have thought to arm himself with one of the three guns they carried in the cart.

When Lynch got within twenty metres of the body he could see that it was Smith hanging there like a sack. Lynch jumped down from the cart, running and he pulled Smith's body off the fence. He could see the wound to Smith's chest, he could see the blood-spattered shirt of his workmate and friend. He knew Ron was dead, dead as any man could be.

Lynch's further inspection of the body showed him that Smith had been speared. Lynch heard himself say, ''E's been speared. That means there are blacks out there in the bush, maybe they're after us. I'd better get out of 'ere, back to Harding, but first I'd better put Smith's body on the cart.'

Lynch grabbed hold of Smith's body under the arms. He dragged the dead weight towards the cart and horse. The horse stamped its legs nervously as though he sensed that something was wrong. The horse seemed restless. Lynch hurried to get the body onto the cart. He slipped two or three times as he trundled the body along, half dragging, half carrying it, blood pumping almost audibly through his brain as he worked.

After what seemed an eternity, he finally reached the work cart, turned and looked back to where he had found Smith's body on the fence. A sudden fear caught hold of him, taking his breath away. There, where only a few minutes ago he had found his friend, less than ten to fifteen metres away, stood a rigid, silent, fearsome-looking black man, armed with a menacing barbed spear. The black man had his barbed spear in his *woomera* almost ready to throw.

Lynch had known cold fear before. His mind flashed back to the time when he had been caught by the troopers for resisting arrest at a fight in a public house; the police had put him in jail for the night at Fremantle. The police had punched and kicked him for resisting them. They placed him in a small, dark room. Lynch hated the darkness. It was terrifying, and even more terrifying to feel the large rats crawling over him. He was sure that it was only a matter of time before the rats would start to eat him alive. Lynch vowed he would never let anything like that happen to him again. But here he faced a greater, more chilling fear.

This was in broad daylight. He was out in a paddock, he had his work cart and horse with him. He knew there were firearms in the cart, just out of reach. His foreman was only a couple of paddocks away from him. But this new fear held him, he could not move. Lynch knew that this black man had killed Smith. Lynch guessed like Smith that this painted shadowy being was there because they had raped and murdered the black woman and man some five days earlier.

'Listen, boy', Lynch shouted out. 'Listen! I didn't kill that woman or 'er man, I only kissed 'er a bit.' Lynch somehow had reached into the cart. Grabbing a musket, he tried to get it aimed at the black man to shoot him. It was in this instant that the barbed blood-stained spear shot its way through the front of his shirt. Lynch dropped to his knees, his eyes filled with terror as the barbed spear forced its way out of his back. Bulmurn's movement was as quick as that of *dugite* the snake. In his death throes, Lynch could not comprehend the accuracy or the strength of the tall ebony being who had speared him. Lynch could only writhe in pain as his life's blood drained from his body. He uttered no sound, it was as if his body was being constrained by some evil force.

Bulmurn hung the bodies of Smith and Lynch back on the fence. Then he went to the cart and looked in. In front of the vehicle, he saw more of the hated pointed sticks that made a noise like thunder and shot out metal balls that killed the black people without any effort at all. Bulmurn reached into the cart and took the firearms out. He took them and hid them in the bushes on the other side of the fence. Bulmurn knew that without the pointed sticks he had more chance of righting the Law of his river people and to avenge his family.

Bulmurn knew his task was unfinished. There were two more men to deal with before his job was done. He knew what he had to do. He had to make the other *wadjbulla* on his own down the fenceline come to him. He would wait for him as he had with the others. He turned towards the rear of the cart. He walked towards the horse and, raising his spear, drove its point into the animal's rump, causing it to rear and squeal out a terrified neigh of pain. The horse bolted back down the fenceline back the way it had just come, in the direction of the foreman, Jack Harding.

Bulmurn took his spear and *woomera* to a woolly bush, where he sat a few metres from the fence. He knew it would not be long before the other *wadjbulla* would come back to this spot looking for his men. Maybe he would think they had gone hunting when he saw the guns were taken out of the cart, mused Bulmurn to himself. All he had to do now was to wait until the other *wadjbulla* found the bodies of the other men on the fence, and when he did, Bulmurn would be ready for him.

When he heard the galloping of the horse and the clattering of the cart heading full pelt towards him, Jack Harding stood up and moved away from the billy can.

He saw the cart was without a driver, yet the horse's bolting, galloping action meant it was frightened or hit by someone or something. His first thought was that Lynch and Smith were playing a trick on him, playing him for a fool. Those bloody idiots were hiding in the tray of the cart! 'I'll fix them good if they wreck that cart', he cursed.

As the horse and cart drew closer, Harding could see the fear in the animal's eyes. The horse was wild-eyed, totally unconstrained in its galloping action. Harding could see that it wasn't going to stop, so he took evasive action. He dived to one side so he could grab hold of the trailing reins and stop the crazed horse from damaging the cart or injuring itself.

Catching the reins, he ran alongside the vehicle, trying to restrain the animal. Finally he was able to get aboard and could use his strength to bring the horse under control, but it would go another two hundred metres before he could achieve control.

Suddenly everything came to a standstill. All Harding could hear was the bellowed labour of the horse's breathing as it sucked oxygen into its near-bursting lungs. Harding looked into the tray of the cart half expecting to see Lynch and Smith hiding there. But they weren't and when he saw nobody in the cart, he said, 'Where are the men? Where are the guns? What in the name of heaven has happened? First Smith, then Lynch. I'll get to the bottom of this. I'll get even with them!'

Harding still held the reins tight on the horse as he got down from the cart. Harding spoke soothing words to it, he walked around it, stroking it with his hand, letting it know that he was a friend. He walked around the horse one more time, reassuring it. That's when he noticed blood running down the right hind leg. There was a deep wound there which puzzled Harding. He didn't know what to make of the wound. One thing was for sure, Jim Rows wasn't going to be pleased with today's events.

Harding waited for nearly half an hour, wondering what may have happened to his workers. 'Haw, they probably went hunting or maybe they had a fight. Maybe they're just playing me for a fool. But one thing's for sure, when I find 'em, I won't muck about with 'em. I'll give 'em a good tongue lashing. I'll get to the bottom of these pranks if this is the last thing I do.'

He climbed upon the cart, jigged the horse to a walk and turned him back towards the others. He looked at the horse's wound again. He said, 'It's quite deep. Maybe he backed into a sharpened fence post. I'll have to treat the horse, I'll have to put salve on the injury or the blowflies will get to the sore.'

Harding back-tracked along the way the horse had galloped. He never realised his life was in danger as he made his way to where Smith and Lynch had met their fate. As Harding's anger began to subside, he started to relax, and as he did this, he let his mind go back to the scene they had come across five days earlier. He allowed his thoughts to go back to the first impressions he had had of the black woman. 'Jesus, she was beautiful. Her body was gorgeous. God, how I wanted to have her first, before the other men touched her. Then Rows pulled rank, saying he was the boss, he would be the first to have her. I had to go second to the boss. But I beat him to the gun . . .'

The horse walked its own way, no longer did he drive it along. Harding just let the reins go slack, letting the horse limp along in the direction it had come from. He had experienced looking for lost men before. He was not worried, they would turn up sooner or later. Harding let the horse go; he knew it would find its way back to the last place of work.

Harding swore. He noted the horse's limp was worsening. 'Now I'll have to unharness him. I'll have to walk him back to the farmhouse to get another horse for the work cart so we can continue the fencing. Damn those two! It's all their fault.'

Harding took the harness off the horse, leaving only the bridle on him, so he could lead the limping beast. After he unharnessed the horse, he began leading it back along the fenceline towards the homestead. Harding showed compassion for the horse, more than he would for his mates, Lynch and Smith.

Harding walked in front of the limping cart horse. His attention towards the horse turned to concern, because the animal now seemed to favour the injured leg more than it had some twenty to thirty minutes ago. He knew the boss wouldn't be happy at the state of the horse. Even old hacks were valuable in the colony at the time.

Locked in his thoughts, Harding approached the converging fenceline without noticing the bodies of Smith and Lynch hung over the wire. It wasn't until he was within a few metres of them that the sudden buzzing of blowflies alerted his otherwise inattentive mind. Harding looked in the direction of the noise and was horrified when he saw the bodies of Smith and Lynch hung over the fence like sheep skins, hung out to dry.

Bulmurn had observed all. He had watched Harding's movement as he led the injured animal down the fenceline. He could see that the big *wadjbulla* was concerned for the horse. He also noted how startled the man was when he saw the bodies of his mates. Bulmurn knew, too, that this man was the same man who had hit the other man he had killed. He had hit him, knocking him from the cart. Bulmurn's instinct told him this man was potentially a danger to him. He knew with this man he would have to be very careful, he felt this man had more power than the other two. Bulmurn had deliberately given the other men a chance to see him. He had given them a chance to do something to prevent their deaths. He would not give this man the same chance.

Bulmurn's body became tense as he watched Harding get closer. He saw the horrified expression on the *wadjbulla's* face, his instincts told him to spear this big man as soon as he was within striking distance. Now, now was the time to strike. Now! Bulmurn took one step forward with his arm raised high, he threw his deadly barbed spear, propelling his *woomera* with tremendous force to hit its target. Again, Bulmurn had struck with swiftness of *dugite* and the cunning of *mokine* the *dwerrt* dingo.

Harding did not know what had hit him. He backed away from the searing pain in his rib cage, but the spear kept on going through to the other side of his body. The spear shattered bone and tissue as it holed his heart. Down he went, his body shuddering out of control. He twitched in a final frenzy of movement, then moved no more.

As Bulmurn kneeled over the body of Harding to remove the spear, he felt no remorse. His only real thought was that he still had one more man to bring to justice, their boss, the leader of this mad dog pack that had raped and killed his sister after they had killed her husband. The man who now owned the land that the Nyoongar people owned. He had been granted land without sitting with the Council of Elders to see if they would allow it to him.

'You, too, will die, you, the leader of the pack. You do not have the right to live anymore. You have lost it because you committed a great crime. You will die like the other bad men. You never owned this land of ours, neither have you the right to rape and kill. I have been asked to take revenge upon you and right the Law. Soon you will join the other three dogs. You will die, too.'

Bulmurn looked at Harding's body, then he looked over at the other two bodies of Smith and Lynch. Again he felt no remorse, only grim determination for what lay ahead of him. He knew what he had to do. 'I will make my way to Jim Rows's house now', Bulmurn thought out loud. 'I will kill this man quickly, at his own house. Then everyone will know I succeeded in my mission. The tribal elders and the river people will know I did it. They will not be blamed because I will show myself to his woman. Then she will not blame any of the others. How can she when she sees only one man? She will see my face and she will give the police troopers a description of me. She must convince them that it was only one man, so they won't retaliate against my river people.

'The police will go to my people at Guildford asking who it was who killed those men. Jubuc will tell. Jubuc will deny tribal conspiracy. Jubuc will point out that it was Bulmurn, the blood brother to the woman who was raped, then killed after her husband was killed by them. They will find out it was Bulmurn, the outcast of the tribe, who did it. Jubuc will tell.'

*   *   *   *   *   *   *   *

Jim Rows had a very busy morning doing his rounds. Looking for fly-blown sheep was not an easy task. Cleaning the blown area on the animals was arduous.

Rows toiled hard to clean the sheep. After three and a half hours, he was satisfied that he had cleaned all the infected sheep in the mob. Now he would set off to the fenceline to join the workers. Rows called his sheep dog upon the buggy seat with him. The dog sat high on the seat looking for all the world as if he should have been the driver!

Rows felt a little tired as he drove his buggy along. Instead of heading towards the fenceline immediately, he remembered his wife's request. He pulled the reins, turning the horse towards the homestead and lunch with Julia. Thoughts of Julia occupied his mind as his horse trotted on towards the house. He wanted her. Perhaps she would come to bed with him before lunch. He would join his workers down the new fenceline later. Yes, Rows thought. Julia first.

Julia was expecting him. She liked it when Jim took time from work to have lunch with her and today was a special day. She would tell him the news that they both wanted to hear: she was pregnant. Soon she would have their child, an heir to their farm and their dreams, but for now it could wait like her garden work could wait until later in the day.

She thought of making love to her Jim. Her excitement grew from the time he entered the cleared patch between the paddock and the homestead.

Jim Rows was not hasty as he washed himself in a tub of water that Julia had drawn for him. It was almost a ritual, her getting the bath ready, with the towels and the fancy talcum powder he had bought for her. She had helped her husband take off his grimy clothing. When he had climbed into the bath, Julia helped to soap his body, helped to rinse the soap off his body.

Julia even helped to soap and rinse his hair with clear water. Rows stood up and kissed her, pulling her close to him so that her dress got all wet and she had to take it off. Jim Rows watched with fascination as she exposed her shapely body to him, a sight he would never tire of. This part of their lovemaking excited them both. Rows kissed her tenderly with passionate love, then he lifted her into his arms and carried her into the bedroom to continue their lovemaking.

Julia was setting the midday meal onto the table when Jim came out of the bedroom fully dressed in a set of clean clothes. His appearance was quite different from the man who had come from the paddocks a short while ago, nearly exhausted. Rows had a renewed spring in his walk, plus a gleam in his eyes and quick smile on his lips when he caught Julia's eyes with his own. Rows told her he would be off soon to join the others working on the new fenceline. He asked if the men had been back to the farmhouse to pick up fence posts. Julia told him that she had not seen them come back, neither had she heard the horse and cart creaking past the house. 'But then', Julia added, 'I cut them good lunches this morning. They wouldn't need to come back unless they really needed the posts.'

'Maybe they've cut a few posts out of the bush near the new block to keep them going for the rest of the day. Perhaps you are right. Either way, there is a stockpile of fence posts along the fenceline they will probably use. Do let's eat', he said light heartedly.

After lunch they sat and yarned about the farm, about the work, the sheep and cattle. They talked about how lucky they were to have a good producing farm. Julia was about to change the subject when Jim rose from the lunch table and patted his stomach. He said, 'Loosen my belt'.

'Jim', Julia said, 'you've got a look of temptation in your eyes. Come here', she said, as she reached out her hands to undo his belt from where she was sitting, 'I have something to tell you', but he moved towards her and covered her mouth with his own.

Bulmurn had been near the homestead when Rows plodded up on the buggy. Rows's sheep dog did not notice or smell the intruder. The dog didn't bark or give a warning to Rows that a stranger, a black man, a heavily painted man, was sitting near the house waiting for the right moment to strike. Bulmurn had gone to the shack where he guessed the other workmen slept. He knew the dog wouldn't be able to warn his master if it could not distinguish his smell from the other workers' smell. Bulmurn sat alongside the cottage where he waited and watched for the unsuspecting Rows to appear from the house.

Bulmurn had a clear view of the homestead. When he saw Rows tie up the dog, he smiled. He knew his task would be much easier. He knew he could make his attack unhindered from the front of the house. It was to be quite a long time before Jim and Julia Rows opened the front door onto the porch of the front verandah. Both the Rowses were happy, they played like teenagers together for a few minutes, embracing each other affectionately. It was at this precise moment that Julia chose to tell her husband the good news. Suddenly Bulmurn appeared, seemingly from nowhere.

When he saw the Rowses embrace each other, Bulmurn pictured his own sister and her husband. He saw their child born from such lovemaking. Now he knew only burning anger at the two people who stood before him. He had no quarrel with the woman, only with her man, the leader of the pack.

Bulmurn jumped upon the front of their verandah and said out loud, 'I am Bulmurn, I am here to kill you white man. I am here to kill you for the murder of my sister and her husband. Now it's your turn to die.'

Jim Rows had just enough time to loosen his grip on Julia and turn to this sudden apparition, when a barbed spear of the *Mobarn Mamarup* tore its way though his clean shirt, in the middle of the left breast, through the rib cage, tearing the heart, bursting the liver, lung and bone apart as the barbs sought their way to the other side, then out into the open air. Blood spurted down the shaft of the spear onto Bulmurn's hand. Blood oozed out of the wounds of Rows's chest and back, staining his shirt red.

Jim Rows was indeed a strong man, but all he could do was grab wildly at the spear in a vain effort to pull it out of his chest. His eyes rolled as he shrieked out a cough. He died, writhing, at his wife's feet. Julia had not even had time to believe what had happened. Her mouth was agape and her eyes were staring in complete horror.

Without thinking, Julia began screaming at Bulmurn, telling him to get away, to stop hurting her husband. She grabbed at the spear trying to pry it loose from her dead husband's grasp. The barbs would not be pulled backwards. With all her strength she tried to pull it out, pulling and tugging, causing her husband's body to jerk like a rag doll.

From a few steps away, Bulmurn watched the woman's

pathetic attempts to save her husband's life. Then Julia stopped her futile attempt to pull the spear out. She turned all her attention fully on to Bulmurn. She flew at him in a rage, punching at him. She screamed at him, 'Killer, killer! You killer! Get away!' Then Bulmurn hit Julia on the side of the head with a rock-like hand. She reeled there, staggered off the verandah onto the ground. She fell and lay very still. Bulmurn's thoughts were racing fast, never before had a woman attacked him in such a manner as this. Not even his beloved Lulura would be foolish enough to make an attack on him.

Although he had found the hunt exhilarating, this last frenzy by the woman was something he had never experienced before. He looked at Julia. This woman had the courage of a wounded animal and courage was something Bulmurn admired in people. Bulmurn knew he hadn't really hurt the woman, his blow to her head was only to stop, not hurt her. His fight was not against her. His fight was against her husband and his workers who raped and murdered his sister and brother-in-law.

Bulmurn knew Julia would remember this for the rest of her life. He turned the dead man into a sitting position so he could remove his spear from his still body. He soaked his hands in human blood as he pulled the shaft of the spear through the back of Rows. Bulmurn wasn't to know that he had prevented Julia from the most intimate moment with her husband. She had not been able to tell him she was pregnant.

Bulmurn said in his own tongue, 'This is a good hunt, it is only right it should end like this. Now the Law is righted. Now I feel satisfied that I have carried out the task asked of me by the Council of Elders. The elders' faith in me is justified. They chose me, I was the right person to do the job. Now my sister and her husband's spirits have been avenged. Now Binyu, my nephew, can rest easy. Come next daybreak at first light of dawn, his parents' spirits won't roam anymore, because the spirits of the Dreamtime will be welcoming them into the Dreamtime world.' This was the last sound he made, before leaving the Rows homestead.

As Bulmurn left the farm, he heard the sheep dog barking. It had at last caught the smell of him, the intruder. The horse hitched to the buggy gave a whinny. Bulmurn smiled as he heard the cawing of the *wardang* giving him a sign from the spirits his mission was finished, now completed.

The scene at the farmhouse looked quiet indeed. The farmer, Jim Rows, looked as though he had fallen asleep against the verandah post. His wife, Julia, lay with the side of her face in the dirt, at the edge of the bottom step of the verandah as though she, too, had just dropped off to sleep.

Jim Rows's spirit would never return to his broken body. His spirit would wander in the Dreamtime until it found a home. Julia's spirit would return to her body. She would regain her sense later in the day when the sun dropped low into the sky, when the temperature fell.

Julia Flees

Julia opened her eyes. Terror could still be seen in them. Her first movements were very ungainly. She rolled to the left side of her body, then to the right, which caused her head to spin. Then she rolled on her back, holding her forehead as she tried to remember what had happened. Julia's head ached.

Even though Bulmurn had not hit her hard enough to kill her, she was concussed. The past events came back slowly into her mind, then rushed into the realisation that Jim was dead. She felt for her tiny baby to reassure herself that the child was unharmed.

'I am alive — that big black man didn't kill me, although heaven knows why he didn't', she thought. Julia struggled to a sitting position as her eyes surveyed the scene around her. She moaned. Then she pulled herself to her feet. She swayed and staggered a little here and there before she caught hold of the verandah post to steady herself. Then her eyes came to rest on her husband Jim. She did not want to touch him because she knew he was dead. He had to be dead — he was sitting leaning on the verandah post with lifeless eyes that could see nothing.

But Julia's courage prevailed. She bent over her husband and cradled him in her arms, putting his head on her breast. She clung to him, crying out the words she wanted her Jim to hear even though she knew he could not. 'I love you Jim. I'll always love you. I'll always remember you loved me, too.' The tears ran down her face as she remembered their lives together facing a new frontier; clearing the land, practically living in the dirt like the natives. 'Now I'm all that's left. Our house. Our sheep. Our cattle. Our land. Our farm. Our family. It's no good to me now that you've gone, Jim. Why? Why did this have to happen to us, Jim. Why us?'

A gentle breeze blew into Julia's face, bringing her mind back to the present situation. The breeze also heralded the coming of darkness, and a new fear. Her husband was gone. She realised that she would have to get help.

Where were those workers of ours? Why hadn't they returned from the fenceline? 'He's killed them, too', Julia cried out in fear and anger. 'Lord in Heaven he's killed them as well.' She got up and looked around her, fearful for her own safety. She had to get away as fast as she could.

Julia ran to the horse and buggy her husband had used around the farm earlier that day. She climbed upon the seat, grabbing the reins at the same time and jerking them so that the horse reared back and around on its hind legs. She did not know how or where she had found the whip, but it really didn't matter, she found it. She slashed the whip as hard as she could down on the horse's rump. The animal lurched forward into a gallop nearly tipping Julia out of the cart as it raced away down the track. Julia giddyuped the horse as hard as she could, driving off in a frenzy, racing through Guildford towards the main township of Perth.

Julia never looked back towards the homestead. She never looked into the now darkening paddocks or the bush around her. She just drove down the track. The only thing she could see was the face of the man who had killed her husband, the face of the man who had caused all these new problems she would now face. She would see the painted face of the big black savage for as long as she lived. 'I'll never forget that horrid black face. Never. I'll never ever forget.'

The only thing Julia had was courage. She kept thinking of her husband, of how much they had put into their lives together.

They had come from England six months apart and met one night at the Governor's ball in the new settlement. She had seen him across the ballroom floor with other girls around him all waiting for the opportunity to accept an invitation to dance. Even though she felt she would faint as she realised he was treading across the ballroom floor towards her, she had to look around to see if it was really her he was going to invite and not some other of the beautiful girls nearby. Rows bowed to her asking for the pleasure of the dance. She accepted shyly, placing her hand in his and soon she was gliding around the dance floor in his arms.

From there on their romance had blossomed into love. Then one night he asked her to marry him and she gladly accepted. She remembered they had spent a week in the new settlement of Perth, staying in one of the finer rooms of the Royal Hotel in St George's Terrace. Julia remembered the wonderful time they had buying things for the new farm in the Swan Valley. After the week was over, he had brought her out to the Rows homestead, built on land granted to him by the Governor.

They had to work hard together to build up their farm to grow wheat, to grow sheep for wool and mutton, and cattle for beef; to grow extra vegetables so they could use the money from market to hire farmhands to clear new land and build fences around their property.

Julia knew now that her life was shattered, and that she would have to rear her child by herself. She knew her life would never be the same again. Never. No, it would never be the same, not without her Jim.

She looked towards the heavens, silently vowing to kill every black man in the country if she had to, to avenge Jim's death. Why did this black man spear Jim? Julia questioned her husband, and the others, Harding, Lynch and Smith. Were they dead, too? Did this have anything to do with the killings of the natives at other areas of the settlement?

Her fear now began to turn to hatred for the black people in the region. Julia's crying became more and more unsteady as she sobbed unashamedly. She gulped for air; the big lump she had in her throat seemed to choke her. Her tormented body was being bounced across the buggy seat, her head ached with each stride the horse took.

Again her thoughts focused on the Aborigines: they didn't want to work, they didn't understand anything about the white settlers nor did they want to. No, no black man was worth keeping. They wouldn't cut down the trees, they couldn't look after the sheep and cattle, instead they wanted to kill them. Their women wouldn't learn how to cook or to work in the house. Their children were always sick. They always hid in the bushes from the whites whenever they passed their camps. These black people were no good.

Julia paused to wipe the teardrops from her cheeks as she approached the scattered dwellings of Perth. She was always going to remember the face of the killer who shouted at them, accusing them. Julia would always remember he blamed her Jim for something in his native tongue. She could not understand what it was the black man had actually said, but she promised herself she would find out. Then, as though it was placed in her mind so she would search in another direction for the answer, she asked, 'Why didn't he kill me, Jim? Why did he only kill you? Even though I don't really know why, I think the others are dead, too.

'Why? Is there something I should know, Jim?' Julia slowed the horse down to a walk, for it had become suddenly clear to her that the horse was balking and breathing very badly. She slowed it down to a walk, while she tried to let her thoughts gain a bit more semblance of order and cohesion. It wasn't that she was afraid she would drive the horse too hard or that it might die. It was the thought of walking down the road to Perth at night all alone that made Julia feel afraid.

Dizziness began to taunt her senses. Slowly, she began to drift off tiredly into semi-consciousness, until she slumped along the seat of the buggy, leaving the horse to plod onwards towards the settlement on its own without Julia to guide it.

Late afternoon the next day, a police patrol of mounted troopers was headed towards the outskirts of Perth. The patrol was on a tour of duty about the settlement and was led by Senior Constable George Clamp, followed by Constables Thomas Bowler and James Bell. In the company of the police officers were three black trackers: Jacky Jack, who answered to 'Jacky', Jimmy Jim Rankin and Wheelbarrow Long.

Jacky Jack's name was given to him by a colonist who considered he was comparable to the donkey or jackass. Jimmy Jim Rankin had been given the names of three settlers whom he had guided around the new settlement to help find land allocated to them by the Governor. Jimmy Jim was proud of the fact that he had been given the names of his bosses for helping them find their farms.

Stories were told around the campfires about how the black trackers and other natives had got their English European names, how the settlers used to laugh at them. Each European name given to an Aborigine was good for a laugh.

Wheelbarrow Long was right proud of his name and everybody took delight in how he introduced himself. The settlers laughed with great mirth when he said, 'Me dis wun boss, me Wheelbarrow . . . Long'. When the others laughed, Wheelbarrow Long laughed with them, their pleasure seemed to give him pleasure as well.

Black trackers were usually Aborigines who were recruited by the police to help capture renegade blacks who broke the English law. The black trackers were paid for their services in flour and tobacco, also a drop of rum here and there, sometimes gin. The rest of the pay was made up with left-over European foods. Sometimes the troopers gave them a small coin like a threepenny bit, for a job thought to be well done. Usually, their payment in coins or food was much lower than the work was worth.

The senior officers also used them as their batmen, as personal servants. They also served as boatmen, as their knowledge of the Swan River was invaluable to the police. Sometimes the European vessels were under threat of an attack from the Aboriginal river people. Sometimes the river people were reluctant to throw their spears at the boat travellers for fear of hitting the trackers, however this was not always the case. Some attacks went ahead regardless of who was in the boat; sometimes respect was lost for the black trackers.

The black trackers were highly skilled bushmen who were needed to find lost settlers, many of whom wandered only a few hundred metres away from a main track, but became very confused. The authorities also needed the trackers to find other Aborigines who had to be brought before the British court of law for crimes committed against the settlers. As the colony expanded away from the river areas and more traditional hunting grounds were taken over as farms for settlers, Aboriginal resistance grew. There were many individual cases of sheep theft, vandalising of property and even attacks on settlers. Black trackers were used to locate their offending countrymen.

Farm stock killed by the Nyoongar hunters were critical losses to the settlers. Poultry stealing was another offence blamed on the Nyoongars. Even vegetables were taken from the growers' gardens and the offenders were often tracked right to their *miamias* where they were arrested. Most of the offenders had to face the colony's court of law which often meant they were sentenced to Wagemup, the feared black man's jail at Rottnest Island.

Without the services of the black tracker, the colony's authorities would never have been able to reach beyond the town's limits to retrieve offenders or people who were lost. The settlers for a time did not know or understand the new environment they were now living in. There were no markers to give them directions, making it easy for inexperienced people in pursuit to get lost in the bush. Not only could the settlers get lost, they could not see what trail an Aborigine left because they were not trained to do so.

The officious but likeable George Clamp said to Bell and Bowler, 'Jacky Jack and the other trackers report of a rumour around the town. They say that some important blacks were found dead. The Mooro people have moved to a new location a half a mile or more away from their old camping areas.'

'Senior Constable, can we still find those people if we have to?', Bowler asked.

'Of course, Constable, our black trackers would know where to go', Clamp said.

Bell retorted, 'Those blacks of ours are like bloodhounds. They can find anything you want them to.'

'All right men', Clamp said to the others. 'It's getting late, let's get back to the barracks. All's quiet here today. We shall see what the morrow brings. I've had this day. This saddle I'm sitting on gets harder as the hours go by.'

As the six men began their journey back to the police barracks, a rider appeared in the distance before them. The rider was on a galloping horse. As he got closer, he called out and waved: 'Hey there! Hey there! I've a message to give to Senior Constable Clamp.'

'It's Constable Allen, Senior, he's in a mighty hurry, too', Bowler said.

'I can see that', said Clamp. 'I've got eyes too, Constable.'

Allen reined his horse to a halt. Hurriedly he saluted Clamp and said, 'Senior Constable Clamp, I'm Constable Ben Allen, with orders from Inspector Isaac Johnson for you, Sir. You and your men are to go out to the homestead of the settler Jim Rows, as soon as possible. His wife came into town this morning all blood-spattered, in a terrible state, saying her husband was dead! She said some black man killed him and for all she knows as she told it, there's a good chance their foreman and two hired hands are dead as well. Rows was speared at the house, in broad daylight.

'Mrs Rows says the native just ran a barbed spear right through Rows. The killer held the spear in both hands, putting all his body weight behind the thrust. It was a surprise attack. Mrs Rows says her husband had no chance.'

'Was she attacked too? Why didn't he kill her?', somebody asked.

'I don't know', Allen said, 'but according to Mrs Rows, the black man hit her to the side of the head with his fist, knocking her unconscious. But she fought him first. After the savage knocked her down, it seems she lay unconscious for many hours before she came to.'

'Lord Jesus', gasped out Bell.

Bowler said, 'What happened then?'

Allen continued, 'She grabbed the horse and buggy, and raced as fast as she could towards Perth. She says she never looked back. You know, she nearly killed that horse. She ran him most of the way into town.

'This all happened yesterday, Mrs Rows says', Allen said. Then he added, after he had caught his breath, 'The Rows have a homestead somewhere out near the Swan River up-stream from Guildford.

'The Rows were saying goodbye, just after lunch. Rows was about to leave for the back paddocks, to join a fencing crew. The poor blighters were standing there on the verandah of the house when the black killer struck. Mrs Rows holds grave fears for the lives of their foreman, Jack Harding his name is, and the two hired hands, Ron Smith and Norman Lynch. Mrs Rows said the workers were out fencing a new paddock. She thinks they're dead, too. She just left her husband where he died, then she fled to Perth because she feared for her own safety. She just left him there. Not a pretty sight in this heat.'

Clamp was thinking out loud: 'We had better get something to carry him back into town on or bury him out there on his farm. Maybe that would be best, bury him there, especially if the others are dead. Rigor mortis has probably set in by now, the weather being so warm, so the body would be in the process of decomposing already. It will be a grisly job if all you say is correct.' Then Clamp asked, 'Tell me, Allen, did Mrs Rows give a good description of the man who killed Rows? I need a description of him so we will know who we are looking for.'

Allen replied, 'Yes, she did. I was just coming to that part, Senior.' Then Allen gave as much of a description of Bulmurn as he could possibly remember from Julia Rows. He tried hard not to miss any details.

'Here's a map of the upper reaches of the Swan with the Rows homestead and farm on it, but ask the way at Guildford. The property is well known. Your orders are to take your men to the Rows homestead immediately to report on the unpleasant situation there.'

Clamp wanted more details from Allen about what had taken place.

'Well, Sir, Mrs Rows says that an enormous black man covered with spots and stripes appeared out of nowhere, in broad daylight, too. He just stuck a barbed spear right through Jim Rows. The blackfella didn't use his spear thrower either. He held onto the weapon.

'Also, Senior, you are to get fresh provisions from the depot at Guildford, then you and your men are to continue on tracking the murderer. You are not to come back without him.'

'Thank you, Constable', Clamp said. 'I'll take it from here. You just tell Inspector Johnson back at the station that I'll be out at the Rows homestead tomorrow. I should have a report by then, also with an ounce of luck we might catch the killer, too.'

Then Clamp turned to his men. 'You heard what our orders are. We are to investigate a murder or murders at Rows's place. When we find out what has happened, we have the murderer to find.

'Now let's get cracking. We'll camp at Guildford on the river bank over night and at first light we will head for the Rows homestead.'

Clamp whistled his horse into a gallop as he turned him towards Guildford along the main track. The Senior Constable knew that he and his group were in for a few difficult days, especially if it were true that all the white men on the Rowses' farm were killed. Usually if any killing was done within their tribal structure, the blacks used a hatchet man, Clamp thought. 'I wonder', he thought, 'if this bloke is like that. I wonder if this savage is a witch doctor? If he is, then somebody in the river tribe must know about him. Getting them to help is going to be a problem. But', Clamp thought, 'I'll use my black trackers, even though they could be in danger for helping to bring a tribal man to British justice.'

Clamp looked at the written order given to him by Constable Allen for the arrest of the murderer or murderers of Rows and possibly others. The order was signed by Inspector Johnson on the assumption that the workers were dead also. Clamp realised that the document he was carrying had the potential to inflict great retribution and pain on the Aboriginal communities of the Swan River area.

Clamp knew the extra rations they always packed when they were on patrol would now be needed for the night ahead. Trailing a black offender who was in a hurry would be extremely difficult and more food would be procured for the search. He looked at his men. He knew the two troopers would be all right because Bell and Bowler were veterans from Van Dieman's Land. It was the black trackers he worried about. It could be very dangerous if these people showed signs of fear, especially if these fears impeded or confused their search for the murderer.

Clamp had heard stories of other white posses who were lured into the bush by their trackers, only to have them light the bush to burn the pursuers alive. He knew that he and his group would have to be alert at all times, that unwary people could be trapped by their own stupidity.

Clamp said to his men as they slowed their horses down, 'Once at the homestead tomorrow, we'll make our headquarters there. Inspector Johnson will see to it that the Officer-in-Charge of the West Swan Barracks despatches a detail to come out to the homestead and check the stock while we do the investigation of any killings on the farm.'

The three police troopers and three black trackers disappeared into the night. They headed towards Guildford, their roadway totally deserted. Occasionally an owl fluttered past their heads. The sounds of the night settled in around them. The night sky was mirrored in pools of the swamps the party passed. The men lost themselves in thought about what had really happened, about the horrors they would find in the days ahead.

Although the three black trackers were ill-informed, each knew that they were going to be in the middle of a tribal killing for a reason they did not know at present. They felt a twinge of excitement at first, but then their concern grew as they realised that whoever killed these *wadjbulla*, he was indeed a very powerful man, one they had to be careful of. They could not know what to expect from such a being.

'Boss', Jacky Jack said to Clamp. 'You no dis mob at dis camp neared Guildford. Dey moob oser day cause sumbody dey die, dey *norch*, sumwum, who portant. Dey always moob wen sumbudy die. Maybe, dis fulla who die gut sumting to do wood dem bosses been kilt.'

'Hm', Clamp thought, 'you could be right Jacky. I shall have to keep that in mind. Only time will tell if you are right, Jacky Jack.'

Clamp called a halt: 'We'll camp here for the night, near the water's edge.' Soon they had a fire going, the smoke drifting though the bush. The smell of smoke caused a couple of kangaroos to move away from the area. Soon the billy boiled, and the men ate some of the rations, washed down with freshly made tea. Then they laid out their bedrolls and slept away a troubled night.

At the first light of dawn, Jacky Jack and Clamp were awake at almost the same time. Jacky Jack stirred the fire to boil the billy for a fresh brew of tea. The others were up by now. When the billy boiled, they took tea from it then turned to the hobbled horses and began saddling them. Clamp was the first to mount his horse: 'Shake a leg men, we have a fair way to go to reach the Rows place. There will be no rest for us this day.'

The Investigation

The police troopers and the black trackers arrived at the Rows homestead about noon, about the same time as Rows had been killed two days before. Rows's body was still on the verandah where it had fallen, blowflies buzzing around it. Rigor mortis had now set in, the bloodstained body was beginning to smell.

'An ugly scene, even for the toughest of us', Senior Constable Clamp said out loud to his charges.

'The poor blighter', agreed trooper Bowler. Even Jacky Jack, Jimmy Jim Rankin and Wheelbarrow Long were affected by the sight of the farmer's dead body. Each one of the three looked uneasy.

'Jacky Jack', Clamp said, 'we know this boss, Rows, here, he was killed with a barbed spear'. Before Clamp could say anymore, Jacky replied, 'Yeah, boss. Look lik'n dis boss *norch* rite, dis boss he good'n dead boss. I recun this fulla hoo kilt im, he lik'n 'is *keitj*. He'n like 'is spear rite boss. Cause dis wun hoo spear him no leab it in dis boss 'ere.' Jacky Jack pointed at Rows's body, 'Yeah, dus it rite'. Jimmy Jim Rankin joined in, agreeing with Jacky Jack.

It was Wheelbarrow Long's turn to talk. 'Look 'ere boss', he said. 'Dis killer fulla he wipe'n he spear dare boss.' The black tracker pointed at a verandah post which had dried blood marks upon it.

Jacky Jack, eager to be in control of the other trackers said, 'Hey boss, you wun us to look for dis black fulla hoo kilt dis boss 'ere?', looking at the dead Rows. 'How he'd come 'ere to dis boss's *miamia*?'

Wheelbarrow Long didn't want to be outdone and said to Clamp, 'Senior Constable, you wunten us to lookt dis blackfulla sign, boss. Recon we should fulla dis wun togeser. Dis wun he look like he blenty tuff. He gut magic to kil'd besides his *keitj*. Yeah boss, dis wun hoo kilt dis boss gut blenty magic.'

Wheelbarrow's chatter made the men uneasy. Then Clamp cut in, 'Wheelbarrow, that's enough of your foolish jibbering about magic. This fellow is only a dirty killer and he's got no magic.'

Wheelbarrow said what Jacky Jack and Jimmy Jim Rankin were thinking: 'You rong boss, dis wun hoo kilt dis boss 'ere, he'm gutem magic brite he'm gut magic brite'.

Then Clamp snapped them out of their thoughts when he said, 'Jacky Jack, you take Jimmy Jim Rankin and Wheelbarrow along with you. I want you to find out what happened to the other three bosses. Whatever you do, I don't want any of you three to miss any details, not one thing.

'Now I've given you three trackers a most important job to do, so I am telling you three men, don't go off anywhere on walkabout because this job I'm giving you is very important to me. You boys hear? If you get scared of anything out there, you come back and tell me. If you don't come back, and I have to come after you, I'll give you a taste of my whip.'

All the black trackers had seen what the Senior Constable could do with a whip. Each felt a shudder run up and down his back. They had seen other Nyoongars get the flesh cut off their back and shoulders, some had died. Those that lived to recover were never the same; most were broken men.

After the black trackers had departed, Clamp said to Bowler and Bell, 'Now that these black heathens are gone, let's give Rows a decent Christian burial. Take his body out the back. We'll bury him, perhaps three to four hundred yards away from the house. His body is too far gone to bury him elsewhere.'

Constable Bowler looked at Clamp and said, 'I reckon Mr Rows would have wanted to be buried close to his home, Senior. I'm sure Mrs Rows would approve of us burying him near the house.'

Clamp said, 'I'll get the good book from the house. There should be one there. Then we can get it over and done with immediately.'

The burial ceremony would have made Julia Rows very proud had she been there to hear the reading the Senior Constable so dutifully carried out. Clamp read the Twenty-third Psalm. He concluded the ceremony with a prayer of his own: 'How hard it is for our settlers in this new land to find peace and reward. Lord take this poor man's soul into your heaven and may God's mercy be given to his wife if she ever returns to this place to live.'

The other troopers admired their senior for his solemn comment, for the manner with which he had taken care of this final act of recognition for the life of the settler Rows, and his prayers for Rows's wife.

After covering the grave, they left the site and trudged back to the house. 'You two had better clean this mess off the verandah now', said Clamp. 'When you are finished, call me, then we'll get out and have a look around the house. I noticed that the cart horse looks very lame.'

When Bell and Bowler had finished their chore of cleaning up around the scene of the crime, Bell said to Clamp, 'You had better come with us, senior, to check the horse.'

Clamp joined them as they went out to inspect the lame cart horse, the one the workers used two days previously, just prior to their deaths. 'Looks like he's been jabbed in the rump with something sharp, Senior', said Bowler. 'Look. As he moves away from us, he limps badly.'

'You're right, we probably will have to put the poor animal down. The flies have got him, too', said Bell. 'I wonder what happened for him to get such a horrific wound.'

'There's no two ways about it, this horse has to be put out of its misery. Take it away from here men, away from the farmhouse, over there.' Clamp pointed towards a clump of trees well away from the house and in an opposite direction to where they had buried Rows. Bell was given the unpopular job of disposing of the unfortunate cart horse.

Two hours passed before the black trackers returned. Clamp could see the excited look on their faces. He knew he wouldn't have to wait long before they told him what they had found in the outer paddocks.

Jacky Jack wasn't going to let the other two black trackers beat him to the story, as he felt he was the more senior one amongst them. He was more experienced. Even though the other two were good bushmen, he was slightly older than them. Being their elder gave him the right to speak first.

Clamp walked towards the trio. 'What have you boys found out there?'

Jacky Jack spoke first. He said to Clamp, Bell and Bowler, 'We tree, we fine dose oser fulla, dose oser bosses dey *norch*, dey dead. We seed dem frum long wade off. Dey alld hung on der fence like cheep. You no wen der bosses kilt den cheep dey hang dem up. Weed no urry dose boss dey dead, *norch* for sure, weed noed dut boss. Speart all a dem dus how he dood it boss. Dus how dis wun kilt dem bosses for sure, speart dem in der art.'

Jimmy Jim, eager to have a say in the matter as well, called out, 'Boss we fine out wear dut blackfulla hoo kilt dem bosses hide. He hide in der bush near der fence, den he kilt dem wid a spear. He der same wun hoo kilt der big boss. Dut boss hoo own dis place', he said pointing at the Rows homestead. 'He hide'm nest to dis oser *miamia* dare. He come frum dut bush ober dare. He go by dut big house dare un he sit dare for a long time. I teld you boss, dis wun he got patience, he sit dare still wait he time for der big boss for he walk from der house, un den he kill dis big boss. He berry farse dis wun hoo kilt im. He kilt im den he goed berry farse way frum dis place.'

Wheelbarrow Long saw his chance, now it was his turn to talk. 'Dis wun for sure is blackfulla, byen his foottrack his big fulla ow he walk long mark on der groun. Musta bin he wachen den big bosses missus all'a time. He mite be stay lung time or diddle bit of time. Mite be he don wait lung time atall, jus waiten for der big boss to come.'

Jimmy Jim continued on, 'Dem bosses all deadt dis wun he powful wun. He jis wait on dem boss for he kilt dose bosses wun by wun'.

Jacky Jack chipped back in saying to the listening troopers, 'You no boss, dis fulla, he cant speared all'a dem at der wun time. He wait on tem tull he git 'is chance. Dis wun hoo kilt dem. Wen he git his chance, he do it rite. Den he speard dem wun by wun wen he catched dem,' and he pointed to his own heart to show where the workers had been speared. 'Den wen he kilt dem he hung dem bosses on dey own fence. Sos he can seed ow he kilt dem. He mean dis fulla bos. I bettun dis fulla gut magic. He cleber too. Tomorrow boss, we black trackers will showd you ow he kilt dem bosses in der back padic ober dare.' Jacky Jack turned and pointed towards the back paddock.

'Boss, we do dut morrow', Jimmy Jim Rankin said. Wheelbarrow Long nodded his head in agreement with the other two trackers and said, 'We can't go out dare it neard nite now boss. It gettun too late now. Soon it git dark dem bosses spirit will be back dare near dem cause dey nut buried properly yet. If we go near dare dey spirit mite take revenge on us, cause dey git kilt by a Nyoongar liken us. We sure don wun to get mistook for sumwum else.'

'Dus is true boss,' said Jacky Jack. 'Dey'd git us for sure, but we nut gunna go to dut place ware dose bosses die till morrow wen der sun he rise in der mornen sky.'

As the three troopers sat around the loungeroom fire of the Rows homestead after a meal, their discussion revolved around the type of person they were pursuing. They knew the black people believed in magic, and so far everything they came across looked very much as if this man had 'magic' or more than his share of luck.

The actual killing of Rows was done in such a ferocious manner that the strength of the victim did not even figure in his defence. Yet this murder had happened in the middle of the day, at the very front door of the homesteader's house, without warning, according to Mrs Rows. The sheep dog hadn't barked or otherwise warned the farmer of the stranger's presence in the yard. It was strange and frightening.

After much discussion, the three troopers tired and bedded down for the night. Morning came quickly. It seemed they had only just gone to sleep before they were awake again, but the troopers felt fresh and well.

The black trackers had slept well, too. They had gone some distance from the house, in the opposite direction to Rows's grave, so his spirit could not find them. They had built a large fire. It was blazing merrily when Clamp and the other two troopers found them in the morning. The warmth of the fire lifted the men's spirits. A busy magpie flew through the air to join its mate on a high tree. Together they caroled a melodious tune in harmony on the high jarrah tree. As if it were a sign, a *wardang* called out its warning for them to be wary of the days to come.

Nevertheless, the investigating party didn't notice the warning because all they were interested in was breakfast — tea was brewing and a fresh lamb's carcass dripped fat into the fire. Jacky Jack had come across the young sheep earlier, hanging in the shed where it had been slaughtered. He couldn't resist taking it down to cook on the fire for them to eat. Usually Clamp would have disciplined him for stealing, but in these circumstances, the food was necessary after the experiences of the last thirty-six hours.

After they had eaten, Clamp was the first to move. The Senior Constable gave crisp orders. 'Listen men, while it's still early we have to make sure that all the animals are watered and fed. I'll check the house to see that everything is secured. Be thorough, and careful. When Constable Allen or others come from Perth I'll have my report ready on the killing of Rows and those other dead men.

'After we secure the house, we will go out to the paddock where those bodies are, and study the scene for as many details as we can. Then we'll bury them.' He despatched the troopers to attend the livestock, then walked back to the house.

Clamp had to plan how he was going to pursue this killer of farmer Rows and his men. Clamp knew he could rely on the black trackers' skill. He knew that they would have a lot to say about where to go or who to speak with when they actually found the fugitive's trail.

'Why', Clamp thought, 'I could get a promotion out of this, if I catch this murdering black.' And he saw himself rising through the ranks. 'I could even be knighted. Me, Sir George Clamp! Hm. Sounds good. Imagine me, the youngest knight in the colony!'

As he walked though the empty house, Clamp shuddered at the unwanted thought that they might fail to capture the killer. It would be bad for him if they failed. He would be ridiculed by the rest of the police force, even demoted and assigned to barracks. Clamp imagined the worst — cleaning and feeding horses, sweeping out the offices, cleaning other officers' boots.

Closing the heavy front door, Clamp met Bell and Bowler on their return from the sheds. He informed them he had made an inspection at the house. He was careful not to miss or disturb anything of importance. He had even left a few pound notes untouched on Jim Rows's desk. He wrote in his report that he had done so, and noted the exact amount of money he had found.

The black trackers sat huddled in a tight group, talking low among themselves. They had not been too anxious to go looking around the homestead. Nyoongar did not touch dead folk's things, and searching amongst the belongings once used by the dead men was not to their liking. The police senior knew this, so he allowed them to cool their heels while his men did the work that was necessary.

'All right men, when we get to those bodies out there, I don't want any of you people to foul up the evidence already seen by Jacky Jack and the others. You are to study the whole scene as we see it. We'll be going out there as experienced police officers, not like some greenhorns fresh out of school', Clamp concluded. 'Hurry it up then men, let's get on with it.'

The police troopers saddled up, followed by the three mounted trackers. Nobody seemed eager to reach the grisly scene of death; nevertheless, they rode on until they reached the site. They all took in the details, each trying to come to terms with what had happened.

Clamp broke the long silence. 'Jacky Jack, you take Jimmy Jim and scout around for any more signs of how these poor fellows were killed. I know you told me yesterday how it all happened, but now I want you trackers to look again. I want you to go over this place with a fine toothed comb, I don't want you to miss a single detail.'

'We go, Boss', said Jacky Jack to Clamp. 'Us not gunna miss wun sing. We dood a goot job you see.'

'I'm depending on you', Clamp said. 'Now get a move on. While you people are doing that we will look at the bodies of these bosses to see how they were killed by that maniac.'

As the black trackers began their search for signs of the killer, Clamp and the other troopers moved towards the bodies. Bell was the first to speak: 'Senior, any fool can see these poor men were all speared in the same manner. I would say it's clear all three were speared from the front.'

Bowler joined in, giving his two bob worth: 'It looks as though they were all speared from a close range, too. That's why the spear went right through their bodies. The killer had to pull part of the spear through the back of their bodies — it was definitely a close-up attack.'

Then Clamp spoke: 'How could one man kill three people almost at the same time without any resistance from them? It appears that they never even had a chance to get to their muskets, let alone fire a shot at him.'

In less than an hour, the black trackers returned and stood in front of Clamp. Each of them was excited. They had argued among themselves to prove just how much each one of them understood what had happened to the three dead men and how they were killed out on the fenceline. Now each of the black trackers was prepared to argue the point of view to the boss, Clamp. They all wanted to be heard by him.

Jacky Jack pointed out to Clamp, Bell and Bowler how each of the workers had been killed, how each man was killed nearly in the same spot, but not at the same time.

'Boss,' Jacky Jack continued, 'see dut boss, dut wun dare he der ferse wun kilt,' he said, pointing his finger to Ron smith. 'Him der furst wun kilt by dut blackman. See dut Boss dare, he'd der ness wun kilt.' Jacky Jack pointed to Norman Lynch. Then he pointed at Jack Harding. 'He'd been der larse wun boss. He'd beed kilt larse by dut killa *marman*, sure nuff boss.'

'How do you know Jacky Jack?', Clamp questioned.

'We'd nose ulrite', Jacky answered back to Clamp. 'Dut ferse wun ob der boss kilt, he'd be coming frum dut way boss. He'd walk frum der big house way we'd seed he track coming dun dis way before we'd gut to ware dey all kilt. He track gut nowd furser dun dis place ere. Dos oser bosses dey go off un leab him walk. Dey track goed pass dis place boss.

'Den dut boss in der middle he'd beed ness cuss we'd alld agreed dut dis boss 'ere come back looken ford der ferse boss. Den dut larse boss he'd come back to look ford dose oser bosses cuss he'd beed wurrit ford dem oser bosses. Weed all noad dut he walk 'ere larse frum dut way boss, weed seed ware he'd tooked der uness an cart frum dey horse. Den der larse boss leed him 'ere till he gut kilt be der killer.'

Wheelbarrow Long said to the investigators, 'Dis killer he hid in tree difrunt place boss beford hed kilt dem. He'd beed goot wood spear ulrite, dis wun beed goot wun wood 'is spear boss', he repeated.

Wheelbarrow Long stood near where they estimated the killer to have thrown the spear that killed the three men. The short distance from the spot where the body fell made Clamp catch his breath quickly in fright.

'Good God', Clamp thought to himself, 'the victims wouldn't have had time to get a gun up ready to fire, the killer's ambush was too well executed. They wouldn't have known he was there hiding.'

Clamp set about writing what the black trackers had told him. Clamp finished the section of his report and in the last paragraph, he wrote, 'The killer of these people is very agile and quick. He has killed these men from a distance of roughly no more than fifteen paces. It seems this frontal attack occurred in the brighter time of the day.'

Jimmy Jim Rankin then said his piece, saying how he supported the other trackers. He pointed out how sure they were that only one man had done all the killing at this spot. 'Dis fulla hoo kilt dem bosses 'ere had been bery strong. He'd taken 'is spear back out ob dose bosses he'd kilt, corse dut spear 'im goot spear too boss. I'd bet'n dis killa fulla recon dis spear it magic *keitj*.'

Then Jacky Jack cut in again, 'Weed ull greed Boss dut dis killa fulla he'd nut trite to hide anysing. He'd nut hide anysing wut 'appen 'ere. No'd fear boss, he'd dun dood nutten like dut ut all. He'd only wun us to no he only wun man do dis killen. Heed tull us heed dun it ulrite.

'Boss us is gut to fine out wut dis fulla kilt dem bosses for. Heed tull us heed dun it. But heed nut tull us why. It mite beed easy to fine ount un it mite beed 'ard too.'

The sky was crystal clear blue when Clamp inspected the graves that the dead men would be buried in. He took out his Bible as he told his men to inter the wretched bodies of Smith, Lynch and Harding, all God-fearing men deserving a Christian burial. After the brief service, the six men returned to the Rows homestead to await the other party of troopers from West Swan Barracks. No doubt Constable Ben Allen would be with them to collect the report.

Sitting at the dining room table, still half-cleared of the dishes from that last lunch two days before, Clamp busied himself with the task of finishing his notes of the killings. Clamp went over his notes one more time, talking to himself, not expecting an answer. It was certain that only one man, a single powerful person, had lain in wait for his victims, singling them out one by one to kill them. This man had attacked with a swiftness and viciousness that had left the victims completely defenceless. It was clear that the man they were after was very intelligent because he had used cunning and guile as he brought about the premeditated deaths of the four settlers.

Each victim was as strong as any man in the new colony. Each was killed instantly with a barbed spear that tore through them. Each man was hit through the heart and liver which meant death was very swift for them. Rows was the only death in which the killer held his spear in his hands as the weapon penetrated the victims. Each time the man killed, he withdrew his spear from the bodies of his victims. This meant he valued his weapon. This savage clearly had a reason for killing these four men. But what was the reason?

It was getting towards the dark of the evening when the party of police troopers from West Swan arrived at the Rows homestead. There were seven troopers in the company, laden with extra provisions. Another small party from Perth, accompanied by Mrs Rows, would come with a wagon to collect her belongings and those of the dead men. Julia would send the sad parcels to the closest relatives.

Constable Ben Allen was the courier from police headquarters. Allen was there to get a report. It was he who first galloped into the homestead clearing and went directly to where Clamp and his men were seated around the fire outside. Saluting, Allen said to Clamp, 'Senior, I'm ready to deliver your report to Inspector Johnson as soon as possible'.

Allen told Clamp and his men that the whole colony was in an uproar. He said that most white settlers were terrified of some black killer with magic powers. 'You see, Senior, that's why your report on what has happened out here and what you intend to do to catch the culprit is so important. We have to keep the other settlers calm. The Chief is concerned that other settlers may abandon their new farms and move into Perth. It's not unheard of. Or they might take the law into their own hands and retaliate against other natives, regardless of who they are. We need to say that you and your men have already investigated the killings of Rows and his men, and also that your people are already on his trail.'

Clamp looked at Allen saying, 'Sit down Constable, have a hot cup of tea. You'll have to stay here with us tonight. You don't know what's out there do you?', he added, chiding the young policeman about his lack of knowledge about the black people and the bush. 'The last thing we want to find in the morning is you hanging on a fence, too. Do I make myself clear?'

'Yes, Sir', said Allen, as he sat down with the others and filled his mug with tea. By now all the other policemen had arrived and joined Clamp's group around the fire. The newcomers were led by Senior Constable Ken Davidson, who introduced himself to Clamp. Clamp offered them tea and told them what they had found out about the killing of Rows and his workers. Everybody sat quietly as he unfolded the horrifying details of his investigation thus far.

Davidson then spoke: 'This is bad, bad business, I mean, how those wretched men were killed. I wonder what provoked such an attack, by what appears to be one man only? There are usually two or three of them or a group when they attack whites.'

'I don't know why it was done in this manner, but I can tell you it was an effective way of killing them. I also believe this man had a good reason to do what he did. When we go after him, we'll have to be very careful and very wary. The way he's killed makes him a most dangerous individual,' Clamp replied.

'However', said Davidson, 'now we are out on the Rows place to protect it, until it's been decided by Mrs Rows what she wants to do with her property. I reckon she'll probably sell the place. I cannot see her working it on her own.'

General chatter began to flow through the campsite, quietly amongst the troopers. The naturalness of the scene made them almost forget there was a killer out there in the dark of night. Maybe it was the enlargement of their numbers which made them all feel safer. They promptly fell asleep.

Morning came quickly to the group. Clamp stretched himself and yawned, others did the same. Clamp commented on how clean and fresh the morning air felt. It was not like the previous days when the air was filled with the pungent smell of death.

'Seems peaceful enough now', Bell responded.

'Yes', Clamp said to Bell, 'Yes, it is at that, peaceful indeed. It's almost as though nothing has happened at all, but we know differently, don't we.'

Clamp called the men. 'Look sharp, men. Let's drink our tea and eat what we have to, but let's not take all day about it. There's a lot of hard work ahead of us today and tomorrow, until we catch that killer wherever he is.'

'I'll move my men out shortly', Clamp said to Davidson. 'The first thing we've got to do is go to the Aboriginal campsite near Guildford. I have a strong suspicion that they know the killer. Once we know the identity of the culprit, it will make it easier for us to track him down, so we can hang him high. He'll swing for these murders!

'Allen', Clamp said, 'you can accompany us to the Aboriginal camp to strengthen our ranks. After we have finished our business there, you are to ride on to Chief Inspector Johnson at police headquarters in Perth.

Clamp, his men and Allen headed out from the Rows homestead, making their way back to the Aboriginal campsite near Guildford to continue their investigation, leaving behind Davidson and his party at the homestead to make an inventory of the Rows property. Davidson and his men counted the chickens, ducks, pigs and milking cows. They estimated everything Jim and Julia Rows had accumulated or built on their property. They assessed the condition of machinery. They looked at hand tools which Jim Rows had fashioned himself. Everything was placed on the list. Davidson and his men were very thorough.

It was mid-morning when Clamp and his men moved out, making their way to the Nyoongar campsite near Guildford, south-west of the Rows homestead in the Swan Valley. The black trackers knew the area well. Clamp liked the open spaces, he like this part of his work-riding in the sunshine, resting in the shade and sitting by a fire in the bush. But he was becoming impassioned by his current assignment, excited at the thrill of the chase. He knew there would be no rest until he caught the killer.

Clamp prepared himself for the meeting with the Nyoongars in their camp. He knew they would have something to say to him. He and his men would have to be careful with them. They would have to be careful not to offend, as they only had a small number of men. Clamp knew he had to make the Nyoongars understand that he only wanted to know who the killer was. He needed to know his identity and why he had killed four white people. He needed to know if there was any difference between the killer and the rest of the Mooro people of Mandoon.

Wadjbulla *Speak to Jubuc*

That afternoon as the sun peaked overhead before beginning a downward course to meet the sea in the west, Clamp and his men arrived at the campsite of the Guildford Aborigines. Carefully, he led the way inside the Nyoongar camp. Clamp looked at Jacky Jack. 'Ask them who's the boss man here, Jacky Jack, and tell them I want to speak with him.'

Jacky Jack leaned towards Clamp. 'See dut wun, dut big fulla be dare trait in frunt of us, dus der wun boss. I no'd is name, it Jubuc. He *mobarn mamarup* dis fulla boss. He gut der magic.'

Jacky Jack straightened himself in the saddle, then he looked towards Jubuc and said to him, '*Bidara Munatj*. This is the boss policeman. He wants to talk to you Jubuc. There's been a bad killing of the *wadjbulla* out at Rows's farm.' Jacky Jack pointed north-east of the tribal camp, back the way they had just come.

Jacky Jack leaned over his horse towards Clamp, the rest of the group straining to hear his whisper: 'Boss. Dis fulla Ise talk to is dey leader ulrite, he talk for dey Council of Elders an' der ress ob dis Nyoongar group 'ere. He be dey boss man ulrite, he name Jubuc and he *Mobarn Mamarup* too. Better be careful ob dis fulla. Jus wun word frum dis fulla an weed dead for sure. Dey'd spear us wid dey *keitj*, dey'd gib us no chances if weed nut be careful boss.'

Clamp showed no fear, but he didn't dismount. He presented himself by moving his mount one step closer to Jubuc whom he looked straight in the eye.

'Jubuc', Clamp said, 'I've heard that somebody died amongst your people. What blackfella died? How did he die? I also want to know the name of the person who killed those white bosses, Rows and his workmen.

'You explain what I said in his native tongue, Jacky Jack, so he fully understands what we have come here for.' Jacky Jack then translated all this to Jubuc, everything that Clamp had said.

Jubuc looked the troopers over, then he eyed the black trackers. 'Scum', he thought to himself. 'They get the *wadjbulla's* leftovers. They get clothes to wear like the policemen, a big horse to ride. Yes, these black men, they think like the *wadjbulla* too. They think they're superior to us. One word from me, they all die, but because I love my people, I've got to tell this mob of scum who it was who died.'

Jubuc turned his eyes to look at the big white man Clamp who sat on his horse waiting for an answer. Jubuc was no coward, nor was he going to be intimidated by anyone, certainly not by these white troopers or the black trackers. Jubuc stepped forward a pace towards Clamp and his men. As Jubuc took a pace forward threateningly, the warriors in the group did the same thing.

The warriors shouted, '*Darganan! Darganan!* Kill! Kill! Kill!' But Jubuc lifted his hand high into the air bringing an immediate silence among them. Jubuc was in total command of what could have been a rather awkward situation.

Jubuc looked at Clamp. Then he spoke out. 'One of our warriors and his woman were killed. It is against the Law to say their names after they die, but because the *wadjbulla* doesn't understand this, I will say their names for him. It was Binyung and Munyee.' Jubuc lifted his hand, indicating the number of days that had passed since they were killed.

Jacky Jack translated all the information to Clamp. Clamp said to Jacky Jack, 'Ask him who killed them'. Jacky Jack in turn put the question to Jubuc, who answered deliberately, 'By the *wadjbulla* who come north of here'. Jacky translated.

'Ask him Jacky Jack. Does he know what his people were killed for? Then you also ask him if he knows who killed the *wadjbulla* bosses. Ask him if it was anyone from here.'

Jacky Jack asked Jubuc the question and Jubuc replied, '*Wadjbulla* they shoot Binyung for his woman. They kill him then they rape her.'

When he told them this, the warriors moved restlessly, and they started to chant, readying themselves for the kill. They chanted, '*Keitj dolum wun barminje wadjbulla Darganan Darganan. Dolun wun barminje Nyoongar Darganan Darganan* (Spear and hit the white men to kill kill. Spear and hit the black men to kill kill).'

Jacky Jack along with the other black trackers froze. They thought their days were numbered. Clamp and his troopers were about to react, but Jubuc again raised his arm into the air. Again silence descended over the Guildford Nyoongars. Then Jubuc spoke out in a loud voice breaking the silence.

'We know that *wadjbulla* north of here killed them', Jubuc put four fingers up, indicating four people. Jubuc looked straight into the eyes of Clamp and said, 'We did not kill these *wadjbulla* men. If they're dead, then we don't know who did it, although we have the right to, because they were our people they killed.'

Again Jubuc spoke, this time more rapidly. He told Jacky Jack to tell Clamp about the murders of the man and woman killed by the *wadjbulla* farmers from the country north-east of Guildford. With grim warning to Jacky Jack, Jubuc told him he could not tell him and the troopers everything. He told him how a child had witnessed the whole incident. Jubuc told Jacky Jack how courageously the child had seen it all and was able to tell how his father was killed so he was out of the way, so they could rape, beat and kill his mother.

Jubuc told how they investigated the location where the felony took place. He told how they found the bodies of the deceased people. He told how they had prepared a proper burial for them, prepared by the tribal leaders. Jubuc himself had helped to perform the burial ceremony of the *Bokal D Yaur*.

Jubuc moved his arms across the campsite as though this was

the very place where it had all happened. Jubuc was sad about the man being shot and about how the woman was treated, also about how the *wadjbulla* showed no mercy for her suffering at all. Jubuc spoke for Binyu, careful to protect his identity.

When Jacky Jack finally turned away from Jubuc, he saw the senior trooper had never taken his eyes off Jubuc, that Clamp had shown no hint of being fearful of the situation they were in at that moment.

'Boss', Jacky said. Then he told Clamp all that Jubuc had told him about what had happened, how Jubuc had seen it all, everything from Jubuc's point of view.

Jubuc began to talk again, his voice changing a little. Now there was much more noticeable urgency in the manner in which he spoke. Jubuc talked carefully of how the blame for the killing of his kinfolk was entirely on the bad *wadjbulla*. 'They were the ones to blame', Jubuc continued. 'This was no accidental drinking party which got out of control. The Nyoongar hunting party was at their own campsite. The *wadjbulla* had entered the campsite from a nearby track. Their intentions were to get the woman. When her man wouldn't give her to them, they shot him to get her.

'I'll give you people a warning, our people who were killed by the *wadjbulla* are a sister and brother-in-law to the powerful *Mobarn Mamarup*. This Nyoongar has got plenty of power to kill. He kills by magic. His name is Bulmurn.'

All the black trackers shifted on their mounts uneasily. All had heard of Bulmurn. They all knew he had been banished from this Guildford tribe a long time ago. Jimmy Jim Rankin swore under his breath. Wheelbarrow Long looked nervously around him as if he half-expected the man to jump out of the mob and spear him.

Each of the black trackers had heard tales about Bulmurn, the big medicine man. They all knew the name 'Bulmurn' had strange effects on Nyoongar people all over the South-West. Everywhere this man went people treated him with caution and respect. Bulmurn was a healer of many people with any sickness. Bulmurn was also an elder and a teacher of all ages. Bulmurn was a very strong leader, a decision-maker in matters of culture, lifestyle and about kinfolk law which kept tribal law secure amongst the Nyoongar people and which helped to determine how the Guildford, Darbalyung Nyoongar lived.

Almost in unison, as though they had rehearsed it, Jimmy Jim Rankin, Jacky Jack and Wheelbarrow Long spoke to Clamp, Bowler, Bell and Allen. The black trackers tried to tell them exactly what Jubuc had told them. The trackers added little bits of information, too. They were too startled by Jubuc's frankness to consider that any other person could be strong enough to do the killing other than Bulmurn, the *Mobarn Mamarup*.

Jubuc had convinced the black trackers that what had happened was very bad, very bad. They were convinced it was indeed the powerful Bulmurn who had taken revenge to right the Law by killing all those *wadjbulla* bosses. They were also convinced Jubuc's people never gave any help or assistance to kill Rows and his workers, nor was anyone else involved as they were very much afraid of the troopers and their guns. They were scared for the lives of their women and children. They had heard about how the first Governor of the new colony, James Stirling, had led the charge in the Battle of Pinjarra.

In the Stirling-led charge of the Battle of Pinjarra, troopers tried to kill every Aborigine that stood in their path, including men, women and children of the Murray River Kalyute people who lived along the river. Only a handful were able to escape to live to tell the story of how it happened.

The black trackers pleaded with Clamp and the other troopers to believe Jubuc, to credit him with being honest. They claimed Jubuc was a reliable leader of his people. They also explained that the people were scared of the magic powers of Bulmurn. They added that these people were afraid that Bulmurn might turn his magic powers against them.

Then Senior Constable Clamp spoke very gruffly to Jubuc and his people: 'You tell them, Jacky Jack, especially Jubuc — you tell him that if he's told us a pack of lies, I'll be back with a lot more troopers. Tell him if that happens it'll be worse than the Battle of Pinjarra.

'You tell him Jacky Jack, that we will be going out after this *mobarn* fellow Bulmurn. Tell him that we will kill him if we have to. You tell him that really all we want to do is to catch him so our law, the white man's law, can deal with him, because the white man's law says this man is a killer of our people, and we have orders to bring him to justice to be tried. If he's guilty, he will be hanged, but right now, you tell him, Jacky Jack, no more killing white folk. It must end here.'

Jacky Jack conveyed the message. He told Jubuc the danger of reprisals against the river people, especially if Jubuc had not told them the truth.

Jubuc said to them in what little English he knew, 'Go! Go! All of you, dun tretn oserwise you all join dem old wun in dey Dreamtime. Go!'

As Jubuc said the word, the warriors of his people put forward their spears and boomerangs at the ready. Fighting sticks appeared out of nowhere. All the warriors were poised, ready to strike at the first trooper or tracker who looked a threat. The warriors circled the horsemen, it looked like they were trying to separate the police troopers and the black trackers.

If Clamp noticed what the warriors were doing, he never let on. But Jacky Jack did see what appeared to be a threat to their safety, so he drove his spurs into the flanks of his horse. The horse jumped straight toward the mob who moved apart creating a gap amidst the ranks which enabled him to go through, followed by the others.

'Men', Clamp warned, 'raise your weapons, but do not fire unless I do or give you the order to. The black trackers are all right. That's just what they needed to keep them on their toes. Now we can depend on them to be alert for other dangers we might face in the coming days.

'About face to the Rows homestead. We can pick up the killer's trail from there.'

Wheelbarrow Long rode alongside Clamp. He said in a creaky voice that showed he had held fears for their safety, 'Crikey, boss. Dey bin neard git us, boss. Why you nut shoot dem boss?'

Clamp answered, 'I knew you would get away from them. You

blokes value your skins too much. Without a shadow of doubt, we knew you would make it.'

Constable Bell laughed as he called out, 'We almost had us three white trackers instead of three black trackers, eh, Senior'.

'Ulrite for you to larf, Boss', Jimmy Jim Rankin said. 'Ise sweatin', boss, Ise, really sweatin'.' Then he joined in and laughed with the others.

'Jacky, what do you think of this leader, Jubuc, you know the one we just spoke to?', said Clamp, seriously.

'Ah 'im', Jacky Jack said. 'He goot man, dut wun Boss he goot leader. Eberybody no 'im he kine man, he goot to 'is people, Boss. He goot man. Even though he tull us go, he goot man.'

Jacky Jack told the others that, even though he was from the south, at one stage of his life a long time ago, he lived among the Guildford mob. He told them that's how he knew about Jubuc. He told them how Bulmurn was the most powerful man around the river area. He also told them how Jubuc had come to gain power through his healing and medical powers. He also told them how Bulmurn had lost out. How he faced the trial of spears and how he had been banished from the tribe.

Jacky Jack said to the listening troopers and trackers, 'Mind you, we neber no. But people say Bulmurn kill 'is people — mixt people, maybe full-blood people too.' Jacky Jack continued to tell Clamp and the others what he knew. Bulmurn didn't approve if a husband was trading his woman for booze and other items.

Jacky Jack said, 'Dis fulla we look for is Bulmurn, he danger-ous wun an he got *mobarn buyl* you no boss, black magic. Dis fulla Bulmurn he nut afraid to kilt dis wun. Yeah Boss. Dis Bulmurn he be our man rite nuff I just nose it. Wut you oser fulla say Bulmurn be our man we gutta look for.' Jimmy Jim nodded in total agreement with Jacky Jack.

Then Wheelbarrow Long quipped: 'Me too boss. Ise agree dis fulla Bulmurn, he killer is rite. Dis fulla gut magic power boss, he cun kill.'

'Like what power?', Bowler asked Wheelbarrow Long.

'Hey boss,' Jacky Jack said to Bowler. 'Dis fulla can change into unysing he wunt to, uny bird specley dut *wardang*, uny black boy tree, uny stump, uny bush, unysing boss I tull you. He cun eben turn into a stone.'

'But boss,' Jimmy Jim Rankin added, 'Ise recon is fabrite shape is he turn into *wardang* the crow. Boss, dus is fabrite wun he like.'

Clamp looked at the three black trackers in turn. He could see that they truly believed that the fugitive Bulmurn could do and change into the things they claimed, such was the power the natives believed he possessed. Clamp turned to constables Allen, Bowler and Bell and said to them, 'It's just native superstition, mumbo jumbo. But we know better. We shall humour them for the moment. I believe it best to let them carry on with their beliefs — we'll get greater cooperation that way.'

Clamp put up his arm, calling his party to a halt. Then he said to Constable Bell, 'Tell the others to break out rations and have a billy boiled and take a well-earned rest. I want to stop and make out the remainder of my report, so I can give it to Allen to take to the Inspector in Perth.'

'Here', Clamp said to Allen nearly an hour later, 'is the full report on details about what happened at the homestead and how Jim Rows and his workmen were killed. I now think that they were killed by a single savage, called Bulmurn. I've outlined what I think is the reason why he killed. I've included details about what Jubuc, current chief of the Beelu, has told us about Rows and his men; that they were seen killing a black man for his woman because they fancied her, how they raped her before they killed her, thinking they had not been seen.'

Surprisingly, Clamp also reported Jubuc's denial of the involvement of the people of his tribe in the incident. Clamp believed Jubuc's opinion that only one man, the banished medicine man was responsible for the killing of the four white men. Clamp realised that he could get further help from Jubuc if he reported him favourably. He added: 'I am going to bring back this savage, alive if possible, so he can hang in public for everyone to see that no black man can kill a white and get away with it. But if we have to kill him then, by God, we will. By the grace of God we will succeed.

Then Clamp handed the report up to Constable Allen, who placed the document into his dispatch bag strapped to the saddle of his dun-coloured horse. Allen saluted Clamp and the others, then kicked his horse into a canter along the wooded track leading to Perth.

The Senior Constable looked at the rest of his men. He looked at each one of them thoughtfully. 'You know', he said to them, 'we are going to need all the luck we can get to capture this man. He might be wild, he might kill again. We don't know, but we must assume the worst. From all accounts, he is no ordinary man. It seems he's very clever at deceiving his own people. He is elusive and smart and will be difficult to capture, but by hell, we'll get him, dead or alive. One thing is certain, men, our careers won't be harmed by this hunt. If we succeed, we can all expect a promotion.'

Clamp looked at his men, assessing each one of them as good men, even including the black trackers. 'Yes', he thought, 'I can trust them, too. I can trust all of them, especially when the going starts to get tough. I've plenty of confidence in them all. We'll get this Bulmurn. We'll either bring him back shackled alive, or draped over the back of a horse.'

The Guildford tribe would be spared any exceptional pressure from the police troopers at this stage, as the settlers in the Swan River area would be told to keep their hands off their weapons when confronted by any native in the bush. They all agreed to wait and give Clamp and his men a chance to track down the killer so he could be punished by the authorities, that is if he was brought back alive. Even if Clamp and his men brought him in dead, at least it would show that the authorities were doing their job.

The settlers knew that the main aim of the government was to try and maintain harmony between the blacks and the colonists. The very last thing they wanted was a confrontation that would cause race relations to deteriorate. Nobody wanted another Battle of Pinjarra in which the Governor himself risked his own life. All agreed that the reputation of the Swan River colony was at stake in this matter.

When Constable Allen rode into Perth Police Headquarters, he went straight to Chief Inspector Johnson's office. He knocked urgently, then opened the door when Johnson said 'Come in'. Allen stood to attention and saluted the Inspector, then handed him Clamp's report.

Johnson finished reading the report. 'Constable, you must not breathe a word about what you know is contained in this report. Keep it to yourself, that's an order. This is not news for the settlers, we don't want a riot and racial wars on our hands, now, do we? You are dismissed, but stand by for further orders.'

'Yes, Sir', said Allen as he turned and left the Inspector's office.

At the request of Governor Hampton, Inspector Johnson went straight to the government offices building, to report on the trooper's findings to the Commissioner of Police, and the Governor.

The three powerful men spoke at some length over the matter. They discussed the situation as they saw it, and decided to keep any retaliation against the Nyoongar people to a minimum. They would allow Clamp and his men to chase the killer, but, at this stage, they would not allow any shooting of blacks in order to bring him out of hiding.

All of the facts, and the inventory of her property would be given to Mrs Rows, revealing that the involvement of her husband and his workers in a careless attack on a black man and his wife had triggered the whole unfortunate affair. This information would act in a twofold way: the government didn't want indiscriminate killings of Swan River blacks; and they wanted Mrs Rows to keep quiet about the killings. They knew she would not want to talk too much about it because she herself could become a target of cruel gossip.

Mrs Rows was to be told that the troopers had identified who the killer was. The troopers were led by one of their best troopers, Senior Constable George Clamp, who was an experienced bushman. Senior Constable Clamp led a party of other experienced bushmen composed of three constables and three black trackers. It was to be made perfectly clear to Mrs Rows that these men were instructed to keep after him until they caught him. No matter how long it took or wherever he went, they were to keep at him until they apprehended him.

The letter to Mrs Rows stated that they had not expected to be delayed too long in catching the killer and making his arrest, because they were almost sure that none of his people would help him or protect him from the troopers. They had made it clear that their chief, Jubuc, had been very helpful in giving the troopers information that would help them to catch the fugitive, the man who now was the most wanted in the colony.

Julia alighted from the buggy at the home she and Jim had made together. If she felt emotion, she showed no sign of it. She was accompanied by the Chief Inspector, Isaac Johnson who went with her as she made her way to the grave of her husband Jim. They stood together by the grave. Johnson thought how pretty Julia looked. He thought how stupid was Rows to let alcohol go to his head so that he would actually kill for a black woman.

Julia could not restrain her emotions any longer, tears came into her eyes. Johnson moved to her side to comfort her, but he restrained himself from doing so. Others would do it, Johnson reasoned. To comfort her was not in the best interests of the colony. He wanted her to know that the retaliatory killings by Bulmurn were the result of a savage's lore. He wanted her to feel the worst about this lore.

Julia cried silently beside the tough Inspector. Johnson realised how much the pioneer's life would have toughened this woman. He then recollected the hard times he'd had since he had arrived in this new colony from England. Without thinking, Johnson said out loud, 'Only the good Lord knows how strong one must be to survive in this new land'.

Johnson walked Julia back to the homestead, where she told the troopers to load her wagon with her valuables. As soon as this was done, she said to her escort, 'Thank you, Inspector. I have all the things I need. I want you to know that I've engaged an agent to hire a manager and two workers to look after this property until I decide whether I want to keep it or sell it. Until then, I will lodge in Perth.'

'As you like it, Ma'am,' Inspector Johnson responded. He detailed two troopers to escort Julia back to Perth with her wagon and buggy. 'Good luck Ma'am.' Then he looked at his men and said, 'Guard Mrs Rows with your lives if it's necessary to do so'.

Inspector Johnson told his remaining seven men, including a black tracker named Jurung, 'Men, we are going to pay a visit to the native campsite at Guildford. Each of your troopers will have to be on guard at all times, but let me warn you, nobody is to do anything to provoke them. Nobody is to do anything at all that may cause a confrontation. No show of weapons unless I have the order. I am going there to talk to their leader, Jubuc.'

Inspector Johnson and the black tracker Jurung rode side-by-side ahead of the other troopers who rode in two's. Johnson and Jurung led the party's approach to the Guildford tribal grounds.

Their approach to the camp had not gone unnoticed. They were met by a group of warriors who blocked their entry into the very heart of the campsite. More people began to emerge from the *miamias* and they joined the warriors. Women and children gathered behind the men. They looked questioningly at the troopers and black tracker. Mistrust showed on their faces.

Then all at once, the Nyoongar people moved aside to make way for a reasonably tall man who walked towards them until he stood quite close in front of them. He carried a spear thrower hooked to a vicious looking barbed spear. It almost looked as if he were ready to throw it at the troopers. The man held his arm in a fist. He shouted at the black tracker in his native tongue asking him why he had brought the *wadjbulla*, especially police troopers to this camp.

Before Jurung could reply, Johnson said to him, 'Jurung, you tell him I am here to speak with their leader, the one named Jubuc. You tell him I come here as a policeman on peaceful business. You tell him I am not here to harm anyone nor do I want to cause any trouble or hurt. Tell them the killing is over.'

Then Jurung said to the man who stood in front of them. 'My boss,' he said, pointing at Johnson, 'he wants to know where Jubuc is, so he can talk to him. All these bosses want to do is bring the killer of those *wadjbulla* bosses to face their law so they can bring him to their justice. Jubuc should already know that because the other big boss, Clamp, he came here before to talk to Jubuc. This boss here,' Jurung pointed to Johnson, 'is a bigger boss than the other, Clamp.'

While Jurung talked to the man, other warriors gathered around Johnson and his troopers. All of the warriors were armed with spears or a weapon of some kind, killing sticks, boomerangs, axes or hammers. '*Darganan, Darganan, Darganan.* Kill, kill, kill,' they shouted as they hit their weapons together making a great clacking sound.

All this movement made Johnson feel nervous for the safety of his men. Johnson could see his men were edgy, they all had their hands on their sidearms ready to draw at a moment's notice. The horses stamped nervously. 'Steady men, you know your orders. You're not to do anything unless I give the word.'

The warriors shouted, '*Yoki! Yoki! Yoki!*' voicing their victory shout. As they shouted a tall man stepped out from the warriors' ranks. He pushed the other man out of his way beckoning him back into the ranks. The man who now stood before them said to Johnson, Jurung and the other troopers, 'I am Jubuc. You want to talk to me.'

Johnson nodded his head in acknowledgment. Jurung looked back to Jubuc and he said to him, 'Yes, Jubuc. This man is my boss, the big boss, in charge of all these men here', and he pointed to Johnson and the troopers.

Jubuc said, 'I know, I heard all you had to say when you were talking to my warrior Walunga.'

'Jurung', Johnson said, 'you ask Jubuc who did all the killings of the farmer Jim Rows and his workers. Ask him who killed those four bosses.'

Jubuc said rapidly, 'First let me ask, does the *munatj* have words to tell us about the killing of our people? Does he want to offer a reassurance that the incident be made known to his people? Does he offer sympathy to the Nyoongar families? I do not think so. No, I reckon he knows nothing about it. If he does know, I still believe, he won't do anything about the death of my people at the hands of the farmer and his men.

'Jurung, you tell your boss, nobody here from our *miamia* has killed anybody. Nobody here is guilty of killing any *wadjbulla* people, but I want you to tell your big boss that we had two of our people killed by *wadjbulla*. You know the man, it was Binyung. He was killed by the *wadjbulla widjibandi*. Then they took his woman Munyee like an animal. All of them raped her, then when they had no more need for her, she, too, was shot by the *wadjbulla widjibandi*.

'You know them Jurung, we know you are related to them. You also know Munyee was sister to Bulmurn, and you know also Binyung was his brother-in-law. We told the same thing to the other *munatj*, who came here before you. I have said the names of the dead, but I have done so for this special circumstance.' Then Jubuc told Jurung the story about Bulmurn. He gave as much detail as he could. Though Jubuc did not directly blame Bulmurn, he made sure that Jurung knew that they suspected Bulmurn.

'Tell your boss also, we did not kill those *wadjbulla*. Now that's all I have to say. You tell your boss to take his troopers and go while you are all still able to.'

Jurung looked at Johnson and also at the other troopers, then he spoke to them. 'Let moob way frum 'ere boss. Jubuc he tull me hoo did dis kilen ob dose oser bosses. It wood be safe for us to leab now boss.'

Johnson then spoke to his men, 'Let's move out.' They rode some distance away from the campsite on the track towards Perth before Johnson called a halt to the group. Then he turned to Jurung and said, 'Jurung, who is the killer? Tell me all about what Jubuc said to you, because he said a lot. I want you to tell me everything. I want to know the type of man the killer is. Don't leave out any single detail about this man. And Jurung, tell me more about Jubuc.'

The Chase

Meanwhile, Senior Constable George Clamp, his two constables, Bell and Bowler, and the three black trackers had picked up Bulmurn's trail in the bush near the Rows homestead. It seemed to the party that Bulmurn was heading eastwards over the Darling Range, through the valleys and ravines, towards the small town of Toodyay.

Sometimes, Bulmurn made it hard for Clamp's party to track him and at times he made his tracks easy for them to follow. The black trackers were revelling in their task, getting a great delight out of losing then finding his tracks again. Bulmurn was always well ahead of them, his tracks displaying strength of movement to the black trackers. Bulmurn knew exactly where they were. He was treating the tracking party like players in a gigantic game of chess. Bulmurn was enjoying keeping ahead of his pursuers, enjoying the pleasures of the chase. It seemed like a game they all enjoyed.

Bulmurn took them over and around the high hill near Toodyay, then he doubled back towards Koongamia, the camp on the side of a hill, an area he knew very well. Bulmurn always had to caution himself not to go back to the Swan River area of the coastal plain, his own home area. He realised if he did do this, then the following party had more chance of catching him.

He realised that up here on the hilly slopes, he could dictate the pace of the chase; that's why he had to control his first impulse to go down to the flat country. This insight into his own weakness made him more vigilant and on guard for any unexpected emergency.

Bulmurn headed south along the ridge towards Kalamunda, the place of the big fire. When he passed through Kalamunda, he followed the Bibulmun Trail for a great distance, then he turned south-east towards Boyagin Boya, the place of the huge rock. Once he reached Boyagin Boya, he would make his trail disappear.

At the big rock, Bulmurn planned to give his hunters the slip then he would get his chance to escape. Once he lost them, he knew the black trackers would spend a lot of time trying to work out how he lost them and he would thus gain much time.

Bulmurn would go up around the Boyagin Boya where he could watch the search party looking for him, but never finding his exact location. He would watch them come in, where they came in, and then leave along exactly the same path.

When he got to the big rock, he would walk quite a way away from it, leaving small signs for them to follow. When he got far enough away from the rock, he would put on his feather boots, then double back to the rock where he would wait for them to arrive. 'They will never find me because I am going to put on my *genabuka*, my ceremonial shoes. By doing this I will leave no trail for those stupid fools to find', he thought.

Bulmurn would wait for them to strike out on his false trail before he made his move. Once they were going away from the rock he would leave his hiding place and would go down to the exact spot where the black trackers and police troopers came upon the big rock. Then he would mix his trail with theirs. By doing this, he hoped he would confuse them, leaving them the problem of trying to find his marks on the ground.

Once Bulmurn gave the black trackers and troopers the slip he would leave his home area where he had lived during the last five seasons, the Swan River and Darling Range escarpment. Bulmurn had made up his mind that he would head north to the area of Moora. He would hide out there amongst the Moorara and Walabing tribes.

Bulmurn laughed to himself as he thought about how he would fool those Nyoongar trackers and those police troopers, those *wadjbulla munatj*. Those *munatj* would be the laughing stock of the whole country. 'Maybe those *wadjbulla munatj* who chase me now will be sent back on their big boat, back across the sea, and those Nyoongar trackers who help the *wadjbulla* to track me, will be sent to Wagemup, the black man's jail on the island the *wadjbulla* call Rottnest now.'

Bulmurn laughed out aloud, sending his mocking laughter resounding through the bushland around him. He slapped his thighs loudly as tears brimmed in his eyes. His mirth continued as he made his way to the big rock, Boyagin Boya.

Jacky Jack was speaking to Jimmy Jim and Wheelbarrow Long in their own tongue. 'You know you two men this *Mobarn Mamarup* we've been following, he's a danger to us. We've got to be very careful of him. He's got a lot of magic this one has. You know and I know the stories of how he's able to talk to dream-time spirits to get power. He can kill us if he wants to.' To demonstrate his point he made a grab for Wheelbarrow's throat causing the man to wince and back away.

'I reckon you're right Jacky but you don't have to try scare us', Jimmy Jim said in their defence.

'I'm not trying to scare you two, I'm just trying to keep you on your toes. We all know Bulmurn is no ordinary man. You know those big *wadjbulla* bosses say he got no power but we know better than they do.'

Jimmy Jim said. 'We know what you say is true, Jacky. We know they don't believe what we say but I don't worry about it 'cause I get their food, they give me clothes and a horse and they don't jail me, so I just do what they tell me to do without question.'

'I do what they tell me to do as well', Wheelbarrow Long said, dipping into the conversation after he had gained a little composure. 'I do what they tell me to do, but I tell you I'm frightened of that Bulmurn more than them. If I could, I'd leave and get out, but if I left this party he might get me on my own and catch me, so me, I'm staying here where it's safe.'

Jacky Jack said to Wheelbarrow Long, 'You know you lucky them bosses can't hear or understand what you been saying or you'd be in trouble, don't talk like that no more. If they think any of us are scared they'll probably shoot us.

'One thing we all know is he's been leaving a trail that's not too hard for us to follow. He knows we know of him. We know he wants us to follow him all right but then we don't know why he makes it easy for us to trail him. He's not like any of the other Nyoongars.'

Then Clamp rode up to the black trackers. 'You boys found anything out you should tell me about?'

They almost all snapped to attention. 'Nusing boss, esept wees jus tullen wun nuser bout dis fulla Bulmurn hoo wees sink has dees magic un wees gutta beed bery careful ob him, corse heed bin giben all dis machic by dem drimtime pearit, you nose dem is dose old wuns hoo dies lung time go', was the reply Clamp received from Jacky Jack.

'You no wut I sink boss, dis fulla hoo wee'd been chasen hee'd bin leaben his track so us nose which way he'd go.'

Clamp said to Bill and Bowler as they joined the group, 'You know, you men I agree with these boys', pointing at the black trackers. 'We must be more alert now that it appears we have gained valuable ground on this man, so that's all the more reason we have to be careful. It's true what Jacky Jack says. The killer has been making his trail easy for us to find. This has to mean he is supremely confident in his ability to lose us or ambush us. I say we must catch him and we will.'

'Ise dunno why'd boss, but ifen wee'd eber cutch dis wun mee'd gut dis feelun us black trackers shoonunt look 'im in 'is face boss cause hee'd mite chaint us into wun ob dose black stumps ord a stone, ord a black boy, ord into *wardang* un Ise dunt wunna bee'd nuser *wardang*, ord any ob dose oser sing boss. *Muyang.* Noad blutty way boss', was Jacky Jack's way of demonstrating his discomfort.

Out of a long silence, Constable Tom Bowler said to the

Senior Constable, 'You know, Senior, these poor blighters are scared out of their wits by this bloke we're chasing. If this bloke, this savage, has powers like they say he has, then we have to be ready to shoot him as soon as we get close to him. We'll have to plug him. The last thing we want to show is weakness, because if we do, the blacks might turn on us and that's something we don't want to happen.'

The young constable's remarks stung his senior like a whip. 'Bowler, surely you don't believe their drivel! Surely you don't? What kind of a man are you? Bowler, you and Bell should know there is a logical explanation for this black's so-called magic. It's probably related to some kind of hypnotic trance. The whole lot of it is just a load of mumbo jumbo.'

'But Senior,' Bowler replied, 'surely this witch doctor must be different from the average blackfella. He has killed four white men as quick as any man has been killed. Most of the stories we've heard about him are about his extraordinary skills, how he makes his own destiny. And there is suspicion amongst his own that he kills his own people which makes him a very formidable foe indeed. I say we cannot take this savage alive.'

Bowler didn't stop there: 'According to the stories we've heard about this killer's magic, he can do just about anything he wants to. I've seen these blackfellas who have had the bone pointed at them become sick, bloody sick, I tell you, the poor wretches get awfully bloody sick. Nothing seems to be wrong with them. They develop pain, then they lose their appetites and don't eat properly, then the sickness they have develops more. It spreads right throughout their bodies. Senior, as soon as they get the message that the bone has been pointed at them, I tell you, they seem to wilt. They get weak, they lose their will to keep on living. They just want to die and that's precisely what happens. They die, they give up.'

Clamp, the Senior Constable, chewed thoughtfully on a stalk of weed before he spoke. He looked at the black trackers then he looked at Bell and Bowler, then he said, 'You may all be right, from your points of view, how you see this blackfella's magic is spread around. But all of you must remember we are supposed to be military men. I can understand the black trackers' mode of thinking, it's what they have been taught to believe. But not you Bowler nor you Bell, you're white like me. We know it's their witchery used by medicine men like this man to keep people under control. Remember, we have God on our side. I can assure you all that if this Bulmurn comes into range, then he has to be shot. I'll get him for sure, because I don't want any of you to go screaming off into the bush. Then I'd have to come bloody looking for you men, too!'

Jacky Jack said to Clamp, 'Boss us fulla are glad. Weed plunty 'appy to 'ear you sayed dis, boss, cause dis fulla he need to be shot, dus for sure boss.'

Clamp put his hand into the air commanding the men to be silent. When they obliged he said to them, 'All right men, that's enough. Let's get on with catching this crazy killer before he does it again. I'm not scared of this man and I hope none of you are. Make no mistake, we'll get this savage. We've got his trail, now all we have to do is make sure we don't lose it. We will keep on his trail day in and day out. We'll make sure we don't give him any peace. We'll be relentless. We'll be like bloodhounds. We'll keep after him until he tires, then when he makes a mistake, we'll be waiting for him.'

'When we capture him,' Clamp repeated, 'that's when I'll prove to you that he's just an ordinary man like us. I really don't care if we take him dead or alive, so let's get on with it now, is that clear? If we don't, Inspector Johnson will have our hides. We will all be the laughing stock of the whole colony. Do any of you want that to happen? I don't! Do you men want to be ridiculed, laughed at, right throughout the whole colony?'

Clamp cast his gaze over his men. He could see his words had got through to them. This gave him the comforting thought that they would all support him regardless of what happened in the future.

Buoyed by Clamp's words, they moved back onto Bulmurn's trail with renewed zest.

Bulmurn is Seen

Bulmurn was now starting to feel the strain of the constant doggedness of Clamp and his men, relentless in pursuit. They were gaining on him. In several instances, he could easily have speared any one of his pursuers, they were so close to him, but he didn't want to give himself away. Bulmurn had now decided that he'd had enough of this chasing game of black trackers and police troopers forever trying to pin him down.

He made the decision that the time was right to implement his plan at the rock, so he made a slight change in direction. He went as fast as he could to Boyagin Boya, the huge rock southeast of where he was now. It took half a day, but once there, he circled the rock several times, leaving signs only where he knew his tracks would confuse the black trackers and police troopers. He entered into the bush from the rock at the same place several times. Each time he did this, he tried to mix his signs, then he retraced his tracks in reverse. By doing this, he hoped that his tracks would completely disappear.

When Bulmurn had finished putting his plan into action he worked his way up the slopes of the high granite rock heading towards the top. During the ascent he slowed himself to marvel at its rugged beauty. It was black, grey, brown, changing to a burnt reddish colour with splotches of green rock mould that grew over parts of its massive face. He noted the gulli trees growing in dirt deposits here and there on top of the rock, and at the bottom of the trees, grey-green rushes grew.

Bulmurn didn't hurry because he knew he was some distance ahead of his hunters and he had quite a bit of time to correctly hide himself once atop Boyagin. When he reached the summit he caught his breath and rubbed the tightness out of the calf muscle of his legs which ached from the climb.

Then he settled himself to his vigil of waiting for his pursuers to arrive from the north-west approach. While he waited the autumn sun drifted lazily across the sky bringing the day to late afternoon, then Bulmurn heard a distant snort from one of the horses. Instantly alert, he scanned the horizon. He could see dust rising here and there in the bush as they made their way towards his position.

The riders were silent, the only signs they made were to point the way Bulmurn's trail went. The silence in their approach made him think the whole group was very much alert. To him it meant they had good concentration. They were cautious, perhaps expecting Bulmurn to be laying in wait for them. Clamp expected an ambush.

The black trackers rode close together in front of the police troopers. Bulmurn sneered: 'Look at those black dogs leading their masters after me. If it weren't for those scum those *wadjbulla* would never be able to find me at all, let alone trail me this far.'

Bulmurn watched the party pass under the spot where he was hiding. Then they all stopped as Clamp rose from the saddle to stand high in the stirrup irons, mainly to stretch himself. As Clamp made this movement, he looked directly at Bulmurn's hiding place.

Bulmurn felt sudden fright, he thought they had seen him. But then he realised that he was almost concealed from the ground where they were. He realised that it was only natural for them to look up and over such an outcrop of huge rock. Bulmurn watched them look in awe at the rugged beauty of the huge rock, Boyagin Boya.

Then Wheelbarrow Long was the first to move. Bulmurn saw

him point at his tracks. Bulmurn had made sure the signs he'd made were not too obvious so that they suspected he was trying to trick them. He just left the signs as though he got a little careless near the rock.

Wheelbarrow Long said to Clamp and the others, 'He bin 'ere dis fulla he gun dis way'. He pointed at the ground showing them Bulmurn's tracks. The group moved in the direction Wheelbarrow Long had taken. Soon the group disappeared from Bulmurn's view. They went around to the left of where he sat.

Bulmurn knew now was the time he should move out and lose them forever, but he changed his mind. He elected to stay where he was because he was curious to see what they would do when they realised they had lost his trail. He knew he was taking a risk, he knew there was the possibility they may climb over the rock, maybe right to the place he was hiding, but it was a risk he was prepared to take, so keen was he to witness their confusion.

He knew he would see them come back around the rock to where they first started. When they came into view, Bulmurn smiled. They were now doing what he planned they would do. The risk of being caught was worth seeing the almost comic confusion of his pursuers as they looked everywhere for his trail. Bulmurn knew that they would track him around the rock again. They would do this to try to locate the place where he had left the rock in another direction.

Bulmurn thought that when they left to go around again, when they were out of sight, he would give them the slip, once and for all. Jacky Jack was the first to speak. He said to Clamp, 'Boss! He gone into tin air boss, rite 'ere boss. I tull you boss, he can make 'imself dispear an he dunit rite ere boss, round dis rock.'

Jacky Jack's voice had fear in it. Had Bulmurn heard this fear he would have felt angry at Jacky Jack. Bulmurn did not like the black trackers for what they were doing. He would have despised Jacky Jack even more so for his weakness.

Clamp gave an order in a voice that cracked the afternoon silence. 'Everybody gather around, listen carefully, he may not have left here at all. He might be close by. We've got to find his trail', and he pointed along the way they came and the way they had been. 'He's close by, I can feel it. I have a notion he's nearby. Now, I want you to pick up again the trail where he came to the rock and where he went around it. Who knows, with a bit of luck we may catch him before nightfall, that's if we all work hard — we might catch him now. Let's all look for his signs carefully,' Clamp said with renewed enthusiasm.

Bulmurn sat high above the patrol watching their every move, secure in the knowledge he would leave no trace. Bulmurn counted on the troopers getting tired of the chase, the black trackers continually losing his trail. He hoped they would abandon their hunt. This is what he hoped they would do, but deep down he knew this was a groundless hope. He knew their leader, the big trooper, was a relentless pursuer who would never give up. He would try to keep after him, no matter what.

Bulmurn smiled to himself. Even though the big trooper wouldn't give up, he was confident that he would soon give the search party the go by. He would soon be left alone to head north towards the Moorara people's country of Moora. When he gave them the slip, they would lose his trail completely. Bulmurn sat in concealment upon the top of the rock, not too far from his pursuers below. The prickly bush, the tammar scrub and sheoak's shade hid him from the prying eyes of the men searching at the base of the rock.

Bulmurn silently chuckled to himself, 'I can see them going around the rock for days, from sunrise to sunset. I can see them getting more and more tired, more and more confused.' This thought gave Bulmurn renewed strength, allowing him to become more accustomed to any tiredness he may have felt, so that he rested himself while they toiled on after his trail.

However, he had misjudged the determination of his pursuers. Clamp had, in fact, never gone with the rest of his group. Instead he stayed at their point of entry to the rock, thus Bulmurn could not leave. Bulmurn cursed Clamp. This was not what he had expected. He had expected Clamp to go and direct the others. Now the time in which he had to escape was getting shorter and shorter.

The sun was moving ever so slowly across the sky. It was not as low as he had expected it to be. This was the way all his people read the daytime. Even though he was a little anxious, he reasoned that sooner or later, Clamp would join his men and when Clamp joined them, he would make his escape to freedom. But this wasn't to be so, because it was when the sun dropped a little in the afternoon sky that he could see the dust kicked up from the trail of the company as they headed back towards their boss who sat on his horse inadvertently blocking the fugitive's exit.

Bulmurn remained unperturbed. He was still rather amused, he felt his time would come when he could make good his escape. He watched the procession of the patrol of men as they wound their way among the brush and balgas at the base of the big rock. In and out they went, yelling, pushing, almost shoving one another out of the way as they jostled for position to be in front to lead the way.

First it was Jacky Jack, then the next was Jimmy Jim Ranking and then it was Wheelbarrow Long who led the way. They all wanted to be the one who had found the trail where Bulmurn had left the rock to go in another direction. Try as they might the black trackers could not find another trail. To them, Bulmurn's trail had just completely disappeared. They headed back to the first point of entry, where Clamp sat upon his horse waiting for them.

Jacky Jack and the others of the group began discussing their part in the chase. They offered excuses to one another of why they could not find the trail and solutions of what they should do to find it. Jimmy Jim Rankin had fallen behind the others — not deliberately — he had just become bored with the chase. The others had already arrived when he made his approach through the bushes to join them all.

It was at this time that Bulmurn, watching intently, had a cramp in his left leg. The pain was so severe that he had to stand. Although it was a cramp in the lower part of his leg, it was enough to make Bulmurn move his whole body to stretch his leg against the cramp.

The movement high on the rock did not go unnoticed, it

caught Jimmy Jim Rankin's eye. He had seen Bulmurn move. Even though Bulmurn's body form blended with the shadowy rock foliage, he had been seen.

Jimmy Jim Rankin's heart thumped and his mind raced, but he kept his head. Even though he had seen Bulmurn move, he just kept his attention away from what he had seen.

Jimmy Jim Rankin casually made his way to Clamp and the others. He made it look as though he had seen nothing. He crossed in front of Clamp so that he could position himself with his back to the rock where Bulmurn had hidden.

Jimmy Jim Rankin whispered to Clamp, 'Boss look ober my solder. Derwun we bin looken for he up der on tup ob der big rock, on tup up dere'. He moved his head in an upwards motion to confirm his sighting of Bulmurn.

Clamp reacted with a swiftness that no one in his group could have even half expected. Somehow Clamp had a primed musket already in his hand and all in one movement, he knocked off the safety catch, took one look over Jimmy Jim Rankin's head, then he raised his firearm and fired. Clamp's swift reaction was due to years of training and bush experience which compensated for any error of judgement he might have made due to the quickness of his movements.

With his glance up to Bulmurn's position, Clamp judged the distance. Clamp knew that one hit would be as good as a killing shot because a wounded man wouldn't be able to escape from him and his troopers and his black trackers. Clamp knew his quick shot was a gamble, but he was very confident of his shooting ability. It was vital to get this killer, after all the savagery they had seen at the Rows place. This butcher had to be stopped. All these thoughts raced through Clamp's mind.

Then a rifle shot boomed out in the stillness surrounding the big rock, echoing across the rocky and wooded hillside.

Jimmy Jim Rankin fell to the ground. He was stunned by Clamp's swift reaction. The blast of the gun almost burst his eardrums. His ears were still ringing as he clambered to his feet. Was Bulmurn dead or still alive? Or was the man gone?

All the other men in the patrol were sure they heard the thud of a bullet striking flesh. They all looked at one another and somebody yelled out, 'A man's been shot! A man's been shot!' They laughed and shouted out in joy, 'We got him! We got him!' They all began to climb up the rocky slope to where they reckoned Bulmurn had been shot by Clamp.

None of them could keep silent. Jimmy Jim Rankin could not contain himself, proudly claiming that he had spotted Bulmurn first.

Clamp said, 'I'm sure I plugged him with a good shot. I had to shoot to kill when I saw how clear his body was silhouetted against the sky from down here. It was just for a moment but it made him a clear target. I had to shoot to kill.'

Jacky Jack said that he was sure he had seen Bulmurn fall down. 'I hope dis bad fulla gut a big hole in his head.'

'I tried for a heart shot, but I really can't tell where I hit him at all,' said Clamp.

'Senior, I heard the bullet strike off a rock too, perhaps after it had struck him,' Bowler said.

'Good on you Senior', Bell said. 'I hope that bullet put a big hole in him. If he's dead, he won't give us any more trouble.'

They all still were excitedly climbing to the place where Bulmurn was last seen, eager to see the damage. Was he dead or alive? Was his body up there on the rock?

Finally they all reached the spot where he was supposed to have fallen, but there was no body there at all. Frantically they spread out to look for the missing body of the fugitive. They searched to no avail.

Then suddenly there was a shout. It was Bowler who called out, 'Here he is! Here is he! Hell Senior, he's fallen down a crevasse in this rock, here!' He pointed.

They ran to join Bowler and to look down at the body in the crevasse, keen to see the man they had been chasing for days. They looked into the crevasse, almost as one. There at the bottom lay a big black man. It was indeed Bulmurn. The big man's body was still convulsing. It was twitching in what looked like death throes to the men up the top. Bulmurn had a head wound leaking a large pool of blood. Bell was exuberant: 'Hell, look at him. Look at his wound!' Then he looked at Clamp and said, 'Senior! You've shot the bastard right through the head. What a shot, Senior. What a *shot!*'

The party erupted in cheers. They all started to shake Clamp's hand to congratulate him on his marksmanship. Clamp was modest: 'It was a lucky shot. God knows it was lucky.'

Jimmy Jim Rankin said to the others in an excited voice, '*Ise lucky Ise sawd im oserwide weed neber get im.*'

'You did well,' Clamp said to him. Jimmy Jim you did well', and warmly slapped him on his bare shoulders. In sheer delight, the others did the same. Their actions made Jimmy Jim Rankin feel a proud man.

Clamp said to his men, 'Men, because it's late afternoon, I think we'll camp here tonight. We'll rest up for the rest of the day. Tonight we will get a good sleep, then we'll move out first light tomorrow morning to bring in the killer's body and complete the mission. Hopefully we can do it in a day and a half from here.

'Boss,' Jacky Jack said. 'Less leab dis wun 'ere in dis rock dann 'ere in dis hole in der rock till tomorrow 'fore weed git 'im out. Oderwise weed mus sleep dann dare round der rock so dis fulla spirit come back to look for dis wun budy, and it fine us unstead. So dus wut weed gutta do boss.'

'Dus is true boss,' Jimmy Jim Rankin said, with Wheelbarrow Long nodding in agreement. Weed agree wid Jacky Jack about dis fulla comen back to fine dis fulla budy. Dus why us gotta moob outa site frum 'ere sowd it nut fine us an cutch us. If it cutch us it could kilt us boss.'

Clamp laughed at them, at what they said and believed. When Clamp laughed, Bell and Bowler laughed also. Clamp said to the trio of black trackers, 'I know your beliefs. Nyoongar, black man, magic man or not, he's dead. He's not going to damn well hurt anyone ever again.

'I tell you boys, he's as dead as a door nail. You boys all saw the hole in his head and the blood. That bloke has bled like a stuck pig, I tell you. You all saw him twitching there, giving his last kicks. Even if his spirit comes back looking for him, I tell you this medicine man's going nowhere.'

Everybody went quiet as they stood there, now nobody laughed. Then Clamp broke the silence, when he said to the black trackers, 'Seeing that you men did a good job, I'll let you have your way. We'll go and make our camp over there, further around the base of the rock', Clamp pointed in the direction he meant.

Jacky Jack looked at Clamp: 'Dis is goot boss sank you ford lett'n us stay way frum ware dis fulla spirit mite git us. Sank you boss.'

'That's all right,' Clamp said to the black trackers. 'Anyway you fellows need a break. I know that's what you blacks do when there's a death in your tribe. Now don't you worry, we'll soon find us a place where that spirit can't find us. We'll be plenty hidden from any spirit looking for us for its revenge.'

With a look of relief all over their faces, the three black trackers nodded in agreement. However, as they went to move away, Jimmy Jim Rankin felt a cold shiver run up the back of his spine. He felt uneasy, it was as if it was some kind of warning not to stay nearby. They should go on their way back to Perth. He felt that it wasn't safe to stay the night. They should leave now, get a head start now. They should be on their way.

What they should do was get the body out of the crevasse, Jimmy Jim Rankin thought. Then tie the killer's body to the horse, and get out of here as fast as they could go, so that when the spirit returned to look for the body, they would all be long gone. If the spirit could not find the body, Jimmy Jim Rankin reasoned, then the spirit would not be able to do any harm to anyone. He faltered behind the others as they moved down the slope of the rock. Should he tell them what he felt? But he was scared the others would ridicule him, that those bosses would laugh at him. He reluctantly followed the others down the face of the rock.

The party moved down the slope until they came to the bottom, then they went around the base of the rock until they came to an opening in the brush, quite some distance from where Bulmurn's body lay still in the crevasse.

Clamp was sure the move would please the black trackers, however, had Jimmy Jim Rankin told him about the premonition he had experienced, maybe he would have had reason to worry. Instead, Clamp thought, 'These black trackers are just a crazy bunch of superstitious natives with their stupid beliefs. Fancy, they believed that buck's spirit would come back looking for its body.

'But,' Clamp thought, 'these black trackers are bloody good at their job.' He somewhat grudgingly respected their views, but the Senior was not in the mood to be set back by a few fearful blackfellas. He knew the only way to control them was to be tough with them when he needed to be tough. Nobody was going to spoil this moment of glory for him.

The group found two small clearings that looked a good camping spot for them to spend the night, the trackers separated from the troopers, and well away from the body of Bulmurn.

Clamp said to his colleagues, Bell and Bowler, 'This looks like an ideal place for us to camp out the night. There's just enough room in the clearing for us to move around in. And there's plenty of brush to keep any chilly wind off us when it's cold. The blacks can sleep over there.' Bell and Bowler nodded their approval. Clamp then looked at the black trackers. 'What you boys say? What you three reckon, you agree with us, that place over there is a good place to camp? Do you all agree that that fella dead upon the hill up there reckon we are safely hidden from his spirit when it comes back to look for his body?'

Jacky Jack spoke for the black trackers. 'Yeah boss, dat is goot place to sleep. Weed all agree wid you boss. Nun spirit gunna fine us 'ere dus for sure.'

Clamp said to his men, 'Let's make a fire, a good fire. Then we'll eat together this night. I've got a surprise for the lot of you.'

They soon had a good fire going. A billy boiled and they sat down to eat the evening meal around the campfire. While they ate, Clamp said to all his men, 'I'm proud of all of you. I'm proud of all of us and I think we did a good job, especially you black trackers. That was as solid a job of tracking as I've ever seen.

'You know the man we were chasing was smart, but in the end

his magic did him no good. He just outsmarted himself. He made one mistake. He stood up, and it cost him his life. I don't know why he showed himself to us, but the main thing is, for some reason he did. When he did, that gave us the break we needed to nail him.'

'I'm bloody glad we did,' Bowler said. 'You know, tracking that black was hard work. He had us on the go all the time. You know, Senior, sometimes we must have been very close to him, we could sense he was close, but we could never see him.'

Said Clamp, 'I had my doubts if we were ever going to see him, let alone take him dead or alive. You know, I was half expecting him to double back the way we had come so we would lose his trail. But he made one mistake, he got careless. He made one step the wrong way. He showed himself to you, Jimmy Jim Rankin.'

Clamp rose from his sitting position and walked to where his saddle bags were and pulled out two bottles of rum. 'I brought these bottles of rum for just such an occasion as this, so let's celebrate our capture of the killer who is now lying up there inside this rock, dead as a door nail.

'Bring your mugs men, and pour yourselves a generous shot of rum. 'You too', he said to the black trackers, 'you can drink with us tonight'. They all relaxed around the fire, drinking, pleased with themselves. 'If it were not for old eagle eyes, Jimmy Jim Rankin, we may never have caught that man. You're a bloody hero, Jimmy Jim. I tell you he was cool under pressure, as cool as I have ever seen anyone anywhere. I mean you, Jimmy Jim. You were very smart, placing yourself so that the summit was within my field of view. Yes, you were smart under pressure,' Clamp said to him, giving him a deserved amount of praise.

'A good piece of work, Jimmy Jim,' said Bell in a matter-of-fact tone.

'I'll see that a recommendation of recognition for your service goes forward to Commissioner Ellis,' Clamp said to the trackers. 'You may be paid in money or you may get extra rations. Maybe I can recommend a cask of rum for each of you, you're the best in the business. If others are better, then I need to be told about them, so I can be convinced they are better than ours.'

'Hey boss,' Jacky Jack laughingly called out to Clamp, 'dut wut you sayed bout dut rum, dut tea, sugar, bout der rum, it all soun good to me. All dut tucker, all dut rum to drink, time to go roun on walkabout. Boss dus is goot sing. Us fulla wounent argue bout dut boss, no blutty way, boss.'

Jimmy Jim Rankin grinned, then spoke in a slurred voice. Already the rum was affecting him. He said, 'I agreed wid Jacky, boss. I'd reckun Wheelbarrow, he 'greed too boss. Wut you say, Wheelbarrow Long, you gree wid us?'

Wheelbarrow Long grinned, his white teeth flashing in the firelight. 'Dis bloke ere,' he pointed to himself, 'gree wood all you osers. Dis rum you gibe us goot. It dut goot it make me feelt goot. If I git cask I going to see my *yorga*. Me no she wunt me un she noad I no bout her wunten me too. But you no boss, sumtime she friten me too. But wen I git dis rum in me I git brabe. I'se gunna fix her', and he made sexual movements with his hips, as though he was holding a woman. Then he laughed and everybody else joined in. Their laughter rang out in the still of the night around the big rock Boyagin Boya. Their laughter released all their pent up fear and anxieties into the stillness around them.

The group yarned on into the night about how they had caught Bulmurn. As they yarned a sudden gust of chilly wind blew across the group's campsite, causing Jacky Jack to comment, 'Dis wun gunna blow un howler tonite, boss.' As he looked skywards he said, 'Dut sky it sure is dark, boss, look like it gunna rain tonight, maybe litennen too boss'.

'All right,' Clamp said to the men. 'Let's hit the sack and get a few hours of good sleep. We have to rise early to get the body out of the crevasse. I want to be in Perth as quick as we can make it. We want to let our superiors know what has happened, that the killer is dead. The settlers in the colony will welcome the news and people will sleep easier at night.'

One of the black trackers stoked the fire. The rest of the men found a comfortable place. Then they uncurled their swags and bedded down. The black trackers had built a wind break for themselves and the troopers, so they all had the same comforts. Each member of the search party lay some two steps apart from the others, with a larger gap between the blacks and the whites. As they drifted into a full, rewarding sleep, dream thoughts were on the reward and citations they might receive for the quick timely catching of the killer, punishing him with death.

The sky was black under a cotton ball of clouds that drifted beneath the moonlight over the sleeping party of pursuers. Mar the wind picked up in strength, but didn't blow as fiercely as Jacky Jack predicted. In the distance thunder rolled in ever-lessening rumbles, as whatever storm there was moved away. Lightning flashed across the sky, but it went unnoticed by the sleeping party of men. Clouds drifted over the area. It was going to rain. The rain would be steady, not hard, just light and misty.

13

Bulmurn Strikes Back

The rain drifted down. The bushes caught most of the small droplets of water as they disintegrated into the mists that rose from the damp ground and the outside of the blankets of the slumbering men. The moisture failed to penetrate the warm heavy rugs. The men slept on unaware of the freshness of the air about them or the smell of the wet earth.

But the misty rain had the opposite effect on Bulmurn. The misty rain began to wet his body. The wind blew down on him causing a freshness that stirred a revival of consciousness in Bulmurn's numbed brain. Bulmurn was alive not dead.

In the darkness of the crevasse, he groaned and moved his left arm, sliding his fingers across the sticky mat of his curly, bloody hair. As his fingers moved over the top of his forehead, he winced in pain as he pinpointed the wound. The bullet had creased his skull, leaving a sizeable flesh wound about as long as his index finger.

The bullet had been slowing down over the distance it was fired, so that when it struck, the impact was less than fatal. It had hit the bony forehead, moving upwards and out, leaving a flesh wound. Had it gone in and penetrated the brain, he would have died instantly, as his tormenters believed. Bulmurn was surely a very lucky man.

Bulmurn sensed that something was wrong with his right arm. He winced in pain when he did tried to move it, then realised it was broken just up from the wrist joint. He had injured his arm as he fell down the crevasse in the rock, but Bulmurn did not know the cause of the break. All he knew was that it was broken. He remembered that when he had a cramp in his leg, he rose and was looking at the black trackers and the police troopers below. He thought that he had heard a thunderous noise. Now here he was in some kind of dark place, trapped with a broken arm.

'I remember where I am', he thought, and as if in response, *babbangwin*, the lightning, flashed across *maroo* the sky, lighting *jidaluk* the night, and shining a light into the crevasse showing Bulmurn where he was.

When Bulmurn tried to move, he nearly blacked out. He steadied himself, realising that he was going to have a hard task to get out of the hole he was in. He had to get out or die in a white man's prison, hung by the neck. Bulmurn didn't want to die. He wanted to live.

Babbangwin, the lightning spirit, flashed across the sky to light the crevasse showing Bulmurn how he was trapped. Then its light faded as *mulga*, the thunder spirit, sounded a low rumble as if to promise it would not awaken anyone else. Then everything again was dark and quiet around him. Bulmurn rested while he waited for the lightning again. While he rested, *midjual*, the rain, kept wetting his body keeping him refreshed and revived so he wouldn't slip back into unconsciousness. The rain kept him cool. *Mar* the wind blew gentle zephyrs of breeze on him. The wind spirit was playing its part in keeping Bulmurn cool and awake.

Then *babbangwin* flashed its light across the sky and into the crevasse where Bulmurn lay. The light signalled that it was time for him to move. Painfully he tried. He raised his good left arm upwards, trying to grasp a hold so he could manoeuvre his body upwards out of the rock hole he was in. He caught a hold with his good left hand, then he pushed his legs to one side of the rock wall to jam his back against the opposite wall. Then he grasped another hold with his left hand before he pushed himself towards the rock surface again.

The only time he stopped was when *babbangwin* withdrew its light. When the lightning streaked across the sky, Bulmurn pulled himself upwards. Bulmurn felt that *mulga* the thunder spirit was pleased with him because its low rumble was quieter than the sound it usually made. *Babbangwin's* light lingered much longer than usual. It seemed to concentrate its brightness into and around the crevasse, allowing Bulmurn to see what he was doing, where to hold with his good hand and where to put his feet.

At last Bulmurn reached the top of the crevasse, he was out. He rolled carefully onto his back, not wanting to hurt his injured arm more than was necessary. He lay and rested to get his breath back, then undid his *nulburn*, the human hair belt, to fashion into a sling for his broken arm. When he finished doing this, he lay for a while longer to relax the pain in his bad arm with the healing powers from his mind. He concentrated his thoughts on the arm to stop the aching and to start the mend.

After a while the pain eased from his arm. He allowed only a dull headache from his head wound. He was confident that it, too, would subside.

Bulmurn stood up, the pain temporarily gone from his head. He looked around, taking in the night scene with an alert mind. Bulmurn's first thoughts were for his safety — he had lost his spear when he fell. He began to realise the situation he was in. He knew he must leave this place immediately. He knew his pursuers would come looking for his body tomorrow at daybreak.

Bulmurn looked at the sky. He saw some recognisable stars so he was able to judge that it was around the middle of the night. That gave him time before the daylight to get as far away as he possibly could, so he could look for a place to conceal himself, to let his head and arm heal. He thought he might even have time tomorrow to gather food along the way as he fled.

But then Bulmurn realised that he had to do something more. He had to save himself. He had to kill for self-preservation. 'I must not allow myself to panic', he thought. 'I must not run like a blind idiot. Was it not the dreamtime spirits that helped me to survive? Was not my dead brother-in-law, Binyung, a rainmaker? It was him that sent *midjual* the rain to awaken and revive me. Was it not my sister Munyee, who told *mar* the wind to blow to keep me cool? Was it not *babbangwin* lighting the hole in the rock to show me how to get out? Was not *mulga's* usual thunderous noise quiet, so that only I could hear? Now I must be careful, I do not want to make a mistake again.'

From the spot where Bulmurn stood, he could see the glow of the pursuers' fire. He began to focus his mind on the camp, singing his way into the black trackers' minds, putting them into a deeper sleep than the police troopers. Bulmurn knew that if anyone was to sense he was nearby, it would be the black trackers.

Then Bulmurn moved off in the direction of the firelight. As he came downwards off the rock face, *babbangwin* flashed his lightning opening up the clouds, and allowing the moon and stars to shine so he could see where he was treading.

Bulmurn wanted to take revenge upon these *wadjbulla*. To do this he would need a weapon to kill them. Then he could make his escape unhindered, losing himself in the Moora area to the north. He carefully worked himself around the less steep side of the rock, and seeing the campfire was not too far away, he slowly approached the horses that had been hobbled and tied in the bush. Once among the horses, Bulmurn searched until he found the saddle bags. He needed to find a weapon of some sort. He searched further, then he found a heavy police baton. He had the weapon with him as he approached the sleeping men. Bulmurn would deal with the troopers first.

So quiet were Bulmurn's movements, not even the horses made any sound as he moved away from them. None snickered or snorted. The whole posse was in a deep sleep. Clamp was the closest to the horses. The other two police troopers lay close to Clamp, while the black trackers lay together away from them on the other side of the fire.

Bulmurn struck his first victim across the temple. He barely moved. So quiet and swift were his death dealing blows, that not one of the troopers or black trackers even knew what it was that was attacking them.

Out of the six men he attacked, he killed four, knocking the other two senseless. In just a few short minutes, the lives of the two police constables, James Bell and Tom Bowler ceased. They were followed into death just as silently by the black trackers, Jimmy Jim Rankin and Wheelbarrow Long.

'Boss! Boss! Wake up! Boss, wake up! It's me, Jacky Jack! Wake up boss!', he cried to the Senior Constable as he shook him hard trying to wake the trooper up.

Jacky Jack shook him hard again and again until he at last got a response from Clamp. Jacky Jack felt a little relief when Clamp moved and his eyes fluttered open. Rolling over onto his back, he looked into the morning sky, adjusting his eyes to the brightness of the daylight. He moved again, then rose to a standing position. As he did so, he felt sharp pains in his head. He felt faint. His temple felt numb. Clamp's immediate reaction was to put his hand to the side of his head where he felt an egg-sized lump.

Clamp straightened himself up, then he looked at Jacky Jack, noticing that he too had a lump on his head. 'Bloody hell', he said out loud. 'Bloody hell. What is it Jacky Jack? What's happened? I feel as though I've been slugged. Wake the others up, Jacky Jack. Tell them we've got a lot of work to do today. Wake them up Jacky Jack, while I get my bearings and my breath back.'

'Boss. You bin hit rite on you head', cried out the hysterical Jacky Jack. 'An I bin hit too boss, sumwum try to kilt us.'

Because of the hit on the head, the Senior Constable didn't quite understand the seriousness of the situation they were in at the time, but Jacky Jack kept on with his agonising spiel about the others in the camp.

'Boss,' Jacky Jack said to Clamp, trying to get his attention again. 'Boss, dey all dead! I'se can't wake dos oser fulla up cause dey all dead. Dey all bin kilt, like we spose to bin.' Jacky Jack looked Clamp in the eyes and said to him, 'It no goot boss. I try to waken him up but dey wounent moob for me. Den I lookt at dem I seed dey all *norch*, all dead.'

Senior Constable Clamp began to realise what Jacky Jack was telling him. 'How do you know they're dead, Jacky? How do you know they're dead?'

'Is liken dis boss. I wake wid my head hurten. Den I'se git up holling my head. Me bin talk to Wheelbarrow Long. I'se still holling my head. Den me seed his eye open, his eye nut seed nusen. I lookt at dos oser fulla. Jimmy Jim Rankin he eye seen nusen, he dead too! Den me moob to dut boss ober dare.' He pointed at Bowler and Bell. 'Dey dead, too, boss, dos bosses like dos black trackers, boss. Dey all dead dey eyes nut seed nusen.

'Den me shake you boss, me shout at you and me cry out, Boss! Boss! Me friten you dead. Me shout and shout out at you. Den me shake you gain. Plese nut be dead too. Nut dis boss plese, nut dis boss.

'I recon boss, dut fulla who kilt dem wun is dut fulla we bin chasen. Dus who me recon dood it. Dus who dood dem fulla in, boss.'

Jacky Jack helped Clamp to a groggy standing position. Clamp staggered a little before he caught his balance. Jacky Jack kept up his near hysterical chatter. 'I tull you boss we shounant ob camped nest to dut Bulmurn cause he gut dos magic powers. Nowd he kilt us out. I recon we neber git back to Perth. Me sure he gut dis power he gut frum der Dreamtime 'pirit.

'Dey gib him back his life after you shoot dis fulla. Maybe he gunna kilt us all, hown we gunna stop dis fulla frum killun us. I'se recon he'd gut too much power for us to handle. Too much power is wut he gut.'

Clamp stood his ground with renewed steadiness as back came the training of a police officer. He snapped at Jacky Jack, 'Shut your whingeing mouth'. Then he surveyed the camp scene without moving towards the four dead men. Clamp could see that they had died in their sleep without any knowledge that they were being killed. 'How savage! How savage is this man,' he said to Jacky Jack.

Both Clamp and Jacky Jack turned as one person towards the top of the rocky hill Boyagin Boya. Together they ran the distance up to the place where the body of Bulmurn had fallen into the rock fissure. When they looked into the crevasse, there was no dead body. The hole was empty. Bulmurn was gone.

Clamp looked at Jacky Jack as he slumped onto the ground. His voice became pathetically feverish, and panic rushed across the hillside in the form of guttural admonishments and fear of Bulmurn, the *mobarn* man.

It took some time before the officer made the tracker see that the fugitive Bulmurn was desperate because he was wounded. He had to try to stop them, the only way he could do it was to kill everyone of the pursuing party. Then he could make his escape. No one would know which way he went.

'If we had died, then I'm sure our remains would never have been found way out in this remote area', he said.

'No you rong boss,' Jacky Jack said. 'Ebery Nyoongar no ware dis place Boyagin Boya is. Dis big rock is a sacred big rock to our people. Nyoongar come to dis rock alla time boss. Dey wod fine us sooner or later cause dey come ere for Nyoongar business alla time.'

'Hm,' Clamp said to Jacky Jack, 'I didn't know that Jacky Jack. Anyway, that bloody killer, Bulmurn, probably thinks we're all dead. Right now, I'm hoping he thinks just that. We need time to get reinforcements. We've got to get back on his trail.'

'How we gunna do dis Boss?' said Jacky Jack.

'Well, Jacky Jack, I'm hoping that he thinks we're dead so he doesn't hurry away from this place or cover his trail too well. You know, Jacky, if he thinks that, he'll get careless. You know what they say, careless men make mistakes, even smart men like our magic one here. He left us alive. He sure as hell made a mistake; now I'm sure he will make others, and we will catch him.'

Clamp Sends for Help

Clamp said to Jacky Jack, 'I've got an important job for you now Jacky Jack. I'm going to send you back to Perth to the big boss policeman, Chief Inspector Isaac Johnson, for you to give him a letter from me.'

'Wut dis letter for boss?'

'This letter is to ask the big boss to send us more men, so we can chase the murderous bastard down and bring him to white men's justice. That's what it's for, Jacky Jack. I'm asking him for more police, also for another black tracker to assist you. I've assured the Inspector we can continue the search because Bulmurn is wounded in the head. I made it plain in the letter that the quicker reinforcements arrive, the easier it will be for us to apprehend this mad-dog killer. Now go, go as quick as you can, speed is important if we are to catch this man.'

Clamp watched him go. He knew he could rely on Jacky Jack to deliver his message. It would take two or three days before reinforcements arrived. Clamp felt that even though the killer would be moving away from them, he would take no chances. He would defend himself at a moment's notice should he happen to return. Clamp also busied himself with the task of burying the four men in proper graves. It kept him from being fearful of this *mobarn* magic killer, that the blacks of this country believed in.

In the Aboriginal way, Clamp moved his camp to a new site away from the one where the killings occurred. He made his new camp close to the rock face to give him an advantage of height. He could see clearly every bush. He had ample clearing in front of him in case any attack was made. Bulmurn would not be able to attack him from above, as the rock overhang protected him by fifteen metres or more. It also eliminated the possibility of any missiles being dropped onto him. As long as he stayed close to the cliff face he would be safe.

Clamp decided it was best if he moved the horses where he could see them. He tied them apart, so that he could see anyone approaching them on their way to his stronghold. He placed his weapons, loaded, at arm's length. All the dead men's muskets made him a well-armed man. He placed his food and water with care, so he had easy access to everything he needed. Having done this he settled back to wait patiently for Jacky Jack and the reinforcements from Perth.

Jacky Jack led the new party towards Clamp's campsite, just two days after he had left to get help. Jacky Jack gave the familiar 'coo-ee, coo-ee' call as they approached the rock. Then Clamp acknowledged by firing off a gunshot, followed by a second round to welcome him and to let the troopers know he was still there. As the shots echoed across the hillside, the troopers let out a cheer, relieved to know he was alive to meet them. When they rode into his camp fifteen minutes later, they saw that Clamp was unkempt and dishevelled. He was unwashed, unshaven and so tired that he was almost asleep on his feet. He looked almost comical.

The reinforcements were led by Chief Inspector Johnson himself, followed by constables Ben Allen, Peter O'Brien and Bernard Clarke and two black trackers, Jacky Jack and Jurung. The addition of another tracker proved beneficial because the two would compete against each other at the head of the party to show who was the better tracker, thus putting more pressure on Bulmurn.

Inspector Johnson acknowledged Clamp's salute and the new arrivals dismounted from their horses. Jurung and Jacky Jack unsaddled and hobbled the horses before staking them out. Then they returned to where the police troopers were sitting around the fire. Each had a mug of tea in their hands.

Jacky Jack looked at Clamp and said, 'Boss it goot to seed you gain. It goot to seed you still libe.'

Clamp looked at him with respect and thought he did a good thing by bringing back the reinforcements in the time that he did. 'It's good to see you remembered to come back with the other bosses, Jacky Jack. You did a good job. You did well.'

Then they all settled back to listen to the details of the chase right up to where they were now at Boyagin Boya, the huge rock. They listened quietly to Clamp. When he finished they all began to talk of new strategies they would use in the renewed chase after the killer. They boiled the billy again, had a light meal, and the discussion continued. Johnson told Clamp and the others that the word was out that the search party had been attacked.

'You know, Clamp,' the Inspector said, 'the whole colony is calling this killer, Bulmurn, the black magic man, and most of the people in the colony are afraid to go out alone anywhere now. If they do have to go out, they arm themselves with the best firearm they have.

'He hasn't enhanced our reputation. This Bulmurn has made us the laughing stock of the whole colony. People are saying that we can't do our job properly. They say "sack them, bring better troopers from home — killers like this need to be caught straight away".'

'You know, George,' Johnson continued, 'We ought to try to take this savage alive if we can, so people can see him. They can touch him with their eyes. They can see for themselves that he's not so tough after all. Then they all can see him hang if they want to. Unless we can do that, I feel we cannot hold our heads up in the colony. The sight of him hanging will restore our pride, knowing we have the people's respect and faith once again.

'Clamp', Johnson continued in a matter of fact voice, 'this black's killing rampage has led us to take action against the tribe of Jubuc and Weejup of Guildford. I don't believe they were not implicated. I sent troopers out to their camps with the intention of planning a scuffle between the blacks and them. They were to kill as many as possible, sparing no one. I'll be pleased if they got that black buck Jubuc, the leader. But I'll be surprised if they did.

'We have to show them where our power lies, clear Guildford out. It is unfortunate that we have to crack down in this way, but the strength we display will make everyone in the colony alert to the fact that we will not be intimidated and the police force is not made up of a bunch of fools.'

'Surely they didn't kill all of the tribe?', Clamp queried.

'I imagine that some would escape up along the Bennett Brook. It branches off the Swan River near Success Hill, you know, the place where they tried to spear Governor Stirling's party, stopping them from landing near the beach there. There is a place some ten miles or more away called Gnangara, north of Guildford.

Now, Senior, have you buried the dead men?'

Clamp nodded, gathering his thoughts, 'Yes, Sir. I've buried the troopers down there on the right. The black trackers are to the left.' He pointed to the four grave mounds.

'Now all we have to do, Inspector, is to get on out there after this savage, find his trail and run him down into the dirt, then bring him back to face our justice, British justice.'

The new posse set out after Bulmurn. Jacky Jack and Jurung headed the group after they had found his trail. Even though Bulmurn had a three-day start on them, he couldn't go far because his head wound and broken arm slowed him up. He knew in his mind that the troopers were again on his trail and that they were being led by black trackers. They were catching up fast. He knew they were after him because he had smelt the smoke from their campfire when the wind blew his way. It seems *mar* the wind was still trying to help Bulmurn. The speed of their pursuit made him guess that black trackers were once again helping the *wadjbulla*.

He began to slow down, dogged by injury, so he decided to use his last method of defence to avoid being captured by his tormentors. He began to sing the black trackers.

His message to the black trackers was that they should join him. Bulmurn sang them silently, probing their minds. He was willing his thought to them, that they should join him so they could make him stronger in resistance. The black trackers should lead the search party away from him, then abandon them by giving them the go by, losing the troopers in the bush. When he was safe, they could rejoin the troopers, feigning that they had lost his trail and for a time had got lost themselves. After they had rejoined the police troopers, they could pretend to find his trail again then lead them in another direction.

Because of his wounds, Bulmurn was now close to being apprehended by the police troopers. He could not keep in front of them now. His best form of defence was to resist them for as long as he could, for he had no intention of making their task too easy. He looked down from the top of a hill. He could see the cloud of dust left by his pursuers. They were making good time after him now, and because of his broken arm, he had to leave the high hills and the thick scrub. The thick scrub and bushes pulled, pushed and hurt his arm, sending searing pain through his body. Bulmurn wondered if his powers were working on the black trackers. 'I'll soon know', Bulmurn thought, 'because here they come now. I'll sing them well.'

Both Jacky Jack and Jurung felt the singing. Jacky Jack remained strong. He thought of helping Bulmurn, but because of what had happened to the others, he could not do it, so he resisted even though he wasn't aware it was Bulmurn who was making him think about helping him.

As they got closer to Bulmurn, Jurung whispered, 'Jacky Jack, let's help Bulmurn. You know we can lose his trail and lead them another way. We can lose them for a while, then rejoin them later. We could say we just lost sight of the troopers when we rejoin them after we've given Bulmurn time to escape.'

But Jacky Jack was able to resist Jurung's suggestion. He said to Jurung in their own language, 'Jurung, if that big boss and those other bosses heard us talking about helping Bulmurn, they wouldn't hesitate to shoot us down or hang us. If they didn't do either of those two things, then they would probably put us in chains, ready for jail on Wagemup. I don't want to go to that place. I want to stay out here alive on this land here. Don't you remember that Bulmurn killed Jimmy Jim Rankin and poor old Wheelbarrow Long? Aren't they our people too?' he questioned Jurung.

'Yeah, I suppose you're right, Jacky Jack,' Jurung answered.

Bulmurn's power of singing Jacky Jack and Jurung only partly worked for him. Even though at times their thinking was confused, they worked it out that, in fact, it was Bulmurn singing them. They fought against Bulmurn's near, overbearing power to confuse their train of thought. They tried to clear their minds because he was trying now to make them see things they didn't actually see. They looked at where Bulmurn was hiding and saw only a black stump or balga, a grass tree. These two objects were actually Bulmurn, but the black trackers didn't recognise or see him, even though they looked at the stump and black boy tree as if in anticipation that Bulmurn was there.

Constable Peter O'Brien, the nearest of the police to the black trackers wondered what they were looking at, because all he saw each time was a large black stump and a large black boy tree which hung down like a man with his hair hanging all the way to the ground. While Constable O'Brien was wondering, Inspector Johnson, Clamp and the other constables moved alongside him. Before anyone could say anything to the black trackers, they moved off in another direction, away from where Bulmurn was hiding. The black trackers talked in a native language that even the versatile Clamp couldn't understand.

The trackers took the group around in a circle until they came back to nearly the same spot near the black boy tree, but it was no longer there. Jacky Jack and Jurung looked at one another, they didn't have to say anything. Each of them knew what the other person thought, but they didn't say anything to the police troopers for fear of being ridiculed by them.

The morning drifted into the afternoon and the pursuers had much trouble tracking the fugitive. Each time the party got close, the black trackers led them in a circle. Bulmurn still fought them off by confusing the black trackers with his singing, especially when the party was close to him.

Bulmurn's luck in evading his pursuers was beginning to run out. The hunters were getting closer and closer all the time. What powers he had over the black trackers began to fade because he also had to use will power to keep his injured body going. His head ached from the gunshot wound and his broken right arm was a constant drain on his energy. Bulmurn was to escape from his tormentors' clutches for only one more night.

That night the police troopers and black trackers ate and slept well. They had a big fire to keep them warm; Bulmurn's night was just the opposite. He had no big fire to keep him warm because he was afraid they would sneak upon him at night if he had a light that they could see. He was sick. He was tired of running. What he needed was a good night's sleep.

The very next day, the hunters were up early. They had risen with the dawning of the day. Breakfast for them was brief because during their conversation around the campfire the previous night, Jacky Jack told the group of police what he and Jurung suspected.

Jacky Jack looked at Clamp disregarding Inspector Johnson's rank. He said to Clamp, 'We bin git plenty close to dis fulla Bulmurn, but ebery time weed git close to 'im he just gut way frum us. Me an Jurung weed jus no weed cutch him come tomorrow. Dus true boss un mees nose it.'

They left in the early morning light, the police troopers following the black trackers who led them onto Bulmurn's trail. Again the chase was on. They began their hunt in deadly earnest. It took the group quite some time before they got close to Bulmurn again. The black trackers stopped to look at a large black stump through some trees in front of them. To the black trackers it was Bulmurn, to the troopers it was just a stump. After a pause, the black trackers led off in another direction. Bulmurn was safe for the time being. Again he had stalled them, but time was running out.

Jacky Jack and Jurung led them around in a circle and they

came back to where they saw the large black stump. Jacky Jack put his hand up to signal for the party to stop, then he called Clamp and Johnson forward. Then Jacky Jack said to Clamp, 'Boss. You watch dut black stump ober dare dus im, dut stump ober dare near dut bush. You no, boss, he sayed to me in my head, he come out from were he is wen we goned way frum 'ere, he no wunt us to seed you cutch 'im. Me and Jurung we go ober dut hill wile you do it. Nuser sing boss, we dunt wunt to seed 'is eyes look at us. Wen you capture 'im, put blinepold ober 'is eyes, den he can't harm us. If he can't seed us, he can't harm us boss. Me un Jurung weed arst you do dis for us boss.'

Senior Constable Clamp looked at his Chief Inspector and said, 'Sir, to us he can't harm anyone just by looking at them. We know that, but they believe otherwise. They have been damned good trackers, those boys. In their culture they believe in these things. It's their hokus pokus. I recommend we follow their advice, otherwise we won't get them to track for us again and we might need them in the future.'

'All right, you have convinced me, Senior,' said the Inspector. 'Permission granted, Jacky Jack. You can go away and wait while we go to make the capture.'

Jacky Jack and Jurung rode over the hill away from the scene of the capture. When they were out of the way, Clamp, Johnson and the other troopers looked towards the stump which the black trackers said was Bulmurn. Clamp said to them, 'Have your firearms at the ready just in case we need them. We can't take a chance with this man. If he makes a wrong move, shoot to kill. Now, I'm going to call him out of where he is hiding.' Then Clamp moved his horse forward, and he called out to where he thought Bulmurn was hiding. 'You in there, come out with your hands where we can see them, drop any weapons you have. If you come out armed, we'll shoot you. Don't do anything foolish. Come out now.'

Everything around the scene was quiet, the birds made no calls, no wind rustled the leaves on the trees, even the horses stood still. Clamp, Johnson and the other police troopers looked in amazement when Bulmurn came out of his hiding place. Each of the mounted police troopers thought the same thing: 'Are my eyes deceiving me? Did I see him just step out of the stump?'

Bulmurn stepped out towards his captors from the direction of the black stump. Even though he was weakened by his wound and his broken arm, he was still defiant and proud. He had his right arm tied up towards his shoulder. His head wound looked infected. When the police troopers saw his swollen broken arm, it made them wince.

'Good God!' Inspector Johnson said to Clamp. 'Senior, no wonder he couldn't outrun us: he must have been constantly knocking his broken arm on hanging branches and bushes. He's had no time for any healing to take place. Nor could he treat his wound properly because of the pressure we put on him. He's had no time to make a dressing for himself.'

'Yes Sir', Clamp replied. 'I noticed the change quite a way back, that he was running in a lower scrub area. Jacky Jack and Jurung mentioned he might have an injury by the way he was travelling. By crikey they were right.'

Sentenced to Wagemup

A group of townsmen were standing in St George's Terrace gossiping. One man said to another, 'Do you people know that the police troopers have caught the Aboriginal witch doctor, that native who killed six white men and two black trackers? Why, he's even killed members of his own tribe, this fellow has. They say he was mistreating his people, he was banished from his tribe near Guildford.'

'The word is that he was killing his own people,' said another. 'He's a real killer, this fellow. They say he's in the Perth lockup at present. Later, he will be taken before a magistrate, but he'll go to a higher court — he's injured you see, has a bad wound on the forehead and a badly broken right arm.'

'The police have confirmed it, he will be sent to the black's jail on Rottnest Island', the first speaker said.

Another man said viciously, 'Yeah, I reckon they'll push hard for a guilty verdict, then hopefully, they will hang the black bastard, as he deserves. Did he kill six men? It's a pity he can't be hung six times for the six whites he killed. It's a pity', he repeated.

'But you know what I heard', said a fourth, 'they say the reason he went on a killing rampage is because he had to punish the first four, a settler and his workers who got horny for the killer's sister. They killed her husband and before they could get to her, they shot him then they pack-raped her.'

Bulmurn watched as Clamp came into the cell he was in. Clamp knew Bulmurn saw him, even though he displayed no sign that he had. To Clamp this didn't matter a damn. They were well-prepared if he tried to escape from custody. Clamp had no doubt they would kill him this time if he tried to.

Outside the cell Clamp had placed an armed trooper with a rifle at the ready for any emergency. Clamp unlatched the chains from the wall, leaving them locked on Bulmurn's body. Clamp wasn't going to take any chances with Bulmurn. If he tried anything, they would shoot him, a situation to be avoided because if they did, it would rob the public of the pleasure of seeing Bulmurn hung.

Clamp thought about the unbearable — Bulmurn escaping. 'Lord, what would happen to me? What would the authorities do to me? Christ, they would probably hang me in his place instead . . .'

But Clamp's fears of Bulmurn escaping from custody were unfounded because he was too ill to move. Clamp had been ordered to make sure the prisoner was suitably dressed for his first public appearance in the Perth Court. To do this Clamp had brought some hand-me-down clothing from the store in the jail.

He showed the trousers and shirt to Bulmurn and used actions to show him how to put the garments on. He said, 'Boy, you've got to wear these clothes into the court today because the Inspector said you have to. As far as I'm concerned I'd just take you in as you are because you're scum, nothing but a murderous savage.'

Bulmurn couldn't understand what Clamp had said but he could see he wanted him to wear the white man's clothing. He resisted but resistance was useless because Clamp and another guard put them forceably on him. This revolted him, he felt suffocated in them.

'My God,' Clamp said to the other guards, 'he looks out of place with clothing on him, almost human. Then he hand-cuffed Bulmurn to himself and led him outside, flanked by the other guards.

Once outside they took him to the courthouse for his court appearances where Bulmurn would have all eight charges of murder read out against him plus one of assault against Julia Rows.

As Bulmurn was led into the courtroom by Clamp, he hobbled after him, even though the weight of the chains impeded his movements. Everybody in the courtroom could see he was in ill health. A crescendo of noise arose from the gallery. Clamp guided Bulmurn to the prisoner's dock and placed him inside the dock. Clamp stood by holding the chains that held the captive. No chance was taken with this prisoner — he was too dangerous to even be released from his chains in the courtroom, even though he was surrounded by police troopers.

The Clerk of the Court told everybody to rise as Judge Harold O'Sullivan entered the courtroom to take his place behind the bench. The Clerk announced, 'This Court is now in progress. Please sit.' Then he moved forward and placed Bulmurn's hand on the Bible to take the oath, even though Bulmurn did not understand what was said to him. Nevertheless, the Clerk spoke it out for him.

Bulmurn listened but understood little of the white man's language and even though he was in ill health, he stood with defiant dignity. As the Clerk continued to read out the charges against him, Bulmurn let his eyes drift ever so slowly as he began to take in the courtroom scene. He gazed over a sea of white faces. Bulmurn thought these people looked alike. Moving over the crowd, his gaze came to rest on one face. That face belonged to a certain woman that he had only seen once. It was none other than Julia Rows.

Julia Rows locked her eyes with Bulmurn's. She did not call out. She didn't have to, her eyes said it all: Murderer. You murdering savage. You murderer. Killer. You heathen.

Bulmurn could not speak her language, but he guessed what she was thinking from the accusation in her eyes. Bulmurn felt pity for her because he had killed her man, but he felt no remorse for her husband, Rows, and the others he had killed. They deserved to die for what they had done. He believed he had brought them to justice for the crimes they had committed. Bulmurn upheld the Law of the Darbalyung Nyoongars of the Swan River.

He reflected on how he had killed the police troopers and black trackers. He did this for self-preservation, cornered, out of a will to survive. He saw it as self-defence.

'Now', Bulmurn thought, 'the roles are reversed. Once I was the law man when they broke our Law. Now these white men think I broke their law. How can this be when I am a law man who brought to justice the wrongdoers who broke our Law?'

At last all the charges were read out, unfolding to the court, as well as to the observers in the public gallery, how everything had happened, the police rendition of how the accused had brought about the recent killings of the Swan settlers, the police troopers and the black trackers. After all the charges were read out, Judge Harold O'Sullivan rapped his gavel on the bench to bring order into the court. He rapped it once, then he rapped it again. 'Silence,' he commanded, 'silence in the court'.

When the judge was satisfied he had control of his courtroom, he said, 'Who represents this man? Has he not had a lawyer appointed to represent him?'

The judge's question brought an outburst from the whole courtroom. This outburst was soon quelled by the judge banging his gavel on the courtroom bench and his booming voice as he commanded, 'Quiet in this court! I'll have no more outbursts like this. Otherwise, I'll have everybody removed from the court. Now, as I said before, who represents this man?'

'I do, your Honour', said a man rising from a sitting position. 'I do. I'm going to be his lawyer, your Honour. My name is William Shenton, and I am representing this man here. Mr Bulmurn, I believe, is his name. We have proof he belongs to one of the Swan River tribes near the Swan Valley area near Guildford.'

'Your Honour,' the young lawyer William Shenton continued, 'I've spoken to the police who brought him in, and I've also spoken to the medical practitioner, Dr Paul Reid, who was asked to treat the prisoner because he was ailing. I will be using his medical advice as evidence. Dr Reid has advised me that the accused is not a well man because of the injuries he has received during the time he was pursued by our patrol of mounted police and black trackers.

'Your Honour,' Shenton continued, 'this man, Mr Bulmurn, is too ill to enter a plea. Until such time as he is well enough to do so, I recommend to this court that he be held in custody. Perhaps we can find an interpreter who speaks his language to tell him what charges he faces. Therefore I am hoping he comprehends the seriousness of his situation.

'Your Honour, the accused is clearly unable to enter a plea. It is Your Honour's decision, whether this man should plead or not and whether the court should proceed now or support my recommendations for an adjournment to a later date for him to be properly tried.'

Then the judge turned to Bulmurn and said, 'Mr Bulmurn, I've taken into account the recommendations made by your lawyer, Mr Shenton. On his evidence, I will not ask you to make a plea. Instead I will remand you in custody of the authorities of the prison for natives on Rottnest Island, until such time as you recover from your illnesses, until you are in good health. Then you are to be brought back here to face this court.' The judge nodded at the Clerk who called loudly 'Court adjourned. Please move out in an orderly fashion.'

Bulmurn stood in the dock not really sure what was said to him. All he knew was that people were on their feet, looking at him, pointing at him, talking about him. He knew in time he would find out what it was all about. He hadn't understood the adjournment or the reasons for it.

The chains on Bulmurn's body made him feel uncomfortable. Nevertheless, he stood in a proud erect manner as though nothing bothered him. Once again he found the eyes of Julia Rows. Once again he read her hatred. Then as though their eyes meeting was a signal, the Senior Constable, George Clamp, pulled Bulmurn's neck chain as though he was a puppet. 'Move!', ordered Clamp. Bulmurn nearly fell as Clamp jerked the chain, but he checked his balance, righted himself, then went the way Clamp indicated.

Clamp took Bulmurn out to where police troopers were waiting to escort a horse-driven jail coach to Fremantle and the Roundhouse Jail. From there he would be transported by sailboat from Arthur's Head across to the native prison, the Rottnest Island jail.

Just near the coach stood a large crowd of civilians waiting for Bulmurn to appear. When they caught sight of him, they began to shout, 'Nigger, killer, black bastard, murderer, killer!'. After the abuse, they pelted Bulmurn with stones. Some of the missiles made Bulmurn wince in pain. Clamp urged him on along into the carriage. Once in the coach, Clamp shouted to the driver, 'Get this damn vehicle moving away from this mad crowd of people before they lynch this man'. The driver needed no further orders. He giddyuped the horses as quickly as he could, anxious to avoid the angry mob. Clamp felt much the same. He was glad the escort was with the coach, because they were able to push the mob back as they went, before they could do much damage to the vehicle or its passengers.

It took just two hours to reach the Round House lock-up. Bulmurn sat the whole journey uncomfortably locked in his prison chains, his arm burning with pain. He sat to one side. On the other side sat Clamp and Trooper Allen, both were heavily armed. Both sat alert but Bulmurn sat quietly, not moving or speaking. The two troopers made idle conversation to pass the miles away. It was late afternoon when they finally arrived at Fremantle. They drove on down through High Street until they neared the Round House jail at Arthur's Head, where the mouth of the Swan River met the Indian Ocean.

At last, Clamp said to Allen, 'We're here. Now we can lock him up under the supervision of the Round House prison guards for the night. Our orders are to stay here the night. In the morning, we have to make sure he gets safely put onto the prison ferry, so they can be put straight into the island's holding cell.'

'Where's that Senior? I mean, where's the holding cell?', Allen questioned Clamp.

'Close to the jetty. It's just a dark hole, one long cell with only a single door. The only ventilation comes from the guards' peek-a-boo opening in the door. You wouldn't even need a guard because the poor black bastards can't get out without being let out. They have no hope of escaping from it', replied Clamp. 'No hope. None whatsoever.'

Bulmurn was taken out of the prison coach to be put into the Round House. His chains rattled as he clambered down from the coach onto the ground and Clamp beckoned him to follow. As Bulmurn did so, he tripped over his leg irons. Fortunately, he didn't hurt his injured right arm. As he picked himself up, nobody moved to help him.

Bulmurn presented a forlorn figure of a man. He looked helpless, but that didn't bring him any sympathy from his captors. Instead it brought him a push from a Round House warden, who said with an Irish accent, 'Hurry it up me boyho, we haven't got all night, have we now?'. He pushed Bulmurn again, causing him to shuffle along to the jail's door a little faster. Finally, Bulmurn was locked up in jail. He was never let out of his irons.

'Paddy O'Reilly is the name,' said the guard to Clamp and Allen, who in turn introduced themselves. 'Look after him', Clamp said to O'Reilly.

O'Reilly looked at Clamp and Allen, then said, 'Is he the killer? Is he the one, this boyho?'

'Yes', said Clamp, 'that's him all right.'

'He don't look so tough', O'Reilly said. 'It's hard to believe he's killed at all.'

Clamp almost shouted back at him, 'Looks can get you killed mate, so don't let his appearance fool you. He's a killer all right. He's a bloody good killer at that. That's why you have to do a good job of guarding him for the night', and Clamp poked O'Reilly in the chest. 'We will see you first thing in the morning to make sure he gets on that boat to Rottnest.'

'Then we'll be happy, won't we Constable?' Clamp said to Allen.

'Yes, Sir!' Allen answered back to Clamp. 'We most surely will be. It will be a load off our minds and shoulders. I'll be glad to see this black bastard go.'

Clamp looked at Allen and said, 'Let's go to the nearest hotel to get us a room each and I'm for a few tots of rum tonight'.

'That's an excellent idea, Senior', Allen agreed, 'an excellent idea'. Together they walked off the jail premises into High Street, their destination the newly constructed inn, the Sailors' Rest.

*   *   *   *   *   *   *   *

The night had passed all too soon for Clamp. He shook his head trying to clear the alcohol that had affected his brain. He staggered into the bathroom, to the wash basin, filling it with cold water. He then dipped his head right into the basin for as long as he could, coughing and spluttering as he withdrew from the cold water.

He drew a towel. Drying himself he smiled as he remembered his boozy night. He and Allen had been drinking in the lounge. A few drinks later they noticed two 'working' women seated at a table alone. Clamp looked at Allen. Allen looked at him. Both rose simultaneously. Each had the same idea. Together they approached the women.

Clamp was the first to speak. 'Evening, ladies, do you mind if we join you, that's if you're on your own and not busy. We'd like to buy you a drink or two', Clamp winked at Allen. The redhead smiled while the brunette whispered in her ear. They could see the look of approval in the eyes of the redhead.

At last, the brunette turned to look at Clamp, then she said, smiling at him, 'We would be pleased to have your company. Take a seat, pour a drink, I'm Nora.' Then she pointed to the other woman and said, 'This is Joan'. Clamp introduced himself and Allen. Then they sat down. Allen poured the drinks.

Their conversation and merriment would last until they were told the bar was closed, then they would take the women up to their rooms to continue a good night, in bed.

When Clamp awoke, he was only mildly surprised Nora wasn't beside him. During the course of the night she had left while he slept. He checked his purse and realised she had taken her fee.

Well worth it, he thought. His thinking came to an end as Allen knocked on the door. 'You there, Senior? It's time for breakfast. We have to make sure that damned black prisoner gets on that boat today.'

'I'm ready.'

After breakfast, they made their way along High Street until they reached the Round House jail. 'Good morning,' Clamp said to O'Reilly who was still on duty.

'Good morning, Sir,' O'Reilly said.

'Prisoner give you any trouble?'

'Nary a thing. That black man was as quiet as a church mouse, wasn't he now!'

O'Reilly unlocked the cell door and Clamp stepped in. He looked at Bulmurn as Bulmurn rose from a sitting position tossing his blanket aside. It was the first time Clamp noticed how tall he was. 'He's near as tall as I am. I'm six feet two inches. Good Lord, this bloke's not as skinny as he looks, and he's stronger than he appears to be.'

Clamp looked Bulmurn in the eye. He said, 'I don't know if you understood me or not, but where you're going is a place I wouldn't like to go. Rottnest Island is a death island for you blacks. Even though they want to bring you back for a public execution on the mainland, I think they'll hang you over there. The devil's keeper is the superintendent over on Rottnest Island. My guess is that he'd have heard you're on the way over, and he can't wait to get his hands on you.'

Clamp and Allen moved Bulmurn out of his cell guiding him down to where an escort party of crewmen and guards were waiting to take the prisoner on board, to transfer him to a lugger gently bobbing up and down in the sea off Long Jetty at Arthur's Head.

Clamp looked at the guards and crew. He said to them, 'Don't lose him. Don't give him a chance to escape, because if he does, he's a hard man to catch.'

Clamp was about to leave, when he thought he heard the black man say his name. 'Clamp!' Clamp turned and looked at Bulmurn. Their eyes locked. Clamp felt a new strength in

Bulmurn's gaze. It was as if he was laughing at Clamp. Mocking him, saying 'I'll be back'. Clamp shook his head and walked away, telling himself he was only imagining these thoughts. 'He has no chance of escaping from Rottnest', he told himself.

The crew and guards were in no hurry, they had done this before, ferrying prisoners over to Rottnest. Soon Bulmurn was on board the lugger sailing out to sea out towards Rottnest Island. Bulmurn looked back, he could see Walyalup disappearing behind him. He looked back for as long as he could at the now distant mainland. If his heart was heavy, Bulmurn was not showing it.

Bulmurn looked ahead of the boat, it was sailing nearer and nearer to Wagemup. 'Soon, I will be on Wagemup, the *wadjbulla* call Rottnest. While I am at Wagemup, I will always dream of my *Bujara Ngunung*, my motherland. *Ngnung mehalburit Bujara Ngunung.* My eyes will look for my motherland. '

Bulmurn watched with interest, though he showed no sign that he was alert to all around him.

The Hanging

Bulmurn's first night in jail was bad; the cell was damp, chilling his body, making him feel cold. How he wished he could light a fire to warm himself. But he couldn't because he was in a white man's prison. Bulmurn stood up, then looked out of the cell's small window, pressing his face against it trying to get a look at his beloved homeland across the blue sea water.

It was a clear morning and he could see the land in the distance. The only sign that people were over there was the evidence of smoke from the white man's fire coming from their buildings. This thought saddened Bulmurn because it only seemed like yesterday when other elders used to say no white man was living on this land. Now they were like their diseases, spreading evil everywhere, killing off the black people who were once the sole occupiers of this great country.

He watched the other prisoners walk past with warders supervising their every move. Here on this Wagemup the menfolk, including Nyoongars and men from other tribes, were forced to do the gathering work that the women used to do. They were forced to use the white man's digging sticks to dig the ground to grow their plants for food. Stupid fools, he thought.

One day an old Nyoongar named Bunyun came to his cell and told him all about what the white men made them do; how they were mistreated, how they were whipped for little or nothing. A lot of prisoners died through mistreatment. Nothing was ever done by the big bosses on the mainland to bring equal justice for the black man on this here Rottnest Island. No, nothing was ever done nor was any recognition given to this courageous patriotic race of people. When they died they were buried in unmarked graves so that their spirits would never return to their homes on the mainland.

Old Bunyun told Bulmurn how much the other prisoners feared him, for they all knew that Bulmurn possessed special powers. They all knew he was a *Boylla Gudjuk*, they were all talking about what he did. 'Even though we all agree you were right, you're on your own. No one will help you because we are all scared of the *wadjbulla* boss. Too many of our people have died here for us to forget. You know Bulmurn, there is no champion or speaker here on Wagemup or over there on our mainland who is prepared to try to bring equal justice for the black man.' Old Bunyun was not young when he had been transported to the island and now he was too old. He told Bulmurn he had been here for many summers and winters. He felt he would never see his people again.

Bulmurn looked old Bunyun in the eye through the cell door bars. Then he said to the elder, 'I know what they say and it saddens me, but I have not given up the hope of freedom.' Then he paused before he said, 'Leave me old man'.

Bulmurn had been on Rottnest for almost two weeks. During that time, with the exception of Bunyun, other prisoners either shunned him or crept past his cell. Most of them tried to get a glimpse of him when he wasn't looking. Most dared not look at him or into his eyes, because they were all scared of him. They were scared he would turn on them by casting a magic spell on them, by pointing the bone at them. Nobody befriended him. They crept past him, shading their eyes from him.

Sometimes they would gather in a group at meal times to yarn to one another. It was Dehan who spoke first, 'Listen you mob I just bin walkin' past that Bulmurn's cell, you all know him, the one they keep locked up all the time because I tell you, old

Vincent, he scared he might escape. Not that he could, but you know what he bin doin'. He gettin' ready to do it any time now. Escape I mean.'

'How you know dat?', Yettap, another of the group queried.

Dehan said, 'Me I know it all right. I see 'im moving 'is arm up an' down, he exercising the arm he broke, I tell you mob, he gunna turn into *wardang* and fly away.'

Dehan continued, 'Anyhow, how I know this is because I was able to sneak up close to his cell and peep inside and he couldn't see me looking at him. He was singing to himself how he gunna get out of dis jail.'

Dulap, from the desert country said, 'I feel sorry for this fulla Bulmurn because he got no chance of getting away from dis island jail. If he does git out he got to swim across the sea. We all know a lot of our people who try get eaten by *bilo* the shark.' Dulap made his point by making the action that he was swimming, and then he shaped his right hand so that it looked like a shark fin cutting through the water, grabbing the invisible swimmer, pulling him under the water.

Everybody in the group shuddered at the thought of being eaten alive by a shark. '*Choo warra, choo warra*', the Nyoongars in the group said as one.

'Dats true, dis happen', Yettap said. 'We know sometime they just shoot our people in the water so the sharks can do this. Or they just follow the person who escaped, let him keep swimming all the way across the sea to the mainland then they just put him back in the boat and bring him straight back here. It really bad, it bad when this happens. They have no good feelings to our people at all.'

Ballyeen, an older man from the Beeliar mob spoke for the first time in his Nyoongar tongue, 'I've been here a long time. All you say is true. They do it all right. We all know that just about two or three of our people die here on this island by every new moon. We all know this is true because we have to bury them here. They catch them then they bring them all the way here in chains. Some of these men come from a long long way away from here never to leave this island of death. They never see their wives and children ever again.'

There was a silence for a while. Then Dehan spoke in English again, 'Wut you tink we should do? You tink we should help Bulmurn escape or not?'

'Not me', Yettap said. All the others agreed with him. They weren't going to help Bulmurn escape. Bulmurn was on his own.

Just as they were concluding their talk Superintendent Vincent came along, in a foul mood. He had heard Dehan mention the word 'escape' and this alerted him to a plot. Livid with rage, he looked for a scape-goat.

The group broke up to try and get away from their tormentor, Vincent. But Vincent was not to be denied the pleasure of punishing someone; that someone was Dehan. Dehan would feel the full force of his evil.

Vincent called out Dehan's name. 'Dehan, stop where you are!' The superintendent approached the stationary Dehan.

'Dehan you heathen, did I hear right, did you mention the word "escape"?'

'Nut me boss. I neber sayed wun word bout scaping from here boss.'

This denial from Dehan was not going to get him any respite. 'Liar. You black bastard, you're like the rest of your mob of animals, you're all liars.'

'Nut me boss. I neber sayed I gunna run away from here boss', Dehan said.

That was the last word Dehan got to say to Vincent because the superintendent grabbed him by his beard and yanked it as hard as he could, pulling out the hair. Vincent then got hold of Dehan's right ear and twisted, and he ripped the ear right away from Dehan's scalp. Then to finish off his evil deed he struck him several times on the head with the keys from the cell doors he always carried with him, knocking him to the ground. Dehan never recovered from this horrible beating. He paid the supreme sacrifice.

* * * * * * * *

'Bulmurn, Bulmurn,' a voice said. Bulmurn recognised it as the voice belonging to old Bunyun. 'Bulmurn,' he said again excitedly. Bulmurn said nothing but Bunyun could tell by Bulmurn's eyes that he could speak. 'All these big *wadjbulla biddairs* are here on this island. You know why they are here. They come here for a hanging.'

'Who are they going to hang?' Bulmurn asked anxiously.

Bulmurn thought to himself while he waited for Bunyun to answer. 'If it's me, I'm not afraid to die. I'm not afraid to hang and die that way. But if I had a choice, I would rather be speared or shot. That's how a man should die.'

'Bulmurn,' Bunyun said. 'Those *wadjbulla jenga* they caught a Yamagee *marman* from north. They gunna hang him because he killed a white man up that way. The hanging is to be held tomorrow at white man time, eight o'clock in the morning.'

Bulmurn said to Bunyun, 'How do you know all this?'.

Bunyun said, 'I know because I'm the servant of Vincent and I heard him talking. He said this man is called Wandabidar. *Biddair wadjbulla* says we can't hang that Bulmurn just yet, he'll come after this blackfulla. That boss he swear like crazy man he is. He say he don't know why they saving you, but he says it won't be for long. He say another two weeks and your arm will be healed, then they hang you. This boss says he's going to enjoy this first hanging and he's going to enjoy hanging you too.'

'What did this man, Wandabidar, do? Why did he kill that *wadjbulla* up north, for I bet he had a good reason to do it,' Bulmurn said.

Bunyun looked at Bulmurn and said, 'I hear the story like this. That man Wandabidar go after the *wadjbulla* because the *wadjbulla* steal Wandabidar brother's wife. This *wadjbulla* used to go to Wandabidar brother's camp all the time his brother way away, then this fulla he would be having sex with her.

'Then this white man he run away with that woman, he take her. But before this white man take her, he hit Wandabidar's brother. He belt him, but first they have a good fight. Then this *wadjbulla* he grab a *kurendee* and hit him over the head. When he go down he lay there bleeding, a big gash on his head. He then grab the woman, leaving Wandabidar's brother to die.

'He nearly did die, only Wandabidar's mother's sister, she came along, she raise the alarm. Wandabidar's sister look after the sick brother. Good job they get a *Mobarn Gudjuk* like you to look at him or he die. Because they get this healer in time, he not die. Then when they tell Wandabidar, he go after the *wadjbulla jenga* and the woman.

'He chase them for many days until he catch up with them. Wandabidar spear the white man, then he make the woman go back to his brother or he spear her, too.

'Then the troopers and black trackers go after Wandabidar. They chase him down till they catch up with him. They arrest him then they jail him. Now they bring him here to hang him till he dead.'

'Bring out Bulmurn', Superintendent Percy Vincent said to Sergeant O'Donnell. 'You help to look after him, too, Mr Jackson', added Vincent. 'I don't want this black here to miss the hanging of Wandabidar. I want him not to miss a single detail of the event, no Sir, by the good Lord I don't.'

They unlocked Bulmurn's chains from the wall of his cell, leaving his body chained. Then they led him out into the circular assembly area — the Quad — where all the black prisoners of Rottnest Island jail stood.

Bulmurn looked around the Quad. Even though he had been in the jail a couple of weeks now, he never really had a good look at what it was made of. Bulmurn knew that black prisoners would have been used as labour to help build this jail. Bulmurn continued to examine the stone and cement work of the walls. The actual jail was built in a circular fashion. There were no corners for anyone to hide behind if they wanted to escape. The circle, Bulmurn noted, made it nearly impossible to escape.

Bulmurn looked at all the black faces. Many were from the Nyoongar river groups, the Beeliar, the Mooro, the Beelu and the Wurerup people. He could see other faces he did not recognise, he knew they were from northern or eastern areas. Nevertheless they were his people. He knew that many of these people standing here waiting for the execution would never leave this island of death. Many would die here like others who lay dead in the dirt of Wagemup. Some would be released, but many many others would die here, never to return to their homes. Their spirits would be on this island in the future. Their spirits would be here for summers and winters without end.

Bulmurn then looked at the others standing around the white man's building in the middle of the Quad. These were the ugly white men, the *wadjbulla* bosses. There was a lot of them. Bulmurn had to count his fingers and toes at least twice to get an idea of the number in attendance, happy at this occasion. They seemed to be glad to see Wandabidar die, Bulmurn observed.

Then his mind was brought out of thought because a white man he didn't know, spoke to the Nyoongar people in the Nyoongar tongue. He tried to make excuses for why the whites wanted to execute Wandabidar for the awful crime he had committed. No black was allowed to kill a white man, he said. If they did kill any white man, they ended up here, he said. After he finished talking, this white man left the jail. Bulmurn noted that he wasn't staying for the hanging.

Everything went quiet, the talking ceased. Even the birds were quiet, the wind was still, the sun dulled by clouds. You could have heard a pin drop as the condemned Wandabidar was led out from his cell. Wandabidar was led out by Warder Will Jackson in charge of the condemned section. As the prisoner stepped from his cell, the clouds moved away from the sun. Wandabidar held his hands to his brow, giving his eyes a chance to adjust to the bright daylight that greeted him on what was to be his last day on earth. Soon he would be reunited back into the womb of *bujara*, the mother, the earth, the land of the black people, of which this island, Wagemup, was a small part.

Wandabidar paused for a moment more. He looked around at the solemn faces of the prisoners, his people. All expected the worst. It was plain to see they all felt for Wandabidar, but each individual was powerless to do anything to prevent the hanging, such was the power of the *wadjbulla* guns.

Wandabidar looked at each of the black faces around the jail.

Some he recognised, some he did not, his eyes came to rest upon Bulmurn. Bulmurn looked back at him, not with sympathy or curiosity but with respect for the man, for what he stood for. Bulmurn noticed how their lives ran a parallel course. Each was a law man, a *Mobarn Gudjuk*, each was an upholder of blackfulla law. Wandabidar's destiny was decided here, now he would be hanged. Would Bulmurn face the same destiny? If Bulmurn would have looked more closely into Wandabidar's eyes, he might have seen what his fate was to be. But he did not look closely.

Wandabidar straightened himself as he looked at the faces of his white captors. 'Hungry *jenga* these *wadjbulla wilbarn jenga*. They just hungry to kill me.' Wandabidar could see they were impatient for him to proceed to the middle of the jail where a man waited near the hangman's noose. He could feel the white men's minds willing him to hurry out to the middle so the hangman could proceed.

As the prisoner stepped forward a stir came from the whites, as if they were glad. Not a word came from any of the black prisoners, and again silence descend on the jail circle with each step Wandabidar took towards the waiting hangman at the scaffold.

Wandabidar moved with grace and strength as if he were going to conduct a meeting with all these members in the middle of the arena. At last he reached the central spot at the steps to the scaffold. He paused briefly, then he grabbed at the step support with both hands and pulled himself up the four steps onto the hanging platform.

All the way Wandabidar was accompanied by Warder Jackson, who pointed at the trap door built into the hanging platform where he wanted Wandabidar to stand. Wandabidar never hesitated. He stood on the square trapdoor awaiting his fate.

Erect and undaunted, he stood looking towards his beloved mainland. As a sign from the spirit of the Dreamtime, *mar* the wind blew cold from the west, swirling around the yard, not affecting the Aboriginal people. It seemed to do its utmost to annoy the white men, making them grab for their hats and plant their feet more firmly on to *terra firma*.

Wandabidar stood calm, tall and dignified. He presented himself to his executioners, a magnificent picture of primitive and uncultured manhood. Each Aborigine recognised his bravery: to them he wasn't primitive nor did he come from an uncultured race. To them he was a very noble and cultured leader.

As the hangman slipped the noose over his head Wandabidar bravely faced his end, alone, with nobody to speak to or for him or to comfort him. Each black man in the jail circle was silently sending their comfort and farewells to a great warrior, wishing him a swift departure into their beloved Dreamtime.

Only the slightest movement passed through Wandabidar's body, as the hangman made a last minute adjustment to the noose and placed a blindfolding bag over his head. Then the hangman hit the triggering mechanism on the scaffold trapdoor with his feet, which opened in an instant, plunging Wandabidar's body into the air, snapping his neck, taking life from a respected warrior and man.

A short time later Bulmurn noted that an official came from among the others to go over to the suspended Wandabidar in the air. When he reached the body, he placed a hand over Wandabidar's neck and heart area. The man nodded his head and crossed his hands over each other with the palms open to make a sign to the others to confirm Wandabidar's death. Bulmurn guessed the white man was a doctor, like himself.

'How strange these *wadjbulla* are', Bulmurn thought, as he contemplated his plight. 'First they want to take everything we have. Now they want to heal me before they kill me. They want to hang me like this brave man Wandabidar.'

Bulmurn looked away from the body as they began to take it down. They would take it to the mortuary cell before interment. Bulmurn hoped that when they buried the unfortunate Wandabidar in his *bokgal*, would be in the slight sitting position facing the east, with his eyes looking past his body to the next sunrise so the rays of *bina*, the dawn, would allow his spirit to ride into the Dreamtime world.

As soon as the hanging was over Vincent said to his men, 'Just to knock the stuffing out of prisoners and to ensure there is no resistance from them because of the hanging, I want you men to put leg irons on every last one of these heathens. There's no telling what might happen. I don't want to take any chances of any kind of rebellion from them.'

Beaten almost to the last man, the prisoners were locked in chains then roughly shoved into the evil darkness of their cells. This surely would obliterate any ounce of courage they may have had.

Bulmurn Disappears

It was three mornings after the warrior Wandabidar had been hung in the Quad. All the prisoners went about their chores in a lifeless manner, living with the memory of Wandabidar's hanging. They needed hope.

Two of the prison warders who helped to guard Bulmurn, Will Jackson and Ben Clarke, were en route to Bulmurn's cell in the Quad to make the morning change. They had the prisoner's breakfast of bread and black tea with them. Jackson moved forward ahead of the other warder, Clarke, to open the cell door. As Jackson inserted the large key into the lock, he made the comment to Clarke that the other warders Thomson and O'Hare should have been there on guard until they relieved them and made the change with them. 'We are late — they must've got fed up with waiting a couple of minutes more.'

Clarke answered, 'I shouldn't worry too much, Will, the black in this cell isn't going anywhere. How could he escape? We've got the jump on him every time.'

Jackson turned the key in the lock and opened the heavy jarrah cell door. Then he and Clarke stepped inside expecting to see Bulmurn in his usual position chained to the wall. The two looked around the cell, in amazement. The prisoner was not there. He was gone! Only his chains remained in the wall.

'Look!' Clarke said to Jackson. 'Look!' he said again, as he bent down to examine the empty chains that had held Bulmurn. 'Will,' Clarke said, 'the locks on these chains are unbroken. How in the hell has this bloke escaped? How did he get free? We're the only ones with keys that could unlock the chains. We've got to tell the Sergeant.'

'You're right', Jackson said. 'You know, Ben, the other blacks here in jail said this man had magic powers. Their talk was that he was just biding his time until escaping. I think they call him a *Mobarn Mamarup*. I think it means he has magic powers to do things out of the ordinary way of doing things, like escaping this way. It's black magic I tell you. Lord knows we've guarded him as well as we could have done.'

'Jesus, Will,' Clarke said to Jackson, 'I reckon old Percy Vincent is going to go blue in the face when we tell him that Bulmurn has escaped from the Quad, from his cell. I tell you, old Vincent will be wild. You and I know, he's mad at the best of times. He's going to be even madder when the Sergeant tells him who it is that has escaped.

'I think the best thing for us to do is to keep quiet about the powers that these black people have. You know if Vincent heard us talking about them like this, he might think we're on their side. Then we we'd be in for a floggin' for sure. If it was up to me I'd say this talk about them having special powers was a load of rubbish.'

'All right,' said Jackson, 'let's not say anything about black magic. It's all rubbish. It's the shock of it that made me panic a bit you know, him escaping the way he did, the prisoner gone like that.' They knocked on Sergeant O'Donnell's door and they heard the sharp reply 'Enter'.

Once in O'Donnell's office they told him their story: how they had found the cell empty, how the cell door was still locked when they had arrived, how the neck and leg chains weren't unlocked. 'Then we looked for the warders Thomson and O'Hare, they're missing too, they can't be found anywhere just yet. We don't know where they are, Sir', Jackson said.

O'Donnell, Jackson and Clarke didn't know that the warders

Thomson and O'Hare had strangely fallen ill with influenza and both were off duty, confined to their beds with sickness. At the time, Superintendent Vincent didn't think it was necessary to replace them and have others guard the prisoner Bulmurn, because he also had two of the best warders treading the roof walk around the Quad keeping an alert night vigil on the prisoners. At the time this situation had developed, nobody else knew Thomson and O'Hare were off work.

It was a black night. Thunder and lightning resounded over the island and rain was falling. All the prisoners were secure.

These conditions allowed a shadowy black figure the perfect opportunity to slip around the inside along the wall of the jail to Bulmurn's cell at the time of the thunder sounding loudly over Rottnest. The shadowy figure slipped inside. When he reappeared there was another black figure with him.

The prisoner put his hand on the shadowy figure's shoulder in thanks, then they parted. The shadowy figure watched as the now escaped prisoner made his way to the wall and vanished over it into the darkness of the unkind rainy night.

The trusted one made his way back to the comfort of his servants' quarters wondering if his eyes had deceived him. Had Bulmurn jumped over that wall — or did he fly?

Two hours after the prisoner had escaped, the lightning lit the black sky along the beach of Thomson Bay, followed by a roll of thunder. *Mar*, the wind, blew the cold night air and rain furiously around the jail making sure everybody in the Quad, including the sentries, sought shelter from the storm. Other officials would lay in the security of their warm beds until the alarm was raised.

* * * * * * * *

'This is bloody serious,' the Sergeant said. 'The first thing we do is to sound the alarm immediately. You ring the bell Jackson', he ordered. 'And when you've sounded it join us to help line up the prisoners.'

Jackson banged the brass bell furiously. The tolling sounded all around the prison, telling troopers and prisoners somebody had escaped. Guards came running. Sergeant shouted out orders and all the prisoners were lined up in the middle of the Quad.

Escorted by Sergeant O'Donnell and the two warders, Jackson and Clarke, Superintendent Vincent approached the prisoners. At Vincent's orders the other jail wardens all stood armed ready to shoot at the first sign of trouble.

Vincent and his guards made their inspection to see if any others were missing besides Bulmurn. Vincent feared others may have gone with the escaped man. But he need not have worried, his fears were unfounded. Bulmurn had escaped on his own. Vincent and company would find no other prisoners missing.

A prisoner in the lineup shouted, 'Bulmurn, he's missing!', and he shouted the Nyoongar word for victory: '*Yoki! Yoki!* Bulmurn, he's escaped.' A buzz of noisy excitement erupted from the prisoners. The Sergeant turned on his heel and struck the prisoner on the side of the head. This action brought immediate silence, but all knew Bulmurn had power, he had strength, his magic was strong.

Vincent heard the Aboriginal word for victory. He was livid with rage at the thought that someone had enough courage to say such a word in his presence. Vincent's colour changed from pink to scarlet. It looked as though he would burst his cheeks. Then he exploded. He shouted at the prisoners, 'So you black bastards, you heathens, approve of his escape. You think it's a victory for you. We'll see who is victorious here — no rations for two days! See to it Sergeant O'Donnell.'

Then Vincent went along the line looking at each prisoner until he drew level with old Bunyun. 'Where is Bulmurn?' he shouted at Bunyun. 'Where is he? Did you help him escape?' Vincent yanked hard old Bunyun's beard. 'Did you?' Bunyun hastily declared through sudden tears, 'Nut me boss. I no help dut wun boss. I dunno wared he gone boss.'

Vincent pushed Bunyun back in line. Then he went down the line stalking another would-be victim. Clarke whispered to Jackson, 'Jesus, he loves to inflict pain on those poor bastards'. Jackson nodded. Vincent grabbed Yettup roughly by the ears.

His action caused Yettup to fall to the ground holding his ear, then Vincent kicked him in the side, saying, 'I suppose you don't know where he is either. Pick him up Sergeant.' Without waiting for an answer, he turned, then he walked out to the front of the prisoners and looked over every one of them.

Most of the prisoners wilted under his gaze, dropping their heads, hoping he wouldn't single them out. Every one of them hated him, but none of them was game enough to stand up to him. They all stood the brunt of his awful brutality. To them he was a *jenark*, the devil himself. To them he was the cruelest man they had ever known.

Just as they hated him, Vincent hated them. He hated all blacks. To him they were animals, so he treated them as such. He personally tortured them. He whipped them with his own cat o' nine tails, always close at hand.

The Superintendent called Sergeant O'Donnell to him. 'Clear this rabble, lock the heathens up. They're not to be released until two days are up, nor are they to be fed.

'Report back to me as quickly as possible. We shall search this island for that black man. I want these prisoners left here to act as black trackers.' Vincent named, Dujan, Jarlung, Meerabin and Bowrell.

All the rest of the prisoners were herded off to their cramped cells and locked in. When every warder had returned, Vincent addressed them: 'Men, today we have lost a very dangerous prisoner. He has killed white men and black men alike. He was put into our security prison here on Rottnest, entrusted into our custody. Now he's gone.

'Prisoners have tried to escape before. If they don't die, we always apprehend them. I hope in this search we shall be successful. One thing is in our favour, that the prisoner may not have gone far, as last night was stormy. The seas between here and the mainland would be high and rough, so I think he's still on this island. I expect you to find him.'

Vincent raised his voice, 'People seem to think that this black man has some kind of magic power to change into different objects. I assure you he cannot! Few people can escape from here. For those who have any sympathy for this savage, I shall say one thing', and he lowered his voice threateningly. 'I'll have you flogged until your backside is red raw. You'll wish you never were born! Now,' he said, 'we'll break into four groups of four men. Each of the four groups will be assigned a black tracker. I want to know if these trackers don't perform well. If they don't then I'll deal with them with the cat. I'll belt the piss out of them, and let them be a lesson to you all. That's all Sergeant O'Donnell.'

This statement caused a shudder of fear to run up the spine of the four black trackers. They knew this madman was capable of maiming or killing them if they failed.

When they had sorted out their groups, O'Donnell informed Vincent that they were ready to search the island. He assured Vincent they would search thoroughly for the prisoner. If he was on the island, they would find him. But Vincent had to have the last say, 'Now, hear this, men. If he's to be found, I want him brought straight to me. Scour every inch of this island if you have to, but make sure you get that black bastard today. We must not fail.'

It was a clear indication that someone would have the hide whipped from his body if the black prisoner wasn't found. They were to search every nook and cranny of the island. No place was to be overlooked. All the boats had to be accounted for. They were not to give this man any easy opportunity to escape. Even though he was missing, this certainly didn't mean he was not on the island, waiting for an opportune moment to make his move to escape to the mainland.

The search went on through the day. The sun set and evening was upon the island but they had not found Bulmurn. The prisoner had vanished. He was nowhere to be found. Land and sea patrols were amazed that a person could disappear so completely. Each group reported to Vincent that they had seen no trace of the fugitive Bulmurn, nothing at all, not even any tracks, nor any trace of the man.

Bulmurn was definitely not in the Gage Roads Channel between Rottnest and Arthur's Head. He had possibly been

201

taken by the sharks, but no sightings had been made at all during the day. Another possibility was that perhaps the current had carried him out to sea.

Superintendent Vincent accepted their reports with great reluctance, then he addressed the tired troops, 'Tomorrow we will search all day again. I have a gut feeling he's still here on the island. I want you to be out at first light.' Then he dismissed his worried men.

That night warders and prisoners alike slept with disturbed sleep, the fears of black magic or vicious retribution in the minds of just about everyone on the island. The next day, Superintendent Percy Vincent had patrols out at sun up. They searched a further day, again without result. Again they reported no success. Now the question on everybody's lips was: 'Where was he?' What had happened to him? Did he swim safely across to the mainland? Was he drowned or eaten by the sharks? Anger turned to puzzlement. Where was he?

None of the search parties was to give the fugitive any chance of escaping by makeshift raft. All were to be on the lookout for such a craft or evidence of one being built. Already Vincent had the boats around the island on patrol, searching particularly those areas where the water currents were strongest, knowing that a swimmer would be caught in the currents. Even then, they had to be alert in the boats, or they could miss a man trying to swim away.

Superintendent Vincent sent word out immediately to the mainland authorities so a patrol could be manned on the shore there. The shore troopers were instructed to patrol the uninhabited beaches a long way to the north. Even though it was highly unlikely that anyone could swim that far north against the Indian Ocean's currents, every possibility had to be checked.

More likely, if an attempt was made to swim the twelve miles across the Gage Road Channel between Rottnest and the mainland, the escapee would head towards Cottesloe Beach or north of Fremantle. However, there was a great risk to the escaping swimmer. The seas were rough, the currents strong and the waters shark infested.

On the third day, near midday, the schooner, H.M.S. *Capture*, the prisoner-carrying ferry, arrived at Rottnest. It was the usual trip with new prisoners, food supplies and mail for the prison authorities.

Captain Owen Simpson stood with Superintendent Vincent amidship near the gangplank. Together they watched the new prisoners being taken by the warders to holding quarters. Later Sergeant O'Donnell would supervise which section of the jail they would go to. Right now, Vincent and Simpson were watching the prisoners and the Aboriginal deck hands unloading and loading the ship. Everything that was big enough to conceal a body was checked by the warders.

Simpson spoke first. 'You know, Percy, that black bastard isn't about to escape on my boat. I have a loyal crew on this vessel, including the blacks who are nearly as good as my own sailors. They know what punishment they get for aiding and abetting any escaped prisoner. They are bound to report any stowaways. Mind you, I keep them in line. They have felt the bite of the whip. It only takes the threat of a flogging to keep them in line. I assure you, that black boy will not get on my vessel, Percy, no way', Simpson said. He shouted out his orders, 'Be thorough men. We don't want the stowaway on this boat. Search all decks!'

Percy Vincent looked at the Captain. 'Now be thorough Owen. The black we're looking for has an injured arm. He broke his right arm when they were chasing him down. It wouldn't have mended properly yet. But then again, it must have healed enough for him to try the swim across to the mainland. Curse him, the black bastard,' he said heatedly.

'This boat may be his only chance to escape, to make it back alive to the mainland, back to his home. You know how it is with these savages, how they try to reach their home territory, some of them more than others. It's their heathen Dreamtime ways. They like to die in their own area, so they can enter their Dreamtime spirit world. That is why they want to return. This fugitive, Bulmurn, is a medicine man of their culture. He's no exception.'

'I sympathise with you Percy', Simpson said. 'I sail at eight hundred hours tomorrow, but under my watchful eyes, I'll have my men and yours make one last thorough search of my ship, and I won't sail until you're satisfied he's not on board the *Capture.*'

'Your word is good enough for me, Owen', Vincent said. 'It's disturbing that he could disappear so completely and easily. You know, he's never seen the outside of his cell, unless it was under strict supervision. It's a mystery. See you before you sail then. Goodnight, Owen.'

Wardang

At seven hundred hours the next morning, Captain Owen Simpson and Superintendent Percy Vincent stood together on board the H.M.S. *Capture* as the final search was made. Simpson said to his sailors, Nyoongar deck hands, and the island's prison warders led by Vincent's right-hand man, O'Donnell, 'Be thorough men, search every inch of this vessel. We don't want it said that we were the people responsible for helping this witch doctor escape back to the mainland, do we now?'

Captain Simpson caught the eyes of his First Mate, James Riley. Riley grinned at his captain, then with a wink he said, 'We sure don't want that to happen. No Sir, Captain, Sir! If that happened, Sir, we would be the laughing stock of the whole colony, wouldn't we, Captain?'

'Be gone with you, mate. Just make sure you do a good job and search this boat from top to bottom. Be thorough, men!' ordered Simpson.

They searched for some fifteen minutes, before each of the searching parties came back to make their report to Simpson and Vincent, standing on the bridge. Nothing unusual had been seen, there was nothing to report.

'I am sorry, Percy,' Simpson said to the Superintendent. 'He's not on board. If he does appear in the next hour or so, it's because we've fished him out of the water of the Indian Ocean on our way back to Port Fremantle. Rest assured, Percy, I'll double my watch on the ship on our way back. I'll have my lookouts alert, looking for him swimming all the way across to the mainland.'

Vincent looked at Simpson and offered his hand. As they shook hands, Vincent said, 'I see you've done your best, Captain. I'm satisfied he's not on your ship now, but I'd be happy if you'd keep a lookout for him.'

Vincent left the ship walking down the gangplank to shore. A sudden noise erupted from the prisoners who worked around the landing dock where the ship was anchored. To Vincent it sounded as though the prisoners were actually cheering. Then he turned to see what had happened.

To his amazement, the Nyoongar prisoners were shouting and laughing. They appeared to be laughing at him. And to top it all off, they were chanting, almost like singing, a drone that sounded like the missing prisoner's name, 'Bulmurn! Bulmurn! Bulmurn!'.

When the Superintendent came into their sights, all went quiet. Then Vincent lunged towards them bellowing, 'Where is he? Where is he?', as he looked to his left and right. Then he spun around, looking back the way he had come, then back again towards the prisoners.

'Where is he? Where is he?', Vincent shouted trying to control his dismay. The prisoners laughingly pointed to the ship's masthead. On top of it sat a black crow!

Vincent was aghast with amazement. 'Surely, surely, those stupid savages don't think that that crow . . . that black crow is him . . .No, surely not. The heathens don't think that bird is him . . .' Anger began to well up inside of him as he realised they really thought the crow to be Bulmurn.

Their chanting began again: 'Bulmurn . . . Bulmurn . . . Bulmurn . . . Bulmurn . . . *Bulmurn Mobarn Boylla Gudjuk jinungin wardang Bulmurn Mobarn Boylla Gudjuk Jjnungin wardang.*' As they sang, they pointed to the crow. '*Bulmurn Mobarn Boylla Gudjuk jinungin barhal wardang. Bulmurn Mobarn*

Boylla Gudjuk barhal wardang', the black prisoners chanted.

Vincent wasn't amused at all. He failed to understand all the words they were saying, but when their laughter penetrated his frustration, he turned to look at the ship once more. There, high on the masthead was the crow, just a plain ordinary scavenging crow. Suddenly Vincent grinned a cruel smile. 'Those stupid black heathens don't know any better. Curse the whole lot of you savages,' he said to the prisoners, but to no one in particular. His amusement was aimed at them all. 'How ridiculous', he sneered. 'How ridiculous these blacks are!'

Vincent's Chief Warder, O'Donnell came on the scene: 'Can I help Sir?' 'No, O'Donnell,' Vincent said, 'but I may as well tell you what's happened, what this rabble here thinks', Vincent pointed at the prisoners, who stood a reasonable distance away from them.

Then Vincent pointed at the moving schooner. 'Look, O'Donnell, up there on the mast. What do you see?' O'Donnell focused his eyes on the mast and answered, 'All I can see on the mast is a black crow, Sir, that's what I see.'

'That's just it, Sergeant', Vincent said. 'That's what these people are making a noise about. They think that crow on the mast is the escaped prisoner Bulmurn. You know how superstitious they are. They believe he's one of those magicians who can change into everything from an ant, to a stump, to a black boy tree and now a bloody crow.'

Then O'Donnell said, 'They're just stupid, primitive natives, Sir. That's what they are.'

There was a pause in the conversation as they watched the sailing vessel cast off and get underway, their eyes glued on the crow, watching to see it if would fly away off the mast. Other eyes watched also. These eyes belonged to the now silent prisoners. The bird just sat there. It never moved.

Captain Simpson was good to his word. He made sure his men kept a sharp lookout for the escaped prisoner, whom they thought might be still in the sea. They looked around at the dark waters of the crossing from the island to the mainland. Captain Simpson scratched his beard thoughtfully, wondering.

Simpson thought back to the night Bulmurn had escaped. According to Vincent, it had been a rough night, the wind blowing a gale. The sea could be heard pounding the island's jetty. This would have been the time the prisoner would have made his move.

Vincent had said, 'His chains were still locked, and we don't know how he got out of them. One of those absent warders must have left the keys within his reach. He certainly didn't get out by magic.'

Simpson was joined by Riley, the ship's First Mate. Simpson told Riley of his thoughts: 'You know, Riley, when they first began to use the island as a jail, many of the prisoners tried to escape by just jumping into the calm waters. It was too easy to recapture them. When they were found missing, boat patrols were put out and they were brought back. Sometimes the boat patrol would just keep the boat next to them, letting them swim all the way across to Fremantle, before they took them back to the island. That really broke their hearts. After they were recaptured, most of them never tried to escape again from Rottnest. But they got smart and now try to escape in rough seas. They have to hope the currents are running the right way to the mainland and they have to do it at night. And then they have to face the sharks.'

Then Riley had his say, 'You know Captain, I ain't one to sympathise with them nor am I likely to help any of them, but I can't help but admire their courage.'

'Yes,' said Simpson, 'I know what you mean, mate. They surely are brave men, but desperate.'

If Captain Simpson had noticed the faces of the returning prisoners they were taking back with them to be released in Fremantle, and the knowing look upon the faces of his own Nyoongar deck hands, he would certainly have been a worried man, because as far as these people were concerned, the crow they saw sitting on the mast was indeed Bulmurn.

The deck hands worked with caution, their eyes clearly bulging, showing the strain they felt about the crow sitting on the mast. The 'freed' prisoners felt the strain also. Whenever they took a quick glance upwards, they saw a man sitting there on the masthead, not a crow. They blinked their eyes to make the first impression of the man's image go away.

Knayel, the eldest Nyoongar, who was looked upon by the other returning prisoners as their unelected leader, spoke in Nyoongar to the small group who sat close together. Knayel said to them quietly, 'I'll be glad when we get to Walyalup, so that we can leave this ship. Then this one up there,' he said turning his eyes upward to where the crow sat, 'he can make his escape. I've got the feeling he's going to wait until we go and these other people go before he changes back into Bulmurn the man.' Everybody nodded their heads in agreement. But, they were not convinced by his words.

Knayel continued to speak to them. 'We all know what he did. We all hope he can escape the *wadjbulla* law, even though he killed six of them. We all know Bulmurn had the right. He's got the Nyoongar Law of the southern tribes on his side. *Kiaya*, we all know he had the right to take revenge for what happened to his sister and brother-in-law. When he killed those four *wadjbulla*, who were guilty, they had the punishment they deserved. He was sure of the identity of the white men who did the killing. A witness who saw the incident made it clear about the identity of the rapist killers.'

Everybody listened to Knayel with intent interest. 'You know the men Bulmurn killed were bad men of the worst kind to the Nyoongar people. Bulmurn was given the tribal responsibility to bring those bad men to justice. He had set about doing just that. He only killed those other two troopers and the two black trackers when they attacked, forcing him to kill for self-preservation. Now he's an outlaw, a killer of the white. Now they want to hang him.

'You know,' Knayel said, 'the white man's law is no law. They are allowed to get away with murder and destruction, without punishment of any kind, even though they all know they are guilty of rape and murder. The smart-talking whites always got away with injustices of the worst kind against the Nyoongar people, no matter how big or small the crime. They always got away with it. Nobody has ever been punished.'

Slowly but surely, Captain Simpson manoeuvred *Capture* alongside the Long Jetty at Anglesea Point in the Port of Fremantle. The *Capture*'s crew soon had the boat securely roped and moored to Long Jetty. The boat would rest until new cargo or prisoners needed to be taken across to Rottnest Island jail.

Captain Simpson called all his men to attention, before unloading commenced. 'Men! I don't want it said that we run an untidy, careless ship. We don't want it said that we have helped a prisoner escape either, now do we?' he questioned.

'No!' his men said unanimously. Simpson raised his hand, the men in turn quietened to let him continue. 'Especially this black magic man who has just escaped from Rottnest Island jail, the one they call Bulmurn'.

Captain Simpson made his voice boom as he said, 'That's why I want you men, all the crew, to search this boat from top to bottom. One more time! I want you to be thorough. Take your time. Do a proper search throughout the ship.' Captain Simpson paused briefly to catch his breath. Then he gave Riley his order. 'Mate,' he said, 'you take the men down into the hold, search this vessel fore and aft. When you've done that return here. If you do a good job, I'll reward you with extra leave.'

Every crew member searched below, around and under what looked like a possible hiding place. They searched the bottom of the boat until they were certain they had done it all, not missing anything that looked like a possible hiding place for anybody. They went down stumbling around the darkest places, every corner of the ship's hold. Some seamen even went to the bilge lockers. They ran their hands along the very bottom planks. Their search was as thorough as any man could make it. Below decks was clear. Riley had them do the same above. It was plain to see that nobody was hiding on the deck of this boat.

Meanwhile, all this time the crow sat perched on the masthead of the boat. Now why that crow had travelled all the way from Rottnest Island to the mainland, was a serious question. Why was it still perched up there even after more time was spent looking for Bulmurn?

There was an even more important question on the lips of the Nyoongar deck hands themselves. Was it Bulmurn or was it really just *wardang*, the black crow?

Every time a Nyoongar deck hand lifted his head to look up at the crow on the mast, a puzzled look came over his face, because what he saw first was the image of a man, before it changed into the *wardang*. For the Nyoongars on board Bulmurn was there for them to see, but not for the white men to see. To them he was displaying his powerful *mobarn* powers. He was showing them he was powerful, showing them he was strong. '*Kiaya!*' they all thought, 'that's what he's doing alright'.

First Mate Riley stood next to Captain Simpson, who had the task of paying off the men. One by one, he paid them their wages, reminding each sailor when to be back on deck ready to sail again, when their leave finished. As he paid them, they made their way off the boat and headed for the nearest tavern for alcohol to wash the salt off their throats. Only the five Aboriginal deck hands were left. These men were frightened about something. Simpson and Riley again failed to notice anything different about them.

Simpson had already let Knayel and the other prisoners off the ship. Now only the deck hands remained. He called the first of the five. He was not obliged to pay them. They were fair workers, he thought, so he would give them a few pence each. As he paid them, he said, 'No going walkabout. No grog. Just make sure you get back here on time when your leave is finished.'

The first four he paid were waiting on the jetty for Korung, the fifth deck hand. He couldn't stand the tension of not releasing his suspicions to the Captain and Riley. 'Boss,' he said to Simpson. 'Boss, I'd seed dut wun you call Bulmurn. He bean riden wid us all dis time. He bean wid us all da time, boss, Captain, Sir.'

'Now, don't be silly, Korung. He's not on this ship. You were with Mr Riley here. You helped to search the boat with him.'

'Captain, Boss, Sir. Wead bean serchen only bottom and dis here deck. He nut in dut bottom or dis deck. He up dare boss.' He pointed to the masthead where the crow sat. 'Up dare, dus him boss, he bin sittin dare alda way ober frum Rottnest, Wagemup, ober der.' He pointed to the island. 'Dus him ulrite boss. Meed sure dut him, yes dut him for sure, boss, Sir.' Again he pointed at the black crow.

Amused, Simpson and Riley looked at one another before Simpson said to Korung. 'You're a bloody superstitious black fool. That's not a man, only a crow. Pass me that musket over there, Mr Riley. I'll prove to this simpleton that it's only a black crow up there. Fetch it to me, Mr Riley.'

'No, Captain Boss, Sir. Me nut rong, dut him up dare ulrite. I nut loud to do nusin gainst dut wun boss his same skin as me.'

'All right Korung,' Simpson said as Riley gave him the rifle. Simpson loaded, then he cocked the gun and took aim at the hapless looking crow sitting on the mast, then he fired. The rifle belched flame and smoke, leaving acrid smell of used gunpowder covering the deck of the boat. The shot echoed all around the Long Jetty and the sand dunes of Fremantle.

Captain Simpson lowered his weapon, thinking he had missed the bird, but then he saw the crow spinning in circles, falling down towards the gangplank of the boat. The spinning bird hit the gangway with a thud.

Everything seemed to come to a standstill for a minute or more. Then Simpson looked at Riley and Korung, 'I knew I hit that bird! I knew I shot it!'

The crow lay as though it was dead. Then it moved, it stood on shaky legs, looking around for an escape route, which way it could go to safety. Had the black crow lost its senses? Instead of flying off, the crow ran off the boat on the Long Jetty, heading towards the sand dunes.

The Nyoongar deck hands who were waiting for Korung to join them, all heard and saw what happened. Now Korung joined the group, shouting at them, 'Cho! Cho! Cho! Did you Nyoongars see that!' 'Kiaya! Kiaya!' they answered him in unison, with excited voices.

Korung shouted, 'Come on!' Then they all ran off after the crow, anxious to see what would happen next. All wanted to keep the crow in their sights.

Simpson said to Riley, 'Look at those silly black heathens go after that bird. I'll be damned if it's only a black crow I shot. I think I must have grazed its wing with my shot. I'm sure I winged it. You know, Riley, I bet they still think it's their medicine man, Bulmurn.'

'I reckon you're right, Sir,' Riley answered. 'Look at them go. Look at them chase after that crow.' Then they both burst out laughing.

'They're stupid all right, these natives. Bloody, bloody stupid.'

As the group chased the bird, it seemed to get faster as it went over and down the sand dunes. The five men began to tire, but not so the bird, it seemed to get stronger. Then it went over a larger sand dune. The men following behind struggled to make the top. Finally, out of breath they reached the top. They stopped, looked in surprise.

To their amazement, there running across the dunes away from them was not a bird, but a tall Nyoongar man. Korung called out, 'It's Bulmurn'. As he called out the name, the man looked back.

As the man looked back, the other four of the group put their hands over their eyes, closing them against the gaze of the running man. They didn't want to be changed into something strange, no way were they going to risk looking into the eyes of Bulmurn.

Korung who said Bulmurn's name, said it again a second time. He could just make out a smile on the face of the man before he disappeared into the distant dunes further along the beach. The four who closed their eyes, now looked again as the figure disappeared. One of them said, 'I wonder if that's Bulmurn from the Nyoongar people of Mundoon area.' Fittingly, Korung, the fifth member of the group had the last say. 'I know. I know who it is.' He repeated, 'I know. I know who it is.' Then he turned and walked back the way they had just come. The others followed, shaken with amazement.

* * * * * * * *

Jubuc looked up. He was startled by the nearness of a circling *wardang*. The black bird cawed, just once. Jubuc thought he recognised the *wardang*, but he thought to himself, 'Aren't all those birds alike?' They all seemed to be the same.

Only Jubuc seemed to notice the crow. No one else really cared. That was until Lulura stepped out of their *miamia*. He then realised that the *wardang* was a messenger. Was it Bulmurn? No, it couldn't be. Lulura shaded her eyes from the sun, then she looked in the direction of the bird. Then, as if it was a sign, she smiled as the crow cawed three times, seemingly at her. Then it flew off in a northerly direction, in the direction of Moora, where the Moorara Nyoongars lived.

Lulura gathered her things and also moved off, following the direction the *wardang* flew. Jubuc didn't try to stop her, although it wasn't as if he didn't want to. Since Bulmurn had been banished and she had been left with him, he had grown very fond of Lulura. But he knew her heart never belonged to him, it belonged to Bulmurn. All the time, he had shared her with Bulmurn. All those times she left him to join Bulmurn, she did come back. Now this was different. He knew she had to go. This time she would never come back.

Jubuc felt sad at her leaving. 'Good luck,' Jubuc shouted, 'good luck!' But Lulura didn't hear him. Her mind was concentrated elsewhere. Jubuc watched her go until she was out of sight. Jubuc felt sad, but he felt good. His heart was glad for Lulura. Now she was free, 'free' he thought out loud. Free to join Bulmurn.

A Note on Nyoongar Terms used in
Bulmurn: A Swan River Nyoongar

ALLIGA	be careful
ALLAWAH	lookout, there's danger
BABBANGWIN	lightning spirit
BADJANG	pus, a festered sore full of pus
BALGA	grass tree, named as 'Black Boy' by early settlers
BALLADONG	York Aboriginal people
BALLAROK	see SKIN GROUPINGS
BARDI	a succulent grub which used to be found in abundance around the Swan River area
BEELIAR	the Beeliar Nyoongar group was led by Midgegooroo and Yagan
BEELU	the Beelu Nyoongar group was led by Mundy
BARHAL	he, he's, him, his
BIDDAIR	father, important person or boss
BIKUTA	the red rock kangaroo
BILO	shark
BINA	dawning of a new day
BOKGAL	grave
BOKAL D YAUR	This is the name for the burial of the dead around the Swan River. The body is layed in the east-west position. The *Mobarn Boylla Gudjuk* is the master of burial ceremonies. During the burial ceremony boughs of saplings are placed in a criss-crossed position in the grave. This is done at three intervals as the grave is filled in. When this is done the *Mobarn Boylla Gudjuk* puts his head and ear on the grave, listening to make sure the body is in the right position and its spirit is content. While he is doing this the grieving people also listen. Not a sound is made. When he is sure all is well, he jumps high into the air and shouts 'it's right', then the family and other relatives wail and cry because they are happy. They know that the spirit of their loved one is in the right position to see the dawn of a new day, the time when the spirit finds its dreaming.

BOYLLA	spiritual magic
BUGAR	champion
BUJARA NGUNUNG	Mother Earth, motherland
BUKA	cape or coat usually made from the grey kangaroo
BULYUT	white spirit
CHO	exclamation of an event that is about to happen or has happened
CHOO CHOO	exclamation about what has happened, also there could be a shame or a delight about what has happened
COOLAMON	wooden vessel that is used to carry food, water or even a baby

DARBALYUNG NYOONGAR	
	Swan River Aboriginal
DARGANAN	to stun or kill
DERBAL YERIGAN	Swan River, Western Australia
DIJIKOK	see SKIN GROUPINGS
DRONDARAP	see SKIN GROUPINGS
DWERRT	native dog, the dingo

GENABUKA	boots
GOORRIT	bag that is tied from the *nulbarn*, that contains the concoctions of the *Mobarn* man
GOTO	bag that is made from the skin of *yonga* the kangaroo. This was the bag the women used for general purposes and to gather food
GUNDIR	another bag the women used to carry their small children. The *goto* and the *gundir* were used daily by the women.

INJI	ceremonial tapping sticks

JENARK	devil
JENGA	evil spirit
JIDALUK	night
JINUNGIN	looking at, staring
JIMBAR	bad spirit
KAABO	dance of the kangaroo
KADJO	hammer
KARTABUKA	hat
KEITJ	barbed spear
KIAYA	yes

KIAYA HAR (HARYO)
                        yes it is, very
KORCHO   axe
KURENDEE   fighting stick
KULUNGA   children
KULLARK   home, the camping area, the *miamia*
KUMARL   grey possum
KURAH   a while ago, a long time ago
KWABBA   good, nice, anything associated with being good
KWABBA JIDALUK a good night
KYLIE   boomerang

MAMARUP   man
MANDOON   Guildford
MAR   wind spirit
MARLEE   black swan
MAROO   sky spirit
MARTAGYN   leg, usually the right leg of a skin group
MIAMIA   hut made of bushes in which Nyoongar people lived
MIDJUAL   rain spirit
MINGA   ant, a black ant
MIRINDITJ   dead, death, it's dead
MOBARN   magic
MOBARN BOYLLA GUDJUK
                        an Aboriginal doctor of medicine and the possessor
                        of spiritual power
MIRO   *woomera* or spear thrower
MOORO   the Mooro was led by 'Yellagonga', the settlers name
                        for the leader Walyunga, or Wuylunga
MULGA   thunder spirit
MUNATJ   leader, boss
MURRN   black or blue
MURRN MORDA   Darling Ranges of Western Australia
MUYANG   Nyoongar word for sex

NAGONAK   see SKIN GROUPINGS
NGOTAK   see SKIN GROUPINGS
NULBURN   waist belt made from human hair or from the grey
                        possum's fur
NORCH   dead
NYOONGAR   Aboriginal of the South-West of Western Australia

QUARN   underground edible tuber

SKIN GROUPINGS:	BALLAROK	1
	DRONDARAP	2
	DIJIKOK	3
	NAGONAK	4
	NGOTAK	5
	WADDARAK	6

These were the important skin groups of the Swan River tribes of Perth, Western Australia. The skin grouping was used strictly by the south-west Aboriginal people, especially for determining wedlock. This system was used to prevent relatives marrying one another so that progeny were sound in mind and body. For example, in the story, Bulmurn is a Ballarak Martagyn and Lulura is a Wadderak Martagyn. These skin groups are the furthest apart, therefore they make the best match. In this way the tribal bloodlines of the south-west people were kept healthy and finely tuned.

WADJBULLA	whitefella, whiteman, the early settlers
WADDARAK	See SKIN GROUPINGS
WAITJ	emu (male)
WARAL	kangaroo skin rug
WARDANG	black crow
WARNBRO	animal skin cape
WARRA	no good, bad
WIDJI BANDI	gun. The gun is named after the leg shank of the female emu, which was thought to resemble a rifle.
WILBARN	the colour white
WILGEE	an orchre type of clay that was burnt in the fire to make a powder. When mixed with grease, it was used as body paint for ceremonial purposes.
WUREUP	the Wureup were led by Weeup
YARKINJE	western swamp long-necked turtle
YOKI	victory
YONGA	western grey kangaroo of Western Australia
YORGA	wife

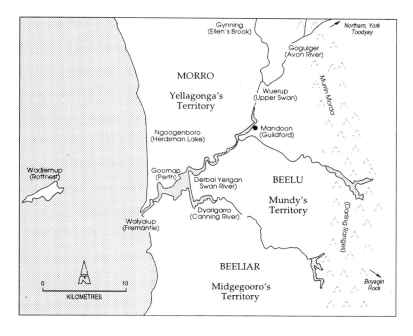

Nyungar – the People: Aboriginal Customs in the Southwest of Australia (p. 27),
edited by Neville Green, Creative Research Publishers, North Perth, was used as
a reference source for this map with kind permission of the editor.